SPOILT CREATURES

SPOILT CREATURES

Amy Twigg

First published in Great Britain in 2024 by Tinder Press
An imprint of HEADLINE PUBLISHING GROUP

1

Cataloguing in Publication Data is available from the British Library

Hardback ISBN 978 1 0354 0791 0
Trade paperback ISBN 978 1 0354 0792 7

Typeset in Sabon LT Pro by CC Book Production

Printed and bound in Great Britain by Clays Ltd, Elcograf S.p.A.

Headline's policy is to use papers that are natural, renewable and
recyclable products and made from wood grown in well-managed forests
and other controlled sources. The logging and manufacturing processes
are expected to conform to the environmental regulations
of the country of origin.

HEADLINE PUBLISHING GROUP
An Hachette UK Company
Carmelite House
50 Victoria Embankment
London EC4Y 0DZ

www.tinderpress.co.uk
www.headline.co.uk
www.hachette.co.uk

For May

'Damn you, spoilt creature; I shan't make you love me any the more by giving myself away like this.'

Vita Sackville-West's letter to Virginia Woolf

'Hate is a bottomless cup; I will pour and pour.'

Medea, Euripides

2018

People looked at the photographs and decided they knew everything about us. Believing in the oil spill of newspaper ink, how it clung to every shadow, conspiring grit and gloom. Always the same photos, of the farmhouse coming apart. Gaping windows, streaks of blood across the kitchen floor where the women had walked with glass in their feet. Walls swollen with damp, an overturned chair. In every grainy shot, the whisper of chaos. Even on the internet, in the blogs and top-ten lists which regurgitated the same information over and over again, the photographs never improved. It didn't seem to matter. People looked at them and came to their own conclusions – about Breach House, and about us. What kind of women we were. They never saw us in the summer, how we dug our hands into the soil. The long evenings spent on the lawn.

They never saw the life we had made for ourselves.

The memory of those first few days after everything happened sat briny in me, perfectly preserved. I could close my eyes and recall what I ate for dinner, what brand of soap I used to clean myself with, scrubbing so hard I left pink contrails across my skin. The constant static of news in the background, waiting for the moment when I'd hear a name I recognised, perhaps even my own. Part of me disappointed when it didn't come. All of my clothes were gone and so I went rooting around in my mother's wardrobe for something to wear, found that it was all too big for me. I twisted in front of the mirror, examining the planes and divots of my body, the bone that now jutted from my hips.

And then, finally, walking past the television one morning and seeing Breach House garlanded in police tape, a series of grave faces peering shock-drunk into the camera. At that point there was so little information that journalists resorted to frantic interviews with locals, only half of whom had known the place existed at all. Those who did could only shrug, their eyes wide and bright, unable to express everything they felt.

A pilgrimage amassed. Only a few at first, people who had watched the news or read the paper and wanted to see for themselves. And then more. They came from all across the country and seemed overly prepared, as if they'd been sat quietly in the dark, waiting for it to happen. At night, they climbed the barricades and entered the house, took home souvenirs to show their friends and family. Someone's jumper, a broken dinner plate. Convinced that what they were doing was more noble than theft: it was preservation.

In the years that followed I went on eBay, searching through listings of yellowed paperbacks, hairbrushes, underwear; shrapnel sellers claimed came from the farm. Some listings mentioned items that contained dark stains, and these usually sold for more. I followed each bidding war closely, surprised by how much someone was willing to pay to feel like they owned a little piece of us. We were collectible. I was hopeful it wouldn't last, that another tragedy would come along and people would forget what had happened. But they continued to talk about us, our story passing from one mouth into another until it changed shape, was chewed into legend.

I began spending more and more time online, searching. Her name appeared in a couple of blogs, but the information was always vague, teetering. Nobody knew her last name and so her first stuck out, rang on the page like a bell. Hazel, Hazel. It gave me a kind of comfort, that the rest of the world knew so little about her. I scavenged through forums, hoping for a sign. She must be out there. At the very least, she must be alive. I would sense that much, wouldn't I?

How easily it returned, the past. There were so many things that could wrench me back to that summer. Heat rising from the engine of an old car, light dappled over water. The smell of jasmine which had the power to tear open an almost-forgotten space in me, flood my body with adrenaline.

Sometimes I wished I'd never met her. That my life had remained dependable and ordinary, leading from one day into the next. The natural conclusion of a career, a marriage, a baby. And other times I'd wake in the middle of the night and find myself grasping for something, my hands splayed as if to say: don't go, stay.

PART ONE:

SPRING

1

2008

It was March, warm and wet, the first time she appeared.

Only segments of her body were visible through the trees, an initial glimpse of waist and hip and clavicle. And then her hair the colour of a burnished penny, brushing lightly against her tailbone. She must have been cold, dressed only in a skirt and blouse, the sort of thing you'd find in a charity shop. A pair of boots that looked a size too big for her feet. As she came towards me, I realised I was holding my breath, waiting for something to happen. She hadn't seen me yet, was busy searching the ground for something. Up close, there was a plumpness to her I hadn't noticed before, a soft sculpt of chin, the band of her skirt cutting into her waist and drawing the flesh out. Her mouth which was red and wet like a wound. Everything about her smacking of excess.

I wouldn't have seen her at all if it hadn't been for my mother and her dog, James. The three of us had gone walking on the downs, something we did not usually do together. My mother had recently become self-conscious about putting weight on, how it made her look, and she was trying to lose it. However, as soon as we'd arrived, I knew it had been a mistake to come. We weren't dressed for the weather. It was colder than I'd been expecting, and the sky hung heavy, threatening rain. At the first sound of thunder, James took off into the woods, and I was sent to retrieve him.

The woman bent over and picked something out of the dirt. After a moment I realised they were mushrooms, porous-looking morels. As she crouched, I caught a glimpse of underwear beneath her skirt, a girlish floral pattern. The knowledge of it was searing, embarrassing – but something else as well. Something that felt like power. She held the mushrooms up to her face, inspecting each one closely before slipping them into the pocket of her skirt.

Suddenly, James burst through the trees, his snout pressed to the ground, hoovering up the trails of other animals. He ran straight for me, barking and slobbering, running excited circles around my feet. Bloody dog. The woman stood up quickly, her pockets bulging with the mushrooms, and looked. Something seemed to pass between us, a kind of fissure. As she held my gaze, I felt the pent-up breath catch in my throat and shoot its way out, forcing me to cough, my cheeks burning with embarrassment. Through a film of tears, I saw the other woman begin to smile. Place a hand around her own throat as if she were the one choking, as if our lungs were the same.

I squeezed my eyes shut to clear them and when I opened them again, she was gone.

*

The house I grew up in was sagging, its white walls pocked with chipped plaster and bird shit, arterial trails across the front where ivy once grew and died. The garden was overgrown, weeds displacing the concrete slabs, making them topple underfoot. Crushed cider cans and crisp packets peppered the ground where teenagers had carelessly tossed them. There was an alleyway behind the house where they sometimes liked to gather, play music and feel each other in the dark. When I was a child, we'd had a family meeting to discuss what colour to paint the front door. I'd voted purple, but my mother said people didn't paint their front doors purple and in the end we'd chosen green. It was a cartoonish hue, like dollar bills, flaking now but still insistently bright.

There was a gust of stale air as we struggled inside, mingled with the lingering smell of fat. My mother wasn't a good cook. Her bacon was always pink and floppy, unrendered curls of rind that lodged in your throat. When she used to make me porridge before school it would sit thick in the bowl like clay.

I went into the kitchen to make sandwiches. There was cheddar in the fridge and a packet of roast beef that had an iridescent sheen to it. I gave it a sniff, thought it smelled okay. Outside, the wind had begun to pick up. It knocked on the windows, rattled them.

'We made it back just in time,' my mother said, following me into the kitchen. She put the kettle on to boil and leaned her backside against the counter. People said we looked alike, but I only saw my father, the same crook in our noses, dry-skinned and short-sighted. It wasn't something I'd ever point out. He'd been gone almost twelve years, buried in pieces because his car had slipped under a truck. I remembered him in vivid bursts – how well he got on with everyone, the tins of mackerel he'd open and then forget about, leaving them to fester in the fridge. When he went on work trips he'd call the house phone and pretend to be someone else, a spy or a criminal who was holding my father hostage, always demanding to know how much I loved him, how far I'd be willing to go to save him.

We took our lunch through to the dining room which overlooked the rear garden. Tangles of mint grew wild, suffocating the other plants, sending their suckers back into the ground. After the rain, I knew, the smell of menthol would steep the air, sharp and clean. Years ago, we used to have a gardener who sometimes left Jehovah's Witness leaflets around the house, until one day they stopped coming and no one had thought to replace them.

'I'm thinking about dyeing my hair,' my mother said with her mouth half full.

This might have caught someone else off guard, but I was used to these diversions of hers, the little trips in logic. I sat back, tipping my head to one side. 'What colour would you dye it?' I asked.

'I don't know, blonde, maybe. With a fringe. Or would that look too desperate at my age?'

'Maybe,' I said.

She pursed her lips, pushed her plate away. 'I don't want any more. The bread tastes stale.'

As I looked down, I saw her touch her thumb and forefinger together in a series of taps, like Morse code. *Tap, tap, tap-tap-tap.* Trying to complete some unknown pattern, a compulsion I'd noticed for the first time a few months after my father died. Other behaviours followed: adjusting the volume of the television in multiples of two or five, eating dinner every night at six or not at all. She armed herself in ritual, as if it might help predict what would come next. Once, when I brought my boyfriend, Nathan, home for dinner, she leaned across the table and adjusted the angle of the fork on his plate, smiling up at him. Afterwards he'd asked me if she was an alcoholic.

It wasn't always this way. When I was a girl she would iron my school shirts very carefully, bake carrot cake for my birthday, the cream-cheese frosting, which was soft and sweet and sat like glue between my fingers. She knew the names of all my friends and, more importantly, the names of my enemies, gleefully cursing them on our morning rides to school. She would sing in the bath, her voice throaty with steam, emerging in great clouds of it, her beautiful pink body.

But that was years ago. I was thirty-two now, the same age she'd been when she'd had me.

'I should go upstairs and sort through the rest of my things,' I said, sitting back in my chair. 'Finish unpacking.'

She looked at me over her cup of tea, the liquid gulping down her throat as she swallowed. 'I've had a think about that. It doesn't make sense for you to unpack everything, especially if something changes. Seems a waste of effort.'

'Nothing's going to change,' I said, the words falling flat with repetition. 'And I can't keep living out of boxes.'

The plates on the table rattled as she leaned in close, sour coffee breath. 'You could speak to Nathan, though. If you spoke, things might feel different. You might feel different.'

'Mum,' I said, a gentle plea.

She turned towards the window. I felt her disappointment keenly, like a lump below the skin. Nathan and I had broken up almost two months ago, but she kept worrying at the fact, treated it like a temporary thing, something we'd get over. I knew she thought I hadn't tried hard enough to salvage my relationship with him, or that it must have been my fault somehow. She worried that my failures were a reflection of her own, that people would look at me and see a continuation of her own humiliation.

Maybe she was right.

I left her and went upstairs before she could say anything else. My bedroom hadn't changed much over the years. The mauve carpet, which my parents had thought was a good idea when they'd first moved in, was now threadbare in several places, worn down to the floorboards underneath. There'd been a brief period of time, after I'd gone to university, when my mother had thought about turning the room into a gym. A stationary bicycle was still pushed up against one wall, functioning now as a clothes horse.

I sat down and began sorting through the pile of cardboard boxes with my name on them. Nathan had done most of the packing, thinking he was being helpful, but the neatly folded dresses and ornaments wrapped in newspaper felt too eager. I thumbed through a stack of CD cases, half of them empty, and thought that perhaps my mother had a point: why bother unpacking, if this was all I had to show for myself? A life that could be gathered in a few boxes, made small. There was something defeating about it too, the suspicion that if I moved back into my old bedroom I'd never leave it again.

I could hear my mother moving around in the kitchen downstairs, the run of the sink as she did the washing-up.

I did not want to get stuck here. I could not.

*

Later that night in bed I thought about the woman in the woods. The moment had been fleeting, and yet I couldn't stop scrutinising it, breaking each second down into its component parts. Her copper hair, the way she'd pushed her body through the trees as if she didn't care what happened to it. She reminded me of something that lived in the water, strange and slippery like an eel: a formless thing that seemed to change shape the longer you looked at it.

2

Nessa's boyfriend, David, was not the type of man to judge things by taste: he needed to know the measurements for everything. Consulting his recipe book as he fixed another round of cocktails, the pneumatic sound of ice churning in its metal shaker.

They'd been together a few years now. I'd been surprised when Nessa had first introduced me to him – so unlike the men she'd dated in the past. Nessa liked big men, broad and loud, the kind who drowned their food in vinegar. But everything about David was slender: his hands, his temper, his mouth.

'What are you making?' I asked.

'Amaretto sours,' he replied, beginning to pour. I could tell straight away he'd overmixed the egg whites, the liquid sitting thick and syrupy in the glass, smelling of arsenic.

Nessa had texted me earlier to say she was hosting, and that I should arrive by seven. She no longer checked to see if I had other plans, knew me well enough to assume that I didn't. Helen and Adam – friends from university – were over as well, already busy exchanging work anecdotes. Stories of misplaced lanyards and deplorable managers, colleagues they prayed would quit and uncomfortable office chairs. I had no stories like that. Sometimes I thought it would be nice if I did, something that would allow me to join in their complaining. But then one of them would talk about spreadsheets or synergy and I'd feel physically ill.

'When did we order the food?' Helen asked, sipping from the drink David handed to her. I noticed the muscles in her jaw stiffen, resisting the urge to gag. She placed the glass down on the table and dabbed at her bottom lip, wiping away the excess foam. 'We should call the manager and complain.'

Helen was very beautiful. She reminded me of the girls I went to school with who used eyelash curlers and were always being harassed by boys. Even when she was being unpleasant you couldn't help but feel drawn to her, in the way all people are drawn to beautiful things.

She turned on the television, scrolling through the channels before deciding on a property programme, the lipsticked presenter showing a retired couple around a villa – somewhere warm, France or Spain.

'How's work, Iris?' Adam asked.

'It's okay,' I shrugged. 'My manager is all right.'

'I've lost the plot,' Helen said, not looking away from the screen. 'Where are you working now, the deli?'

'Off-licence,' Nessa corrected her. Impossible not to hear the judgement in her voice.

'That still qualifies you as the best person to get us pissed,' Adam said. I smiled, grateful.

Helen continued: 'And what about Nathan?' Something threatening in the way she turned to me, her lips puckering with sympathy. 'Have you heard from him at all?'

I shook my head.

'Men can be such pigs, can't they?'

'I keep telling her to get back out there,' Nessa said. 'Sitting around moping is the worst thing you can do. You need to be proactive.'

Helen nodded slowly like a great wisdom had been imparted.

Nessa's desire to corral my life into a size and shape that was similar to her own was nothing new. She'd been trying to map out our futures since uni. We would both get jobs that afforded us houses with patios, perfect for barbecues in the summer. Our husbands would get along, perhaps even play squash together once a week. There'd be a well-behaved dog or cat to dote upon – and later on, children. I knew I should want these things too, and yet I kept finding myself tetherless, slipping further away from Nessa's nuclear ideal and unable to tell whether that was such a bad thing.

The couple on television were crying now. I could see by the camera angles that the presenter had asked them a personal question, something to invoke tragedy. Did these people agree to humiliation before going on the show? Did they know? The woman shredded a tissue between her fingers, a membrane of mucus suspended between her nose and hand. Someone should have cleaned it away for her – her husband – but instead they let her go on like that, sobbing and leaking.

'Another round?' David asked.

'I can help,' I said, following him into the kitchen.

He opened his recipe book and began chopping lemons. He was good with a knife, slicing confidently through the peel. Outside, I could hear Nessa and Helen talking in a hush. Imagined their heads bent low, almost touching.

'She's just worried about you.' David had stopped chopping, was looking sideways at me. 'We all are. We just want to make sure you're okay.'

'Why wouldn't I be okay?'

'How you've been lately,' he told me. 'The break-up with Nathan, moving back into your mum's. It would be a lot for anyone.'

'I'm not about to kill myself,' I laughed.

David flashed a hollow smile and crossed over to the sink. The kitchen was tiny, enough for a fridge and a couple of laminate cabinets, and it meant he had to go around me, his body brushing, briefly, alongside mine. I tried to gauge the closeness of him, if he pressed himself harder than was necessary against me. Lingered a moment too long, so that I felt the shape of him through his clothing. I watched his face as he rinsed the cocktail shaker, but there was nothing there, no hint of knowing.

*

By the time the food arrived it was dark, the moon a ruddy thing in the sky. We'd ordered Indian food, but there were foil cartons filled with portions of chips and onion rings, slack from the steam, which Nessa piled on to her plate. She'd never been an adventurous eater. We crowded round the small dining table, our elbows jutting as David fiddled with the CD player, the gravelled undertones of Stevie Nicks filling the gaps in conversation while we ate. Helen insisted on sharing a main course with Adam and made a point out of serving him herself, giving him the largest chunks of meat so she was left with the onions and gristle, picking at them and smiling like she'd made some personal sacrifice. I wondered if he knew she was in love with him.

'Are you sure you don't want any more of this korma?' he asked her, holding up the foil carton.

She placed a hand over her stomach. 'I better not. I really need to lose weight.' It was obvious she wanted Adam to disagree with her; she was putting herself down so he could pick her back up again. But he either didn't notice or was uninterested in her little game, spooning more curry on to his plate.

David served a third round of drinks, better this time: Nessa must have helped. I drank quickly, without really tasting anything, the edges of my mind gradually blurring into pleasant nothingness. I blinked around the table, watching the others talk but no longer able to follow the thread of their conversation. Somebody must have told a joke because suddenly they were all laughing, so loudly it bordered on hysteria.

My hand felt heavy as I picked up my fork, cumbersome. I let go without thinking and watched it fall on to the table, shattering a poppadom. Helen gave a small cry, rearing back in her seat. Nessa looked at me, her annoyance tamped down by a parental patience.

'Come on then, Iris,' she said to me. 'We were just talking about our plans for the year, what we want to achieve. So: what do you want to achieve?'

I told her I wasn't sure.

'You must have some idea though,' she pressed. 'I mean, you can't carry on like this forever. There will be things you want to do. Move out of your mum's, meet someone new.'

I made a noncommittal noise. Nessa was a good friend – my best by default – but her pragmatism was exhausting. She'd always known the things she wanted in life and how to get them, whereas my desires had no clear shape, sat inside me like a clam, impossible to shuck open. All I knew is that I wanted something different; something more.

'If you're looking for a place to live, I might know somewhere,' Helen said. 'My sister couch-hopped a bit last year after she lost her job. She ended up at this place out in the sticks for a few months and said it was just what she needed.'

'Isn't she a vegan now?' Nessa asked.

'Don't get her started,' Adam said, making a point of rolling his eyes. 'Her sister's a nutjob.'

'Why is she a nutjob?' David asked.

'The last time I saw her, all she did was talk about how my clothes cost too much money and that it was sexist to kiss her goodbye on the cheek.'

David laughed, but I could see the hurt on Helen's face. 'You've only met her once,' she said. 'She's been through a hard time. But this place helped.'

'It sounds like a spa or something,' Nessa said.

'Or a cult,' Adam added.

Helen reached into her handbag, strung on the back of her chair, tubes of lipstick clattering as she searched for her phone. 'It's a place for women who, I don't know, need a change of scenery. I have the number here somewhere if you want.'

She slid a napkin across the table to me. Underneath the phone number were two words: *Breach House*.

'Okay,' I said. 'Thanks.' Helen's helpfulness surprised me. I tried to smile at her, but she'd already turned away, was locked in conversation again with Nessa. I traced my thumb across the napkin, watching as the ink bled into the tissue.

3

There was a memory of Nathan I couldn't quite shake loose. It was during those final few weeks, when we were barely speaking to one another, already living separate lives. I'd suggested going for lunch at our favourite pub, the Wheatsheaf. We liked it because there were three springer spaniels who sat at the bar all day, their faces resting on the counter-top so you had to thread your hand through a tangle of ears and snouts to get your pint. Nathan always ordered the fish-finger sandwich, could eat all of his and mine and still have room for dessert. Over the years I'd found myself leaving the food on my plate for him to finish, even if I wasn't full yet: it felt like the sort of thing a good girlfriend should do.

We sat at our usual table, eating and watching the dogs. Nathan took a long sip of his pint and when he put it back down again there was a foam moustache along his upper lip. I smiled, gestured to it, but he wasn't looking at me. He'd barely spoken a word since we arrived and I wondered if he would have noticed if I hadn't come, if I hadn't got into the car with him at all.

A couple walked past our table and I recognised the man as one of Nathan's work friends. He stopped next to us and punched Nathan gently in the shoulder.

'Small world,' he said.

Nathan sat up, a smile coming to his face so quickly I knew it rang false. He'd been caught off guard and now had to bungle his way into the role of contented boyfriend.

'Andrew,' he said. 'How are you?'

As they chatted, I let my gaze slip sideways to Andrew's girlfriend, who was the kind of woman my mother would have pointed out in the street, all legs and lipstick, her hair an impossible helix. Our eyes met and I felt her quick calculation as she worked out what box to place me in, whether I was someone worth knowing. She did not try to make small talk.

After they'd gone, I drank what was left of my gin and tonic, turned flat from the melted ice. Nathan touched a finger to his lip, the foam still streaked across it. 'For fuck's sake, Iris,' he said, swiping a hand across his mouth to clean it. 'Why didn't you tell me?'

I smiled, uncertain. He was joking, he must have been. But the look on his face. 'It was just a bit of foam,' I said. And then, to appease him, to bring him back to me: 'You looked cute.'

'I must have looked like an idiot.' He shook his head, a wounded expression on his face like I'd betrayed him.

*

There was a pattern in my family, of women losing their husbands. My grandmother, Anne, had been widowed a decade by the time I was born. She almost seemed to take pleasure in telling me how her husband – my grandfather – had died of a brain aneurysm. The suddenness of it, how they'd been having a conversation one morning about what colour to paint the downstairs bathroom when his head had keeled over into his bowl of cereal. Soggy bran flakes stuck to his cheek by the time my grandmother was able to pull him out. It can happen to anyone, she'd tell me. There could be a ticking timebomb hidden away in your head and you'd never know about it until it decided to go off. Nothing to be done except die. Now eat your broccoli.

Anne never remarried, which was a shame, because on her own she was insufferable. To me, she was unnecessarily cruel with her constant wheedling, forcing my mother to check my hair for lice, bending my neck over the bathroom sink and scraping my scalp with a metal comb until it came away bloody. The soft and unsalted dinners she'd occasionally cook for us.

When my father died, I began to see Anne's behaviour repeated in my mother. Little things at first. Synaptic flashes of paranoia, driving to school and then turning around halfway to make sure the front door was still locked. Refusing to eat red meat or fish in case the gristle or bone lodged in her throat. Once, she became so fixated on carbon-monoxide poisoning, convinced that our oven was broken and emitting dangerous fumes, that we packed our bags and camped out in a Travelodge for almost a week. It was the fear of not knowing, of having something taken away without notice. I should have felt sorry for her, but instead all there was was anger. The urge to force my mother in front of a mirror and make her look until she saw something she recognised, a version of herself that lived unhaunted.

The first man my mother dated after the death of my father was an electrician with yellow teeth. He drank his coffee like sludge, thick mugs of it that made him reek. He'd shown up at my school one afternoon and said he was there to take me home. His jumper was stained, gut pressing, stretching the fabric so I caught an embarrassing glimpse of hair above his belt line. I'd gone with him, forgetting every preventative video they'd shown us in class, handing him my backpack and climbing into the passenger seat. No one had stopped us and, besides, I'd been curious to see what might happen. Whether I'd make the headlines if he killed me. He didn't say anything as he drove, which might have frightened me if he hadn't seemed to know the way to my house so well. There were takeaway cartons scattered across the dashboard, glossy slicks of dried mayonnaise stinking the air. I went fishing in the glove compartment, glancing at this strange man to see if he'd stop me, and found a couple of crumpled magazines, more takeaway remnants and one of those multitools used for camping. When we arrived home, my mother greeted me as if everything was perfectly normal. But there was something in the way she simpered, giggling when this man touched her bottom on his way to the bathroom, that made me feel sorry for her.

After the electrician there were others, although they never stayed for long. Men who were kind or not, who smirked when I came out of the shower or tried to help me with my homework. I dealt with each of them carefully, like I would a wild fox that had wandered into the house. Giving them a wide berth, checking to make sure they didn't piss on anything.

*

I waited two days before calling the number Helen had given me. The ink on the napkin had blurred a little but was still legible. I felt nervous dialling, although I wasn't sure why. Held the phone very close to my ear and then seemed to catch myself, going instead to the fridge and helping myself to one of my mother's Diet Cokes, as if the nonchalance of one act could follow into the next.

It rang. I sipped my drink, sweetener washing to the back of my mouth. The fizz from the can almost eclipsed the sound of someone speaking, so for a moment I wasn't sure if it was that I heard or someone breathing.

'Hello?' I said.

There was no response, although I was certain now I could hear a voice on the other end of the line. Breathing or smoking or laughing. 'My friend gave me this number,' I went on. 'She said you might have a spare room available.'

'Your friend,' the voice said. A woman.

'Her sister lived with you for a few months, I think.'

'Good for her.'

I opened my mouth, closed it. This wasn't what I'd been expecting. 'I'm not a smoker.' The inexplicable urge to impress this woman, to gain her favour. 'And I don't have any pets. A single bed would be fine.'

'What's your name?' the woman asked. Something almost familiar about the way her voice rolled up the last syllable at the end.

'Iris.'

'I'm sorry, Iris,' she said. 'I don't think I can help you.'

4

When Nathan and I broke up – properly, I mean: for good – neither of us cried. We were not those types of people. Even when my father died, I didn't remember crying – although perhaps I did and had buried the memory, somewhere dark and quiet where it couldn't be easily accessed. Nathan wasn't one of those men who considered crying effeminate, but nor did he show any grand gesture of emotion either. He'd smile politely at birthday gifts without really investigating them, so you never knew if you had bought the right thing, and never revealed when he was in pain. Once, he disappeared for almost a day, and when he came back I noticed one of his teeth was missing. He shrugged and told me it had been bothering him for a few weeks and he'd decided to have it pulled.

So I didn't cry, although I wished that I had. Wasn't that what bodies were for? Physical commemorations of our emotions, literal outpourings. To cry would have been an acknowledgement of the life we'd built and subsequently dismantled. But that wasn't our style. There was never a world-ending confrontation between us, no clear event I could point to and say: yes, that was the end.

Rather, there were microcosms. Little moments I would pick over weeks, months later, and scour for their portent.

Going for breakfast at the local garden centre and asking Nathan to order for me while I went to the toilet; coming back to find he'd chosen eggs royale even though I was allergic to salmon. When I'd asked him about it, he said it had been a simple mistake.

We broke up multiple times without realising it. A gradual dissection of our lives. Separating our CD collection into mine and his, going to social events alone. Never volunteering the information that I was in a relationship unless asked, so that when he finally asked me to go there was an air of readiness about it.

What I'm trying to say is, sometimes things get away from you.

When I told my mother it was over with Nathan, she asked me if I wanted to put my head in her lap. I told her yes, knowing better than to turn down such a rare offer, and made appreciative noises as she stroked my hair with blunted fingers. She promised things could be mended between me and Nathan, that it was important to try. Of course, when she said those things she was not really talking to me but to herself, making assurances about her own marriage that were years out of date. She'd never taken off her wedding ring and now couldn't: her fingers were fatter than before, the skin growing around the ring so the only way for it to be removed was with some kind of saw.

*

Three weeks passed. I tried calling the number again, but nobody picked up. I'd stay on the phone, sometimes for nearly ten minutes, convinced if I hung up that would be the moment someone on the other end of the line – the woman

I'd spoken to – would notice and run to answer. When no one did, I asked Helen if she could find out more about the place her sister had stayed. Whether it was a hostel, or some kind of retreat. If she knew anyone who lived there now. Helen was eager to help, jumping on my first real attempt at getting myself together, but didn't have any further information, and her sister was now living in Italy.

I began calling at different times of the day, early and then late. Once at three in the morning after drinking too much wine. Not fully knowing why it mattered so much, only that I mustn't stop, that I had to hear her voice again. Could even convince myself it was some sort of endurance test, an appraisal. It didn't matter that it didn't make sense, I just needed an answer.

At some point I left the house to grab a coffee. The man behind the counter at the café handed me a biscuit with my order, even though I hadn't asked for one, told me it was on the house. Something alarming about the way he smiled, slow and wide like he knew what I was thinking.

I sat down by the window and drank my coffee quickly, scalding the roof of my mouth. Turning the saucer around with my other hand, the biscuit taking on a bizarre significance. There was nothing stopping me from eating it. Perhaps I would eat it and tell him how much I enjoyed it, and he would say he was glad to hear it and ask for my phone number. It could be a fun story to tell our friends at dinner parties: the biscuit that brought us together. And yet there was something about the presumptuousness of it that pissed me off.

'Didn't you like it?' the man asked when he came to clear away my empty coffee cup.

'I didn't order it,' I told him.

When I arrived back home, I went upstairs to my bedroom and dialled the number again. Hope a stone in my throat as it rang, and rang.

This time, someone answered. It was the same woman as before, clicking her tongue before she spoke, already annoyed. I ducked my head around the corner, checking to make sure my mother wasn't listening.

'Yes?'

'Hello,' I said, the elation I felt at finally getting through to someone overtaken by the need to keep her listening. 'Please don't hang up. My name is Iris. I called before, about a spare room.'

'Called and called and called,' the other woman said.

'I can pay in advance. If you need it in cash, I can do that as well. I don't have any animals and I'm not allergic to them either.'

'There's such a thing as playing hard to get, you know. You don't want to come across as needy.'

'I think it's probably too late for that,' I told her. I pressed my lips tight, but even then I couldn't stop the noise from leaking out of me. A low, desperate whine.

There was shuffling on the other end of the line, a rearranging.

'Are you free tomorrow?' the voice said.

5

My mother knew Tom, the owner of the off-licence, from church. She wasn't religious but enjoyed going to Mass, having somewhere to gossip and eat biscuits afterwards. There were ten years between them, enough that he didn't think of her in that way but still wanted to be a good Christian, offering me work when I was made redundant from my last job. I could only imagine what my mother must have said about me to him, that I was in need of a strong role model, someone to take me under their wing.

When I started working in the shop, it soon became obvious Tom had a predilection for hiring younger women and that, being in my thirties, I was the anomaly. The age difference only served to heighten my shame. It was clear the other girls viewed the shop as something transitional, a waiting room before they moved on to somewhere more interesting, university or the city. But for me it felt like a terminus, a room without windows or doors. The other girls seemed to sense this about me too, would only talk about the weather or their favourite sandwich filling, conversations they could wriggle out of easily, as if worried my inertia was contagious.

It was Wednesday and I'd arranged to meet the woman on the telephone here at the shop. It was only after I'd told her where I worked and what time I'd be there that I realised

I hadn't asked her name. It seemed trivial at the time, but now I worried I'd fallen at the first hurdle. I'd spent a long time getting ready that morning, curling my hair and then going over it again with straighteners when I hated the way it looked. Putting on make-up for the first time in weeks, mascara clumping my eyelashes together, lipstick borrowed from Nessa that made me look as if I'd smashed a beetroot against my mouth.

The shop door opened, triggering the electric bell overhead – not a delicate chime like the ones you heard in old movies but a synthetic two-note yowl. A woman walked in, dressed in a floral kimono and jeans. An electric current passed through me, the startle of recognition.

'Iris,' she said. Not a question, but a statement. A fact.

'I know you,' I said, an involuntary hand coming up to my throat. The pulse under my thumb beating a frantic tattoo.

'We spoke on the phone,' she replied, speaking slowly like I was a child.

I shook my head and smiled. 'I mean the other day. I'm not sure if you remember. Up on the downs? My dog had run away.'

Her eyes narrowed, taking me in properly now. I got the sense, not that she met many people but that it took a significant event for someone to lodge in her memory. As she came closer, I realised there were details about her I hadn't noticed before, or had wilfully misconstrued to satisfy my own image of her. She was shorter than I remembered and her skin was very dry, flakes of it peeling from her nose. Her hair fizzed with split ends.

'I remember,' she said after a moment.

It was strange, how the coincidence of her being both the

woman on the downs and the woman on the phone didn't seem odd to me, not just then. Rather, there was an inevitability about it, a slotting together of pieces.

'How is he, the dog?' she asked.

'He's fine,' I said. 'He's my mother's, actually.'

'Does he usually run off like that?'

Part of me hoped someone else would come into the shop. I was unused to this kind of scrutiny. Talking to her was like being plunged into a body of water, cold rushing into all my crevices. Every time she looked at me I could feel myself beginning to drown. 'No,' I told her. 'I don't think so.'

She smiled as if I'd told a joke.

I watched as she began walking down the wine aisle, reading the labels on each bottle. 'Do you sell those things that look like flowers?' She cupped her hands together, miming the shape.

'Artichoke hearts?' I stepped around the counter and pointed to a shelf of antipasti, Tom's attempt at appealing to the middle class. She took one of the jars and opened it. Stuck her fingers inside and popped a bristled globe into her mouth. I watched her eat, the tendon in her jaw jumping as she chewed. I realised she didn't intend to pay for it and that I wouldn't ask her to.

'Are you Italian?' she asked. 'Your hair, I wondered.' I reached an instinctive hand up, felt the dry and brittle strands. She was teasing me, she had to be.

I shook my head. 'No.'

She talked with her mouth full. 'I went to Rome once on a school trip. I couldn't believe my parents let me go. Would you trust an underpaid teaching assistant to keep an eye on your child, let alone thirty of them, for a week?' She ate another artichoke. 'I came back from it a stone heavier. My mother put me on a diet.'

'I've never been to Italy,' I told her. The furthest I'd ever got was a long weekend in France with Nathan and some friends. It had rained constantly, so we spent most of the time inside the rental flat, reading the detective paperbacks the owners had left behind.

The door opened again and a man walked in, lumbering towards the counter, dressed in a coat that was large and black and looked as if it contained a multitude of pockets. As he came closer, I saw him look between the two of us, a mixture of confusion and suspicion on his face, like he'd just walked into the middle of a crime being committed.

'I'm sorry,' I told her. 'I'll just be a second.'

Her eyes flicked towards the man and then away. She shrugged. 'Do your thing.'

The man set several bottles of cider down on the counter, the teeth-grating sound of rattling glass. He dug into one of his pockets, searching for coins. I tried not to look at her, but every now and again my eyes would drift towards her as she walked up and down the aisles, eating more artichokes. Her fingers wet and shiny with oil. There was something feral about her, the way she stomped around in her wellington boots, leaving clumps of mud behind. The sound of her breathing, so loud I could hear it from behind the counter. As she rounded the corner, I caught sight of a long scratch along her left leg. A perfect red line, angry-looking.

'The other girls who work here ask about my day,' the man said, glaring at me. I blinked at him as he held his hand out, cupped with coins. I realised he expected me to take them directly from him, rather than placing them down on the counter. He went on. 'Customer service is a part of your job. I come here every week, I give you my business. I don't have to, I could go somewhere else. The other girls, they ask.'

'How is your day?' I asked.

He shook his head, quietly loading his coat with the bottles and walking back out of the shop, rubbing his hands together as if trying to rid them of a stain.

*

If my father were alive, he'd tell me the same thing. That it was important to smile and ask people how their day was, even if you didn't mean it. Especially if you didn't mean it, because then it was worth more. He was an expert in subterfuge, could wheedle his way under anyone's skin – like a splinter – just by asking about their day. At dinner parties – when my parents still threw dinner parties – he would cup each guest's shoulder and ask them very seriously if they suffered from any allergies. And how could you deny a man like that, who enquired about your body's shortcomings in such an earnest manner? Never mind that he didn't bother to check before you drove all that way, or make any effort to set out gluten-free bread. You were just thankful for the glimmer of his attention, a single moment when you felt as if your requirements mattered. After that, how could you deny him anything?

To this day, I didn't know a single person who'd disliked my father. They flocked to him like magpies, drawn to his shine, and it was easier to tell yourself that it didn't matter, that you were content with only the glimpses of shadow left behind.

*

Once the man had left the shop she introduced herself to me. She told me her name was Hazel. Like the tree, the nut, the colour of a person's eye. I asked her if she wanted to come back to my house, where it would be quieter. Nobody would notice if I closed the shop for a couple of hours – Tom's lunch breaks usually overran. And even if he came back and saw the shop was closed, I could always say I'd had an emergency. I'd tell him my imaginary cat had been run over or that I'd got my period. I knew I was being greedy, that I wanted Hazel all to myself, without interruption. But there was a very real sense that if another distraction came along, the next time I looked for her she would be gone. Her attention was like eating a good oyster: delicious, but swallowed in a second.

Under the fluorescent light, I saw her frown before finally rolling her shoulders in a shrug. 'Okay.'

*

The house felt different with Hazel in it. When we arrived, she lingered in the hallway, eyeing the artwork hanging above the coat rack. 'That looks like something you'd find in a hospital,' she said. 'Do you know what I mean?'

I nodded and we went into the living room. Hazel did a lap of the perimeter, one hand brushing along the walls and furniture, her expression that of someone who had only recently arrived on the planet, was still learning the texture and shape of everything.

She went over to my mother's CD collection, wiped the dust from one of the plastic casings. 'Are these yours?' she asked.

'No. They're my mum's.'

'Do you get on with her?'

I wasn't sure how to answer that. She began examining the

CDs at random, putting them back in the wrong order – a very deliberate carelessness, like she was waiting for someone to challenge or stop her. But I couldn't, just carried on watching. This was what it meant to spend time with her, I was beginning to understand. A thousand tiny oversights.

'Do you want something to drink?' I asked. 'I think there's wine.'

Hazel shook her head. 'I don't drink.' She hadn't taken off her boots and the dried mud from them rained in chunks on to the carpet.

I went over to the window and lit a cigarette, a habit left over from university when Nessa and I would split a pack between us, more interested in the way the cigarette looked in our hands than actually smoking it. The flourish of our wrists, overwrought gesticulation. We'd huddle against the side of pubs and bars with the other smokers – the proper ones – waving our arms about as we talked, ash littering the hems of our dresses until someone pointed out that neither of us had taken a single puff of our cigarettes and that they'd burned down to the filter.

Hazel came and perched next to me. I offered her the cigarette but instead she leaned forward, inhaling directly from my fingers. Bending so her hair fell in slices across her face. Her presumption was staggering, made it seem impossible to dispute. I found myself adjusting the angle of my wrist, a slight movement so she'd be more comfortable.

'Don't tell anyone about this, okay, Iris?' Hazel said. 'I shouldn't really be smoking.'

'I won't,' I replied.

'So,' she said, blowing smoke through her front teeth. 'You're looking for somewhere to live.'

'Yes.' When she said nothing further, I scrambled to fill the silence. 'I broke up with my boyfriend a few weeks ago and I've been living here ever since. It's not really a sustainable situation.'

Hazel ducked underneath the window sash so her upper body was leaning outside. We were on the ground floor, but even so I felt a little gulp of panic that she might lose her balance and fall.

'It's good you weren't married,' she said, her voice muffled by the glass so I had to watch the shape of her mouth very carefully. 'Less paperwork.'

Until now everyone had treated my break-up with Nathan like an amputation, something vital removed from me. They spoke in low voices like I was a wounded animal, their pity piling on top of me. But Hazel made it seem as if I had been cut free of an impossible weight, and now there was no telling where I might go. Her assurance was infectious, made me laugh.

'How much did your friend tell you about where I live?' Hazel asked, ducking back into the living room.

'She said her sister stayed with you for a few weeks when she was having a hard time. And that when she came back she was – different. Better.'

A beat of silence. Then, 'Right.'

'Please,' I said, too afraid to touch her. Using my voice instead to carry my craving, the need to know more.

And so, this was what Hazel told me. Breach House was not a hostel. It was not a retreat either, or a wellness centre, or a refuge. It was a place for women. Buried away in the downs where it couldn't easily be found. Not everyone was made for it. Some only stayed for a matter of days, or hours. There was something about being around so much quiet, Hazel explained. People tended to fill the silence with unwanted thoughts, and in the end preferred the white noise of cities and apartment buildings. But, for some, Breach House was a raft. No, it was wet earth. Something to sink into.

'I didn't know places like that still existed,' I told her. 'It sounds perfect.' I smiled, trying to communicate how serious I was, to convince her that I could belong in a place like that. I could – I wanted to – be like her. 'I can pay in advance, if that helps,' I said.

Hazel said it was not up to her. That there were steps to follow, conversations to be had, but she would let me know. She stood up from the windowsill and made her way back to the front door. I got up with her, knowing this time there was no way of keeping her but still desperate to cement myself in her favour.

'When I saw you on the downs the other day,' I said. 'You were picking morels, weren't you?'

She seemed surprised. 'You know about mushrooms?'

'They're rare for these parts. My father and I went picking once when I was a girl, only he ended up finding false morels. They can be hard to tell apart. He was ill for two weeks.'

In the hallway Hazel gave the artwork one last glance before stepping out on to the street. 'Well,' she said. 'Thank you for your hospitality, Iris. I'll let you know.'

I was learning to love the sound of my name in her mouth, the final syllable drawn out and serpentine.

I-rissss.

6

Two weeks passed, and in that time I used distraction as a salve, taking on extra shifts at work and agreeing to assemble a new bookcase for my mother's living room, which took me a couple of days. Somewhere along the way the instructions had been lost, or had never existed in the first place, and I'd had to feel my way into the construction, slotting pieces together and then dismantling them, like a game of Jenga. I kept the TV on in the background, the constant trickle of adverts and credit rolls eventually bleeding into my sleep, kaleidoscoping my dreams. Occasionally a nature documentary would come on and I'd stop what I was doing and watch it, the presenter's calm narration layered over scenes of massacre. Recently in the news there had been a controversy after it was discovered that a camera crew had saved a drowning elephant calf while filming a nature documentary. It was unethical to disrupt nature's course, experts said. That humanity had meddled enough already. The correct thing to do would have been to let it drown. I tried to imagine myself in that situation, poised behind a camera lens with the weight of such a decision, and couldn't. Found that it was much easier to imagine myself as the one drowning.

Occasionally thoughts of Hazel made it through, my mind flooding with her image. Untethered flashes of skin, hair, the sound of her voice. Once it started, there was no stopping it – I had to find the nearest chair or surface and sit down until the moment had passed, until I was myself again. I couldn't stop thinking about the self-entitlement with which she moved through the world. She never would have ended up in my position, I knew. Living a life that was edged in boundary. She was too fearless for that. I had the growing urge to prove to her that I was not meant for this life either, that I'd ended up here in error. I had vivid daydreams about swimming in the sea with her, stealing ice cream from one of those trucks, not able to eat it fast enough, the cones melting in our fists.

Once the bookcase was done, I shunted it against the wall and began filling it with my mother's things, and mine. I was curious to see what my life's assortment looked like next to hers. Most of the interesting objects I owned – my Balinese wood carving of a rabbit, a first edition of *Catch-22* – were still at Nathan's house. Without them, I was a collection of old VHS tapes, unused notebooks, scented candles. I could have been anyone.

*

It rained the day Hazel finally came back.

I was at work, mopping the sage linoleum when the shop door opened – and I knew. Could already parse her footsteps from everyone else's; not loud, but unquiet. There was a difference. I willed myself not to look straight away, my hands tightening around the mop until my knuckles popped white. She remained where she was, not speaking. Finally, I rested the mop against the wall.

'I'm kidnapping you,' she said matter-of-factly.

'Where are we going?' I asked.

Hazel smiled, waded further into the shop. Her familiar wellies printing fresh mud onto the floor. Her hair was tangled in a braid today, revealing the full shape of her face, the hammock of pudge underneath her chin. The rain had silvered her skin, making it appear almost translucent. 'You wanted to see where I live. Here's your chance.'

'Now?' I was alone in the shop, though my shift had only just begun.

She made a point of rolling her eyes. 'I'm double parked. It's now or never.'

Years of caution had been conditioned into me, preventative videos in school of hapless girls being drugged and taken. Stories in the local paper about women who went missing and turned up in pieces. But the truth was: I couldn't help but feel flattered. That Hazel must have been watching me, waiting until she knew I was alone. The possibility of her calculation obliterated by the fact she'd stood outside in the rain for me.

*

What I learned from one of the nature documentaries: the green heron, native to north and central America, lures its prey by dropping bait into the water. Often, it will use smaller fish to tempt larger ones to the surface. No one knows how the green heron developed this behaviour, although it's thought it learned by observing humans.

7

The car she led me to was rusted and filled with junk, wooden crates of potatoes rolling around in the back. I climbed into the passenger seat, my finger slipping through the frayed upholstery into the foam underneath. I was feeling a little drunk, unsure what was about to happen next. Hazel seemed to sense my apprehension, placing the key in the ignition but not turning it right away. Giving me the chance to leave. I put on my seatbelt, and said nothing.

We followed the road that led through town. Hazel was a bad driver, merging into lanes without looking, her hands loose on the wheel. I watched as other drivers slammed their feet on the brakes, swerving to narrowly avoid her, but she didn't seem to notice, or else didn't care. Was used to people bending out of shape for her. I pressed my toes into my shoes, kept tugging on my seatbelt to make sure it worked.

Civilisation gradually fell away, the road swelling and contracting as we sank further into the downs. The feminine spread of land, ribs of forest and the Stour, which ran like a silty vein throughout. I pressed my head against the window, a sense of relief as I soon lost track of where we were. 'Blythe can be intimidating when you first meet her,' Hazel told me. 'But you're going to like her.'

I learned that Blythe ran the place where Hazel was taking

me, that she was in charge. The way she spoke about her reminded me of the way my father used to talk about John Paul Jones, all reverence and magic and a little fear. 'She's creating something special. She sees the world for what it is, you know? It's like she has this knowledge buried deep inside her. You'll understand when we get there.'

'Does she know that I'm coming?' I asked. 'I mean, is it okay that you're bringing me?'

'Don't worry,' Hazel told me. 'You're with me.'

Warm words; honeyed.

After a while a familiar sickness sank into me. I'd never been good in cars. Most people accepted this about me, chalking it up to how my father died, when actually the fear came much earlier – if 'fear' was the right word at all. I was eleven and had just started my first year of secondary school. My mother arranged for me to carpool with a couple of other children who were also starting at the school. One of the girls, Jessica, had been in the same English set as me in primary school and so naturally I gravitated towards her, assuming that our shared capabilities put us in tow. I'd always thought of Jessica as someone like me: quiet, thoughtful, desperate for kin. We seemed like a natural fit. For a week or two we stuck together, sitting next to each other in the back seat, trying to find some common ground. It soon became apparent, however, that we were very different people, and that I'd confused her derision for quietness. She was not my friend but a tourist. And then she was something else entirely, her and the other girls at school beginning to change, a metamorphosis of rolled-up skirts up and Impulse body spray. The lumps under their shirts which began to form. Suddenly the morning carpool was a hostile place, where Jessica and the other girls would surreptitiously pinch the fat on my thighs or else the lack of my chest, babbling about things I did not understand.

It was my first taste of society, the tectonic shift of allegiance.

Hazel slowed the car to a crawl and veered from the main road on to a long, roughly hewn driveway. At the end was a stone-walled farmhouse, smaller than I'd imagined, maybe three or four bedrooms. White flowers grew all along the front, unbloomed so they resembled a string of teeth, drooling along the brick towards what looked like a conservatory. The front door was in need of repainting. On the right-hand side was a placard that read *Breach House*.

It was all so painfully normal that for a moment I wondered if I'd misinterpreted something.

'Here we are,' Hazel said, popping her seatbelt.

I got out of the car. Although we were well away from the motorway, I could still hear the distant roar of traffic. Looked behind me to check if there was another car coming down the driveway. 'Sound travels differently here,' Hazel explained. 'Sometimes you can hear people from miles away, having a conversation like they're standing right next to you. It's weird.'

As Hazel led me around the side of the house, the rest of the farm gradually revealed itself. An allotment frothing with green, a barn which I later learned held a couple of pigs, too old and tough to slaughter. Woodland hemming all of it in, the sarcastic clatter of magpies up in the blackthorn, snapping their beaks. As we passed by the allotment, a couple of women stopped what they were doing to look at us, their arms and faces leoparded with dirt. One of them raised a hand in a half-wave.

We went inside the house, into the kitchen. A few more women were sat around a large dining table playing five-card draw, talking so quickly it could have been a foreign language, the same whiff of bedlam about them as Hazel. They seemed comfortable like this, absent-mindedly shucking the black from under their nails and flicking it on to the floor.

'This is Iris,' Hazel said, sitting down without any further explanation. The others didn't seem to need it, clamouring to make space. I squeezed between two of them.

'We're in the middle of a game, otherwise I'd cut you in,' one of them told me.

I sat and watched as they played but couldn't keep up with the quick movements of their hands, how they slapped their cards down on the table and elbowed each other when they thought someone was cheating.

'What do you think of our home so far?' the woman next to me asked, pressing just below my elbow to get my attention. She was younger than the others, couldn't have been more than eighteen. Her voice was pitched deliberately higher so it sounded babyish. She told me her name was Pearl, the other two Molly and Ambika.

'It's nice,' I said, the words coming out soft and futile, although Pearl nodded, still holding on to me. I was unused to this kind of intimacy, given so freely without expecting anything in return. The realisation that this girl just wanted to make me feel good.

'It can be a lot to take in,' she told me. 'I remember how overwhelming it was when I first came.'

'You find everything overwhelming,' Molly said.

'No I don't,' Pearl said, her voice rising.

'You cried the first time you saw a rat eating out of the bins.'

'Can someone pass me the salt?' Ambika asked, eating a plate of sliced tomato. I got the impression she was cutting in before Molly could say anything further to upset Pearl, playing the mediator. 'Do you want some?'

I put a slice in my mouth, chewed slowly. It was very good, supple and bright, the salt prickling my tongue. 'It's delicious,' I told them.

'We grow everything ourselves,' Molly said. 'None of that processed crap, pumped full of hormones and whatever-the-fuck else.' She placed the last of her cards down on the table. 'I win again.'

Ambika brushed a hand along Molly's wrist, different to how Pearl had touched me. 'Let Iris play, too.'

I felt myself blush as Molly caught Ambika's hand and kissed the palm of it. 'All right then, once more around the block.'

The cards felt slippery in my hands. I didn't really know the rules of the game we were playing, not that it mattered. I was simply happy to be among these women, dirty and loud and entirely sure of themselves. It was intoxicating.

'So, Iris,' Molly began, making a pair of clubs. 'How do you know Hazel?'

'Well, a friend gave me the number for Breach House and I rang it and she answered, but we met once before that, on the downs . . .' I hated how frantic I sounded, closed my mouth.

Ambika smiled. 'Have you met Blythe yet?'

'No,' I replied. 'Hazel told me she's in charge?'

They nodded. 'I wouldn't be alive if it wasn't for her,' Molly said, throwing her cards aside, the game now forgotten. 'I'd be lying in a gutter somewhere.' Ambika kissed Molly's shoulder, but it was clear they all felt the same gratitude towards Blythe, a misty expression glazing each of their faces. Even Hazel sat a little straighter at the mention of her name.

'You should stay for dinner,' Pearl told me. 'She'll be back by then.'

'Where is she now?'

Pearl shrugged. 'She goes walking. There's only one car between us, which we're really only supposed to use for supply runs. Blythe says walking helps her figure things out, puts everything into perspective. Sometimes she's gone the whole day. But she'll be back for dinner. You'll stay until then, won't you?'

'I'd like to,' I said. Pearl smiled, her mouth spreading to reveal a brace of decayed teeth, her central incisors, which jutted out on to her bottom lip. She seemed to catch herself, covering her mouth with one hand. The shame was so familiar to me I couldn't help but look away, which I realised afterwards must have made her feel worse.

Hazel shuffled her cards. 'Iris might have other places to be.' I felt the cut of her words keenly, the possibility that she didn't want me here any more. She'd been quiet since introducing me to everyone and I wondered now if I'd done something wrong, unwittingly revealed some defect that meant I did not belong at Breach House.

The kitchen door opened and a woman older than the others appeared, carrying a wooden crate filled with vegetables. My heart tripped a beat, for a moment thinking this was Blythe but realising that it couldn't be: I would have seen it on the other women's faces. Still, there was a deference in the way they lowered their voices when she came in, Pearl standing and asking if she could do anything to help.

'Do I look incapable?' the woman said, not unkindly. When she saw me sitting at the table, she nodded. 'Looks like you've picked up another stray. I'm Sarah. Has anyone offered you a cup of tea? Sometimes they forget to ask.'

She put the kettle on before I could answer, one of those old ones you boiled on the stove. I enjoyed watching the process of it, the whistle of steam. Sarah, I soon discovered, couldn't help but mother. She did all of the cooking at Breach House, one of the only chores that was not split evenly among the women. Sometimes, if she was overworked, she would allow you to peel potatoes or chop garlic, but even then it felt like she was doing you a favour rather than the other way around. The kitchen smelled perpetually of her good cooking, peppers and tomatoes rendered down to sauce, the warmth of bread. When she served the tea, it was with home-made biscuits.

*

Nessa and I liked to watch horror movies when we were at university. Blockbusters were still around, despite feeling irrelevant even back then, and we would go every Friday afternoon after class, wandering slowly down the carpeted aisles, looking for something to watch. Our favourites were about teenage girls trapped in warehouses who had to escape, or else zombies. We'd start by choosing two movies each, fiercely debating the reasons why we'd chosen them, until eventually the selection was whittled down to two, and then one. Usually we watched whatever Nessa had picked out. I'd learned she was a sore loser and wouldn't properly watch whatever movie I'd chosen, getting up from the sofa multiple times to make more popcorn or shouting upstairs to one of our other roommates, afterwards insisting that it wasn't her fault the movie was terrible, it just was. So I let her choose, and in return she bought liquorice cables.

After a while patterns began to form. The same mistakes were made. The girls ran upstairs instead of outside the house, cutting off any chance of escape. They trusted their boyfriends, who told them it was safe to swim in the lake. It got to the point where Nessa and I could divine what would happen by watching the first scene alone, whether the monster or serial killer would be an avatar for the victims' internal fears (always) or if the girl would survive to the end (toss-up). It was depressing how quickly we became desensitised to gore, the inertia of severed limbs and bashed-in skulls. The same cheesy lines that were delivered again and again. More than anything though, we became scathing. Part of us anticipating the moment when one of the characters would slip up and meet their grisly end just so we could point to each other and say: *stupid, what were they thinking?*

It would be years before I met Hazel. Years before I dropped everything to visit Breach House for the first time, despite knowing nothing about her, not really. Only knowing that I couldn't say no, that I would do whatever it took to stay. The same instinct that drove you further inside the house instead of running far away.

8

After we'd finished drinking our tea, Hazel stood up from the table and looped her arm through my elbow. 'Come on,' she said. 'They start to grate on you if you spend too long with them.'

'Fuck you,' Molly said, pleasantly enough.

I thrilled at Hazel's touch, pliant as she pulled me into the hallway. It was nearly impossible to move without tripping over someone's boots, mess scattered everywhere. A coat rack heaved with wax jackets, foul-smelling from the recent rainfall. Women spilled out of what seemed to be the living room, a few more emerging from the conservatory at the end of the hall. All busy with some chore or other, an infectious sense of industry about them: I found myself wanting to follow, to put myself to use. But Hazel tugged at me again and led me upstairs.

Her bedroom gave nothing away, no artwork or CDs or scented candles. It could have been anyone's. 'This side of the house is better,' she said, sitting down on a double bed. There was a granny square blanket on top, a patchwork of different-coloured yarns. 'Sometimes the pigs squeal at night if something's spooked them, usually foxes. They make a sound like they're being tortured. But it's not so loud over here.'

'That sounds horrifying.'

Hazel smiled. 'Do you want something to drink? I have a mini fridge.'

I said okay and she leaned over the side of the bed, her hair cascading over her face. The mini fridge was underneath. She offered me a glass of what looked like iced tea, a greasy film floating on top. I sipped it carefully, made appreciative noises even though it tasted bad. Hazel leaned against the headboard, stretching her legs out so that her left ankle brushed against my hip. I glanced down, long enough to notice that she didn't shave, her skin covered in a thick down. She reached up and picked the dry skin from her bottom lip, a drop of blood beading forth, dark and shiny. Her insouciance seemed to unlock something inside me, made me feel foolish for the hours spent carefully shaving my legs, finding the right shade of foundation for my skin.

'Are you worried about your work?' she asked. 'Do you think you'd be fired if your boss came back and saw you weren't there?'

'I don't know,' I said.

'If it was me and I saw my employee wasn't where they were supposed to be, I'd be pissed off.'

I scrutinised her face for a sign that she was joking, but she was busy picking at a loose thread in the blanket, pulling until one of the squares began to unravel. She'd told me it was now or never. That if I wanted to see Breach House, I had to go with her there and then. She could have visited me at my mother's house, when she knew I wasn't working, but that wasn't the point. She'd wanted to see if I would drop everything to go with her, I thought to prove, if not loyalty, then willingness. But I was quickly learning that Hazel's intentions were continually in flux. Suddenly, leaving work wasn't an act of commitment, but of flakiness.

As if she could hear my thoughts, Hazel tapped me gently with her foot. 'I'm just fucking with you.' She sat back up and went over to the small desk by the window. A mason jar filled with flowers sat on top. I didn't know what kind they were. 'So, what do you think? Is it what you expected?'

'No,' I confessed. 'Although I'm not sure what I was expecting. Everyone seems nice.'

'Yeah,' Hazel said.

'How many women are there?'

Hazel lifted a shoulder. 'It depends. Some days as many as forty, but there's only about a dozen of us who actually live on the farm. The others have families, or jobs they don't want to give up.'

'And that's okay with Blythe?'

'They bring in more money,' Hazel explained. 'We still have bills to pay.'

'I like Sarah,' I said.

The corners of Hazel's mouth twisted in a half-smile. 'Her and Blythe go way back. The farm was Sarah's originally. She used to live here with her family. And then one day she got sick, the kind of sick you're not supposed to get better from. While her kids were fighting over the inheritance or whatever, she ended up meeting Blythe and – she got better.'

It was unclear exactly what Sarah had been dying of or what Blythe did to help, only that it had happened. Any doubts I might have had were drowned in the cream of Hazel's reverence, the way she spoke about Blythe with such surety. 'After that, Sarah invited Blythe to live with her on the farm, so that they had a place to help other women.'

'And no men?' I asked.

She shook her head. 'No men.'

I watched as she twirled one of the flower stems.

'I feel I should tell you,' she continued, not looking at me, 'I almost didn't come to get you today. I thought for a long time about it and decided maybe it would be best if you found somewhere else to live.'

I tried not to let hurt show on my face. Watched as she continued fiddling with the flower, her thumb and forefinger pinching the stem, harder and harder until chlorophyll began to ooze from it, staining the water green.

Before, I'd viewed Breach House as a simple change in circumstance, moving from one location to another – a way to get out from under my mother. And it was still that, but now I'd met the women, seen how they lived, new possibilities were beginning to unfurl in front of me. The possibility of change, to become someone else. I wanted Hazel to believe I could be like her.

So, then, a spike of courage: 'But you changed your mind in the end. Why?'

I didn't think she would answer. For a moment it seemed as if she wouldn't, was too busy examining her hand, edged in green. After a moment she placed one of her fingers inside her mouth, sucking the residue from the flower. I couldn't tell whether she found the flavour unpleasant.

'You came across as too desperate and I wasn't sure you'd be able to cope, living somewhere like this.' She stared at me frankly, stroking her tongue along the palate of her mouth a few times to get rid of the taste. 'But I'm trying to get better at listening to signs. When you pointed out we'd met before,

I thought someone somewhere must be trying to tell me something. And I like you.'

'Oh,' I said.

'Yes,' she continued, as if I'd asked a question. 'You're a good person, I can tell. Scared, but good.'

I told her that was nice to know, but Hazel was no longer listening. She was staring out the window, her face gone slack. Something crept into the room with us then, a feeling of displacement. I took a step forward just as Hazel pushed herself out of the chair, turning to me and saying, 'She's back.'

*

After university, a few months after I'd started going out with Nathan, I asked him to watch a horror movie with me. His aversion to nearly all media was beginning to grate on me even then, his insistence that most novels were too self-congratulatory and movies were all remakes now. He only bought a television after I begged, unnerved by how quiet his flat was without it, his furniture which had nothing to point at.

I chose *The Texas Chainsaw Massacre*, the one that had come out a few years before, not the original, which he said proved his point about remakes. I could have picked something else – something less severe – but I suppose I wanted to see how he'd react. There had to be something quantifiable about a man's reaction to watching someone being sawn in half.

In the opening scene, a woman pulled a gun out from between her legs and shot herself in the mouth. The camera travelled through the back of her skull so you could see the other victims reacting to it, their faces pulled wide with horror. I glanced sideways at Nathan, expecting him to be upset, but instead he blinked and asked how they managed to achieve the shot, whether a special device had to be created to slide through the woman's head.

If Nathan were here now, that's what he'd want to know. How the special effects were achieved. Because there was something supernatural about the way sound seemed to suddenly cloister, condensing, so that all I could hear was my own breathing, wet and uneven. The light which cracked the sky open. All of it, a heralding.

I stood next to Hazel by the window and looked out. A group of women came rushing from the allotment – the dull rainfall of spades and watering cans as they abandoned their work on the spot – towards the woods, where a figure had emerged.

I'd never seen a woman so large. Even from here, I could tell she stood over six feet tall and was thickly built; strong. Her short hair combed back to reveal the shape of her skull. She was barefoot. I said to Hazel she must have been cold or in pain, but Hazel said that was how Blythe always walked. There were some rules that didn't apply to her.

As Blythe made her way towards the house, trailed by the other women, she looked straight up at the window and smiled, as if she'd been expecting me.

I went downstairs with Hazel. Up close, Blythe's mouth was feline, wide and permanently curved towards her eyes. 'Iris,' she said, already knowing my name. Easy to imagine she'd divined it rather than being told by one of the women. 'Welcome to Breach House.' Her voice was deep, almost masculine. It caught in the crevices of the kitchen, circled back to me in a low thrum. My name in her mouth felt crucial, as if by speaking it she could summon something from deep within me. 'Have my girls been taking care of you?' she asked.

'Yes,' I replied, cutting a sideways glance at Hazel. I was frightened of saying the wrong thing and embarrassing her, sensed that Blythe would only offer her approval once.

'I'm glad to hear it,' she said. 'Did they offer you something to drink?'

I told her Sarah had made tea.

Blythe nodded and smiled. 'That's good.' Without saying anything else, she reached for my hands, turning them over so the palms were facing up. It was impossible not to feel diminished by her, how easily she was able to reposition me, her thumbs which were the same length as my middle fingers. I watched as she conducted her examination, searching for some unknown quality. Her cat's mouth thinning. Finally, she said, 'Too clean.'

*

And so I followed Hazel outside, my too-clean hands flexing by my side as she led me into the allotment. Cucumbers bent the vines they grew on, almost ready for harvesting, dill sprouting nearby for it to be pickled with. Heads of lettuce curled like the undercarriages of snails, planted in neat rows. Everywhere, the smell of dirt – of growth.

Hazel pointed to a patch of ground and told me to start pulling weeds. I blinked, waiting to see if she would say anything further. Getting on my knees when she didn't. It was a test, I understood. Blythe, the other women, they were waiting to see what I was made of. If I would bloody myself for them, or make my excuses and leave. I could see now it took a certain type of woman to live at Breach House, and

I wanted to believe I could be one of them, loud and strong and capable.

I sank my bare hands into the earth, felt my way into the roots. As I worked, Hazel knelt beside me and named each plant, dandelion and smooth cat's ear, fat hen, which required both hands to wrench from the ground. Buttercup leaves with their large, spindly networks that coated the ground and were immensely satisfying to dislodge. I continued to reach further down, straining until I felt my fingernails begin to tear. Crescents of pain which I could almost convince myself felt satisfying. Right then, all I wanted to do was sink into it, away from everything else, this life that had somehow built up around me – cheap takeaways and cardboard boxes with my name on them, the way my mother looked at me when she thought I couldn't see.

'You have to pull out the bulbs as well,' Hazel told me. 'Otherwise the willowherb runs rampant. They bed deeper than you'd think.'

I used my body's weight to press further down until I was almost up to my wrists – my elbows – in soil. Gasping when something sharp dug into my finger, a rock or piece of glass. I quickly snapped my mouth shut, careful not to look at Hazel just then, fearing what would happen if I did. Was she facing me? It was difficult to tell.

One last plunder. Pushing through the pain, a deliverance of sweat and soil until, eventually, I popped a bulb out of the ground, the size and shape of a pickled onion.

'That's good,' Hazel said, and then: 'Show me.' Gesturing for my hand, the one now rimed with dirt and blood. She stroked a clean line across the back of it, brushing along the tributary of veins and tendon until she reached my index finger. An angry red line slashed across it, resembling a mouth. She made a small noise in the back of her throat, sad-sounding. For a moment I thought she might kiss it better, my stomach clenching, before her grip suddenly changed, grew tighter. Squeezing until fresh blood began to run. I felt tears coming but knew better than to shed them.

Finally, she let go. 'There,' she told me. 'That's better.'

9

When Nathan first suggested we move in together, what he really meant was would I move into his uncle's house with him. A dead uncle, not particularly well loved, who hadn't managed to last in either one of his marriages long enough to produce offspring, the house coming to Nathan through oversight rather than any deep affection. After the uncle's funeral, I went with Nathan to see the house, eager to support him, but also to visualise myself living there, to see if I could be the sort of woman I knew he wanted me to be. We'd been together a year by then, long enough that I'd got a feel for his soft bones, the regular dependency with which he returned to his family home for roast dinners and fresh laundry. He liked to be coddled, was considered a good son because of it. Nathan's mother was so unlike my own, rose-scented and large, an overspilling of flesh that was impossibly comforting, suggesting decades of shepherd's pies and birthday cake. Her bathroom cabinet always contained an unopened box of *Nice'nEasy* that promised one hundred per cent grey coverage. She made a point of including me in everything, over-explaining private jokes (which had the opposite effect and made me feel like a stranger) and buying the same number of Christmas presents for me as for her own children. Without me having to ask, she gave me her secret recipe for macaroni cheese, lent me her lipstick on a night out, ironed the creases from my linen skirt. Of course, I knew her suburban love came from a place of self-preservation. She was making sure I could take care of her son, showing me what real duty of care looked like. Good mothers know when to lay out honey instead of vinegar. I could only imagine the stories Nathan must have told her about my own mother, the worry it would have caused: mothers always wanted to see a little bit of themselves in their children's partner.

The house, then. It was quiet and beige apart from the bathroom, which was green. Nathan said there wasn't much point in buying new furniture when the house had everything we needed already, and I found it difficult to argue the point, worried I'd seem callous or ungrateful, determined instead to bask in the fact he wanted to live together at all. It was the biggest step I'd ever taken in a relationship and I marvelled at the banality of it, conversations about boilers and council tax, remembering to close the bathroom door before going to the toilet. I would be the partner Nathan's mother expected, the kind my own had failed to be. I learned how to use an iron, watching daytime reality television while pressing the wrinkles out of Nathan's shirts. Spent weeks perfecting my recipe for baked cod so that I was ready whenever Nathan suggested a last-minute dinner party, an unreasonable euphoria gripping me every time he told his friends he'd rather eat my recipe than a restaurant's. Our perfectly presented life. At night, Nathan's hand mapping the constellation of freckles across my body, insisting he could see Cassiopeia between my shoulder blades, Gemini along my thigh.

It was all right, I told myself, that none of the furniture was mine. The ugly drinks cabinet still stocked with the dead uncle's beer and brandy, his old golf clubs. Sitting down at night to watch television and being hyper-aware of the imprint of his backside in the leather sofa, my hip bones sliding into the sink, always a degree uncomfortable.

*

By the time we finished in the allotment, our hands and knees were covered in dirt. Hazel seemed unbothered by this, wiping her hands on the fabric of her shirt. Tugging her neck towards the house in a gesture for me to follow. I stuck close, pathetically grateful that she would help, that she would help me. As we made our way back, I could feel one of my fingernails had split down to the quick, was beginning to curl at the corner, wanting to come apart. I eased my thumb underneath, levered more of the nail until there was a bite of pain. I looked up and saw the women's faces pressed against the kitchen window, pale ghosts, their breath thick on the glass.

'Come on,' Hazel said, leading me with one hand around my wrist. Was her grip tighter than necessary? I didn't want to overanalyse every interaction between us and yet I was getting so good at it. She guided me into the kitchen, presenting me to Blythe like a nut, something to be cracked open. Blythe made a gesture and the meaning became obvious: I showed her my hands a second time, now bruised and bloodied. The women hadn't left their place by the window. I knew they wouldn't speak or move until Blythe had passed her judgement. Decided whether I was worthy.

She took my hand in her own, thumbed some of the blood away from my finger. 'I used to have hands just like these,' she told me. Her voice a low purr. 'All soft and pale. My mother told me it was important to look after them because they were the first part of your body to age, and if my hands looked old too soon it would spell disaster. I'd slather them in so much hand cream my fingers would chafe.' She looked at me and smiled. I couldn't help but smile back, a call-and-response that she seemed to invoke in everyone. If she'd begun to cry just then, I would have shed tears for her.

'But look at my hands now. Feel them.' She repositioned us so that I was the one holding her hand, so large and rough it felt like a paw. I looked down and saw a latticework of scars covering her skin up to the wrist, nails that were hard and blunt. A chunk of skin was missing from her third finger and I felt along the divot, sensing cartilage. They were ugly hands, and strong. 'It takes work to have hands like mine,' she continued, towering over me. 'Not everyone is up to the task. Everyone who comes here thinks they are. They want to be a part of something special without putting their heart into it, but that doesn't work for me. It only works if all of you is here.'

I nodded, my vision beginning to tunnel until the kitchen and other women fell away and it was just me and Blythe. The hypnotic cant of her voice, how my hands seemed to disappear inside hers. 'I made this place for women like you, Iris. Did you know that?' I shook my head. 'Special women, hurting women. I bet you're sad, aren't you, Iris?' I thought of my mother, and Nathan, and Nessa with her endless optimism that you'd get what you wanted if you just *tried*. I thought of my father and the kind of man he'd been. He would have laughed if he'd seen me here.

'That's okay,' she continued. 'I used to be sad too. It's hard to be happy when the world treats us so badly, isn't it? You can be happy here. Do you want to be happy, Iris?'

Everything she said was beginning to make sense, in the way all things could make sense when spoken with enough force. And there was a part of me that wanted to believe everything Blythe said, that Breach House was the answer to a question I hadn't realised I'd asked.

My gaze searched the room for Hazel. Her eyes narrowed – with doubt, with hope, I wasn't sure. It looked as if a speck of my blood had somehow made it on to the corner of her mouth. She licked it away.

I turned back to Blythe. 'Please,' I said, quietly so that only she would hear. 'Please, yes.'

*

I'd heard so many stories about the uncle – from Nathan and his family – that it was difficult sometimes to remember I'd never actually met him. His idiosyncrasies became familiar to me in a way that felt obscene. The particular way he ate his food, peeling pies and spring rolls apart – anything that resembled a shell – and spooning the innards into his too-large mouth. His decade-long subscription to *True Crime Magazine*, whose headlines always said something like 'Twisted doctor enjoyed watching his patients die.' Each issue explored the life and crimes of a famous serial killer, pages of black-and-white photographs etching their crime scenes in grained detail. From what I could tell, it had never been out of print.

The uncle's presence hovered web-like in the corner of every room. How could it not? I was sitting on his sofa, eating off his plate. An intruder in my own home. And so, after almost a year of living there, I decided to buy a new pair of curtains for the lounge. Wanting to see if it would transform the space, make it feel more like mine. They were not the sort of thing I would usually buy, tropical with a parrot motif – impossible to match with the pine furniture and brown carpet. When Nathan didn't mention them, I bought other things – a spider plant that began spilling out smaller versions of itself, a tumble dryer. He even agreed to replace the sofa. But there was always a part of me that felt as if I was overstepping my boundaries, committing some minor crime. Eventually it became difficult to believe it was just the two of us living there. I found myself starting at any little noise, instinctively turning towards the front door as if expecting the uncle to walk through and ask what we were doing in his house. It became difficult to sleep. At night, Nathan would press his hand into the small of my back and tell me to name all the rivers I could think of until eventually I stumbled into dream with the Cam, the Medway, the Itchen pouring out of my mouth.

*

When Blythe let go, the women rushed forward as if responding to an unspoken command, some frequency I wasn't yet attuned to. None of them had been discourteous, but it was only now I felt truly welcomed, like a permission had been granted. They gathered me into their arms, talking quickly and excitedly, their faces so close to mine I could make out every detail, the sebaceous cups of their chins and noses, split ends rendered somehow beautiful. I looked for Hazel through the press of bodies, the kitchen growing louder and smaller than it actually was, the radio's heavy thrum of music passing through my body in waves. Between a shoulder and an elbow I finally saw Hazel, standing in the corner, watching. Our eyes met and it was just like the first time I saw her, everything else dropping away until we were the only ones left. Her mouth began to move. What was it? She was saying something, but I couldn't hear her over the noise. I felt myself trying to pull away, to get closer so I could make out the shape of Hazel's words, but I soon lost sight of her, was smothered by the press of bodies, the fug of their body odour and sweet-breath, and something else, something that smelled like it came from the ground.

*

When Nathan and I finally broke up, there was no question about living arrangements. The house was in his name: he would stay and I would go. Some days later, I returned to pick up my things. Already the rosemary bush I'd planted in the front garden had grown leggy, its leaves turning pale and limp as it struggled and failed to find sunlight. I remember kicking the recycling bin, half hoping for the tell-tale clink of wine bottles, the suggestion of miserable nights alone. But no such luck. When he answered the door, he looked surprised to see me.

'Did we arrange something?' he asked. Already I'd been relegated to an acquaintance, someone who needed prior permission before showing up. He wore a damp towel around his shoulders and as he opened the door wider I caught a whiff of his deodorant, the purity of steam. He must have just come out of the shower. It still felt strange that I no longer knew when he did these routine things, the chores that made up a life, brushing his teeth and flossing, changing the batteries in the smoke detector. I could no longer earmark his day, predict what room he might go into next.

'I left some things behind,' I told him. 'I can come back another time.'

'No,' he said, making a point of stepping back to let me pass. 'Now is fine. Come in.'

I followed him into the living room, still hoping to find evidence that he was not coping without me. Dirty plates in the sink, unwashed laundry. But there was nothing, no detritus that suggested I was essential to his wellbeing. Nessa had always told me it was a good thing, not having to rely on your partner for happiness, but I'd always been clear about what I wanted: an obliterating symbiosis. A person I could not live without and who could not live without me.

'What happened to the curtains?' I asked.

'I thought you took them with you,' Nathan said. He'd hung the old set back up, a grey plaid that had a suckering effect, seemed to leach what little colour there was left in the room. I noticed he'd also covered the sofa with a throw. 'I know you bought them, so I just assumed you'd taken them for your new place.'

'I would have remembered if I'd taken them down,' I told him.

He smiled, gave an indifferent shrug. 'I'm sorry, I don't know.'

I looked around the room. It was exactly as I remembered it the first time Nathan showed me around, pine furniture and carpet. The golf clubs now gathering dust. Everything I'd bought to make the house feel more like mine had been packed away, forgotten. There was nothing left of me here. It was as if I'd been rinsed clean, as if I'd never been here at all.

10

I went back to Breach House the next day, and the next. Calling in sick to work so that I could spend all day on the farm, waiting by the side of the road for Hazel to pick me up. I was determined to put myself to use. There was always something to be done around the farm, some chore that nobody wanted to do and which I always volunteered for, desperate to prove myself. Taking out the bins, feeding the chickens. Combing the house for fleas, sprinkling talcum powder over the furniture to dry out their eggs, the chalky residue it left behind. It was disconcerting how quickly I got used to their bites, my mother's paranoia shrinking before the other women's confidence – that nothing bad could truly happen to us while we were on the farm. I didn't tell anyone about where I went, not even Nessa. What would I have said? There was no way to make them understand, no word that had the right shape or weight to convey how I felt. Trying to explain any of it would be pointless: it was so far beyond them.

To my mother's credit, she never asked. Hopeful, perhaps, that I'd reconciled with Nathan or started seeing someone new. When I returned home in the evenings she'd smile coyly at me, as if whatever was happening was a private joke between us.

Hazel took me with her sometimes to run errands in the

village down the road from Breach House, which was really just a farm shop, fishmonger's, post office and several brick cottages. Mainly we went to buy toilet paper or fill the car up with petrol – pockets of time when it was just the two of us. That was what I looked forward to the most, even if we did not say much. We spoke in other ways. For instance, Hazel invented a game where she secretly thought of an action and I had to perform it correctly to win, like touching my nose or scratching my wrist. I'd grab different parts of myself until I'd worked out what the action was and she'd nod or shake her head, signalling whether I was close. Occasionally, if she was in a bad mood, the action would be something like punching myself in the stomach or stubbing my toe and I would only be able to guess correctly after I'd performed it.

As the weather grew warmer, we spent more and more time outside, our skin turning red and peeling. I'd stopped going to work entirely by then. Tom had phoned me several times and even left a few angry voicemails, but after a while he'd given up and that was that. It surprised me, how easy it had been, how simple. The women spent hours meditating on the lawn, something they had learned from Blythe, their legs crossed until pins and needles came. Not everyone was good at it, and arguments often sprang from the heavy silence.

'But what are you supposed to think about?' Pearl asked one afternoon, rubbing her feet. 'I'm so bored.'

'You're not supposed to think,' Molly said. 'That's the whole point.'

'But how can you not think?' Pearl pressed. 'I can't stop thinking about how hungry I am.'

'Then go away and eat something.'

Pearl pouted, bratty with youth, and slapped her feet

heavily on the ground. I found it difficult sometimes to like her, but then she would offer me the food off her plate or pick me a bouquet of wild flowers and I'd feel tremendous guilt, want to take her into my arms. 'Maybe you find it so easy to meditate,' she continued, plucking out fistfuls of grass, 'because there aren't any thoughts in your head to get rid of.'

'Shut up,' Hazel snapped, her eyes still closed. She could remain like that for hours, knotted around herself like a pretzel, inscrutable.

In snatches and drips, thrown into conversation like bird-seed, I learned more about why some of the women had come to Breach House. Ambika's father who made her share a bed with him until she was twelve years old, her mother long dead in the ground. Pearl who carried the literal scars of her last relationship in a tidal spill down her front – a software engineer who'd seemed gentle until he threw a pan of boiling water over her. Not everyone was brought here by violence. There were some women who came because they were exhausted – of the nine-to-five, working to afford a house they barely lived in, being passed over again and again for promotions. Women who were tired of bad dates and microwave meals, unsolicited dick pics and getting stuck in traffic. Threading keys through their fingers on dark walks home, keeping one hand over their drink so nothing could be slipped into it, not drinking at all because the bartender had given them a weird feeling. Learning about an Angel Shot, a code word the government developed for people who felt unsafe in bars and clubs, only to ask for one and be met with blank stares. Being called bright or bossy or feisty, words meant to patronise and degrade, to wear down. Who could blame them for wanting something different? Even the women who didn't live on the farm, who went home to their husbands and children, looked to Blythe with a mixture of relief and devotion: to finally have someone who understood.

It was more difficult prising information out of Hazel. Mostly she wanted to talk about me, why my relationship had ended with Nathan. She asked so many questions about him it became difficult to keep straight what I had and hadn't told her. She took an almost savage interest in him, wanting to know what the worst thing he'd ever said to me was, if he snored in his sleep. What he was like in bed. I found it impossible to resist her, revealing the most intimate details in return for her friendship.

As I grew more familiar with the other women, I tried asking them about Hazel, what they knew about her, but could never parse the truth. 'Her father is some kind of aristocrat,' Molly told me one afternoon, rolling her eyes. 'She grew up in a house with a swimming pool.'

'That's not right,' Ambika interrupted. 'She told me she grew up on a council estate.'

The fingernail which I'd torn in the allotment continued to pare away from my cuticle, a gnawing pain that was impossible to forget because it was always there. I peeled it in small increments, a millimetre at a time, too much of a coward to rip it off in one go and be done with it – until finally the nail dangled by a thin layer of skin. When I plucked it free, I noticed there was still dirt clinging to the underside and placed it very carefully on the flat of my tongue. Dirt and blood, but something else as well – soft and sweet, like milk. I imagined my nail brushing along Hazel's arm, gathering some of her skin's cells, a build-up of her DNA that now sat in my mouth. Greedy, I couldn't help but swallow. The sharp point of keratin scratching my throat on the way down.

*

One afternoon I joined a few of the women on a drive to the local village. Blythe had an agreement with the owners of the farm shop there, who bought produce grown at Breach House for a decent price. A dog wearing a high-vis jacket sporting the words 'Follow me for English wine' roamed around the courtyard outside the shop, sniffing at our feet as we walked past.

I helped unload the car, heaving crates back and forth. Building up a sweat, stalactites of damp creeping down my armpits. It was the beginning of May and the weather was unusually fierce, a dry heat that caught in the back of your throat. Later tonight the women would celebrate Beltane, the pagan festival for fertility. An event to usher in new life. From what I could tell, Blythe and the other women didn't follow any one religion or belief, but pilfered where they felt like it. More than anything, it was an excuse for a celebration. 'Wear something green,' Pearl had advised me earlier. 'Or white is good too. But not your favourite outfit because it might get ruined.'

'Why would it get ruined?' I asked, but she wouldn't say, only tapped the side of her nose and gave a smug grin.

Once we'd unloaded the crates, we went around the shop buying things like toothpaste and batteries, our pockets brimming with the petty cash Sarah had given us. I followed behind Hazel, who took her time examining a basket of handmade ceramic bowls dipped in so much glaze the surface was splotched and uneven. She handled them roughly, picking them up and putting them back down again from a height so they clattered against each other, threatened to shatter. Gradually I became aware of a group of shoppers watching us. They moved furtively down the aisle, two of the women whispering something and then smiling. For a moment I wondered if I knew them, if they recognised me, but I was far away enough from home that this seemed unlikely. I began filling my basket with bottles of tomato sauce, just for something to do, trying not to let the itch of their gaze work its way under my skin, their whispering which seemed to grow louder.

'You can't let it bother you,' Hazel said, clocking them. 'If you're with us, people are going to stare. That's just how it is.'

'Do you know them?' I asked.

She shrugged and shook her head, like she didn't understand the question. 'No. But they know us. Most people around here do.' She smiled then, a slow, indulgent curve of her mouth. 'It's like I told you. Blythe is creating something special. A lot of people can't handle it. They'd rather bury their heads in the sand and go on with their small, depressing lives.' She set another bowl down and this time I heard the distinct sound of something fracturing. 'Fuck them.'

As the group edged closer I smelled their perfume, drifting towards me in a noxious cloud, like parma violets. Hazel turned towards them, her bald stare enough to shame a couple of them, their eyes dropping to the cans of soup, the basket of radishes which we had grown ourselves. But a few of them held her gaze, long enough to watch as Hazel lifted a hand to her mouth, parting her index and middle fingers into a v-shape and stroking her tongue through the seam in an overt gesture. The women balked, clutching their shopping baskets to their chests, their smiles now gone, replaced by something that wasn't quite disgust, wasn't quite fear. They walked quickly past, giving us a wide berth as if we might be contagious. Hazel turned to me and smiled, her fingers still pressed to her mouth, glistening.

*

The evening came on mild and warm, an orange streak across the sky so vibrant it looked almost chemical. Pollen hanging in the air, thick enough to choke. We'd decided it was too perfect to be kept indoors and dragged the dining table out on to the lawn. It took five of us to move it, Molly yelling to lift higher, to stop acting like babies and put our backs into it. Meanwhile, more women kept arriving, the most I'd seen at Breach House so far.

The radio was brought outside and turned up as loud as it would go, women dancing in wild circles, flinging themselves about. Their mouths open wide, as if about to swallow something. I perched on the end of the table, the music shuddering through me, a twang in my ribs. Pearl spun herself around and around, arms flung out either side of her until eventually she lost her balance and went tumbling into the other women, who screamed and laughed and swore at her.

Hazel came and sat next to me at the table. Her mouth was bright pink like she'd been eating berries, her hair loose over her shoulders. She smiled and presented me with a lilac flower, tucking it into the breast pocket of my shirt. I tried keeping my face still, not wanting to betray the power her gesture had over me, but even so I felt myself smile. She tipped her head back, soaking her face in the final few moments of sunlight. It was impossible just then to believe she could be the same person who'd provoked those women in the farm shop, the wet slide of her tongue. She looked so gentle. I wanted to tell her but knew it would rupture the moment, spoil something between us. Nobody wanted to be told they were gentle.

Dinner was heralded by the sound of our cheering, Sarah holding a ceramic dish aloft like it was blessed. The sun had set by then and candles were brought out, casting a rough glow over everything. Mosquitoes and fruit flies clogged the air, coating our skin in a horrible lacquer, and we began slapping each other – hard – without warning, claiming to have seen one land on a shoulder, a leg. By the morning we'd be covered in welts and wouldn't be able to tell our wounds apart, what the bugs had inflicted and what we'd done to each other.

Sarah was the kind of cook I'd hoped she'd be, generous and full of secrets. I'd seen her earlier in the day preparing the pie that now sat in the middle of the table, the tough knots of muscle in her arms as she'd kneaded the dough. Sprinkling vinegar on top to make the pastry flake more. There was an almost violent contraction in my stomach, my mouth filling with saliva. Blythe sat at the head of the table, barefoot and solemn, her hands laid flat in front of her. Our bodies drew towards her instinctively, breath held as we waited for her to give the signal that we could eat, a benevolent nod of her head.

Alongside the pie were buttered potatoes and fennel salad, sugar snap peas that were satisfying to chew. A thick slice of bread materialised in my hand and I held it aloft, catching the stream of melted butter on my tongue. Hazel sat opposite me, head bent low as she ate, her elbows jutting into the women either side of her, carving more space for herself. I watched the machination of her mouth as she chewed, was reminded of when she'd shown up at my work and demanded the artichokes, self-assured and greedy. As if she could hear my thoughts, Hazel looked up and smiled.

The other women ate like carrion, tearing at the food with their dirty hands, greedy and fast and indiscriminate. I watched as Molly crammed an entire roasted onion into her mouth, the pulpy excess spilling on to the floor. Insatiable, these women. Again and again they filled their plates, squabbling over the last potato, their mouths glistening with oil. It was as if they were trying to plug something inside themselves, satisfy some unknowable need. Blythe was the only one who didn't eat. I suspected she survived in some other way, was able to sustain herself on light and air: the immaterial.

Afterwards, Sarah brought out dessert. Pears stewed in syrup, the size and colour of hearts. Lemon drizzle cake cut into uneven squares, the frosting so sweet it put stones in my cheeks. Hazel and Pearl fought over a slice, their playfulness turning mean as Hazel dug her nails into Pearl's arm and licked her tongue across the top.

I ate everything that was offered to me, eating until my stomach hurt. Ready to gorge myself on this new life I'd found.

11

After dinner Hazel took me by the elbow and led me upstairs. We went into the airing cupboard and filled our arms with whatever we could find, blankets and towels. An old set of sheets that must have belonged to Sarah's children, pilled and stamped with cartoon helicopters. A few women were standing underneath the hatch to the loft, struggling to pull the ladder down.

'What are they doing?' I asked.

'Grabbing the tents,' she replied. 'We sleep outside on Beltane. The bonfire keeps us warm.' She loaded another set of blankets on to the pile I was holding, pressing down just hard enough that it might have been an accident, my back hunching to keep hold of everything. I looked up at her and caught something flinty in her expression, a challenge. Although I'd been spending increasing amounts of time at Breach House, I still had never stayed the night. A quiet part of me sensed that it wouldn't be something I could come back from if I did.

'You don't have to,' she said. 'I can take you home if you want.'

The women had managed to unfold the ladder and were taking turns passing everything down. I could tell the tents were old and poorly maintained, a smell coming off them that suggested they'd been folded while still wet. Holes poked through the canvas, made by mice or moths.

'I want to stay,' I said.

Hazel looked me up and down in that way of hers, where you weren't sure if she'd really heard you, before nodding.

'Come on then.'

Outside, we spread the blankets and bedsheets on the grass, forming a patchwork beside the unlit bonfire. The women had spent all afternoon building it, heaping wood at the end of the field where the ground sloped upwards. Not just wood, but whatever they could find that would burn – fencing, lint from the tumble-dryer, a children's abacus that someone had uncovered in the shed. By the time they'd finished, the pyre reached at least ten feet high. 'We built it too close to the barn last year,' Pearl confided, smiling so quickly she forgot to cover her mouth. There were several dark gaps where teeth should have been, her tongue peeking between two incisors like a pink eel.

'What happened?' I asked.

'You can't really tell any more,' she said. 'We painted over it, but the flame caught one of the beams, almost sent the whole place up.'

'Were the pigs all right?'

Pearl shrugged as if she hadn't even considered this. 'Nothing died.'

The sky was beginning to bruise purple and copper and unfamiliar sounds echoed from the trees, animals I couldn't immediately identify. I watched as the other women took off their shoes, wrinkled their toes in the grass. There was a sense of great anticipation, nervous laughter ricocheting across the field. Pearl fiddled with a cat's cradle, dredged up from the back of some cupboard, her fingers working quickly to build up the string. I sat down on one of the blankets, squeezing my knees close. It was colder than I'd been expecting and I found myself wanting someone to light the bonfire already, so we'd have something to huddle around. But the moment seemed always around the corner, a lesson in delayed gratification. My nose began to run.

'Here,' Hazel said. She took off her jumper and handed it to me. It smelled a bit like damp, but I wore it anyway, hugging it to my body when she wasn't looking. She sat down next to me, our shoulders knocking together.

'When will they light the bonfire?' I asked through chattering teeth.

'Soon,' she told me. 'When we can't wait any longer.'

Across the field I saw Blythe exit the house and make her way towards us, carrying something in her hand. One by one the other women stopped what they were doing and looked at her, their hands fidgeting nervously at their sides. Even Hazel repositioned herself, her gaze honed in on Blythe, the pulse in her throat quickening. I decided to seize the opportunity, prise information out of her while she was distracted.

'How long have you lived here?' I asked. 'I don't think you've ever said.'

'You didn't ask,' she replied, still not looking at me.

'No,' I agreed, then waited.

A beat passed, two. 'Three years.'

Blythe came to stand in front of the bonfire. The size of it failed to diminish her, instead made her seem somehow taller, larger. An exponential growth as she looked at each of us in turn. I realised now she was holding a box of matches. She took one out of its packet, held it aloft with sacramental importance.

'Three years,' I said, my voice trembling. 'That's a long time.'

Hazel shrugged. 'Tapeworms live longer.'

We watched as Blythe took one of the matches out and struck it against the cardboard box. A flame jumped to life, followed by the smell of sulphur. She pinched it between her thumb and finger, the flame growing taller, eating its way down the match. I felt myself wince as it licked at Blythe's fingers. Wasn't it painful? But, no. She didn't seem to feel it at all. Pearl tossed her cat's cradle on to the grass. Over the course of the night, it would end up trampled into the dirt, forgotten for good.

'How long will the bonfire burn for?' I asked, but Hazel was no longer paying attention to me.

Finally, Blythe flicked the match into the tinder at the bottom of the pyre. There was a good breeze and it didn't take long for the fire to catch, flames climbing higher and higher until it hurt my eyes to look. There was a deafening cheer. The women jumped up and ran to the bonfire, got so close that for a moment I worried they were going to launch themselves on top of it. Molly and Ambika shed their clothes, dancing lunatic around the flames, and it wasn't long before the other women joined them, their breasts cut into sharp relief, stomachs that were round and bloated from dinner. I held Hazel's jumper tighter.

'Are you freaking out yet?' Hazel asked. 'My offer still stands if you want to go back.'

A nervous laugh boiled up my throat. I tried to tamp it back down. 'Why would I want to go?'

She looked at me as if it should have been obvious. 'Not everyone is made for Breach House. The way we live.'

I tried not to let the hurt of that show, that she could sever our ties so easily, when I could no longer imagine a time before her. 'I don't want to go,' I said.

Her eyes travelled down the length of me and back up. 'If you're going to stay,' she said. 'If you want to be one of us, you have to mean it. It's not like a gym membership, you can't change your mind. It's a commitment.'

I told myself she was testing my resolve, wanting to see how easily I'd break. But the truth was there was very little that could have deterred me from staying.

'I don't want to go,' I said again.

It seemed like she might say something further, take me by the elbow and lead me down the driveway. But then she lifted her shoulders in a soft shrug. 'If you say so.'

The bonfire seemed to light up the entire field. The women continued to scream their laughter, dancing as close as they dared to the mounting flames, their faces carved skeletal by its glow. I could see the bats sketching across the sky, dipping every now and again towards the ground, trying to get the shape of us. Some of them flying so close we could make out the shiny pennies of their eyes. My jaw ached from smiling, the delight of nobody knowing where I was except for these women. My mother, Nessa, Nathan – these were problems that belonged in another world, to another version of myself. Here I could be whatever I wanted, the person I should have been to begin with.

*

The rest of the evening unspooled in streams of colour and sound. Molly and Ambika dancing in circles until they fell on the ground laughing. Sarah's feet, red and sore from stepping too close to the fire. Hazel spilling drink into her lap. Hazel clearing smoke from her throat. Hazel, Hazel, Hazel.

I watched as the bonfire reached its peak, the flames running so high they seemed to obliterate all else, scorching my peripheral vision. Every time I opened my mouth to say something I felt the wetness on my tongue evaporate, cutting the words off. My forehead grew red and sore to the touch. And yet I couldn't seem to step away, didn't want to.

Carefully, I stood. Hazel's jumper had shrunk in the heat, stuck to me now like a second skin. I struggled out of it, prising my head from the yoke and in the process momentarily blinding myself. By the time I'd worked myself free, I looked around and found that everyone had gone.

I closed my eyes and opened them again, expecting them to emerge from the shadows. The fire made it difficult to see, that was all. But, no. They had left, I didn't know where.

I stumbled a few steps away from the fire and was surprised to find a stream of cool, fresh air. I drank it down greedily while trying to find the others. Staring into the darkness and manifesting shapes from it – someone's arm, a pair of eyes. At one point I thought I saw Hazel huddled next to some gorse and went to grab her – *got you!* – only for my hands to travel straight through her phantom and into the barbed branches. Blood sprang between my fingers.

Behind me, a noise. Definitive, something I could latch on to. I turned around and saw Blythe, silhouetted by the fire. She crooked a finger, gesturing for me to come. I still wasn't used to her heft, how the grass flattened beneath her. I couldn't have fit my hands around her neck if I'd tried.

'You look worried, Iris,' she said.

'Where are the others?' I asked.

She gave a vague smile, patting her elbow. Up close I noticed several dark hairs sprouting from her chin, a pucker of scar underneath one ear. There was a smell to her which reminded me of the water my mother used to clean the car, cold and brackish. I realised I'd never seen her go to the bathroom, wondered if perhaps she used the garden hose to wash herself with. Blythe could never do the same things as us: she had to be different, in every way.

'They'll be back, don't worry.'

It was the first time I'd been alone with her since my first visit to Breach House, almost two weeks ago. Part of me had expected her to seek me out after I'd proved myself in the allotment, but she'd remained elusive, appearing only at mealtimes and even then not making an effort to speak directly to me.

'What is all this?' The words tumbled out of me before I could regret them. 'I mean, what gave you the idea for this place? Why here?'

Her eyes pinned me in place. 'You're still not sure about us.'

I shook my head quickly. 'No, that's not what I meant. I'm just – curious.'

'Well, I'm curious too, Iris. About you. I want to know why you're here.' She reached down and squeezed my hand, her fingers hard like curls of mineral. Something about the strength of her, the bulk, which drew truth to the surface.

'My father died when I was younger,' I found myself saying. 'A car accident. It changed my mother. I don't know. Sometimes all I am is angry. At them, at myself.'

Blythe nodded as if she understood perfectly. 'You loved him.'

'Yes,' I said, even though the answer was larger than that, thorned with rage and loss and betrayal. 'But he wasn't always a good man.'

Blythe gave another squeeze and a wetness slipped between us, my blood. She held it up to the light. 'I'm beginning to recognise these hands,' she said, stroking the club of her thumb along my palms, the calluses that had begun to form. 'These are becoming good hands. Strong hands.'

There was a sudden banging sound followed by squealing. I turned around and saw a wave of women spilling out of the barn, corralling the two pigs towards the bonfire, their hides rippling with fear.

'What are they doing?' I asked, my heart kicking.

Blythe laughed. 'It's for protection. Farmers used to run their cattle around a fire to cleanse them before putting them out to pasture.' The women chased the pigs around the bonfire, slapping their fat bottoms. Squeals rose into the air.

'Is that what you believe?' I asked.

She smiled, seeming to consider. 'It doesn't matter. It's what we do.'

When the ritual had been completed, the pigs were left to find their way back inside the barn, already forgotten, their dissatisfied grunts going unnoticed as the women turned their attention back to the fire.

The scaffolding which held the bonfire together was starting to shift and snap. For a moment it looked as if someone was caught inside it, trying to dig their way out. A loud cracking ruptured the air as the burning wood finally collapsed in on itself, the rush of embers bathing us in new heat. The women yelled with delight, jumping backwards and then rushing forward again, so close I could see the flames licking at their feet.

Molly was the first to jump, leaping over the grasping fire and landing neatly on the other side, her hands raised in triumph. She called to Ambika, who soon followed – not nearly as nimbly – and collided into Molly, knocking them both over. After that it was a procession, each woman jumping over the bonfire, their bravery matched only by their carelessness, how they barrelled into each other like skittles.

'It looks frightening,' Blythe told me. 'But I promise you won't even feel it.' Her hand was on my shoulder, kneading gently.

I realised she expected me to jump.

Hazel stared at us from across the fire, her face pink and raw from where she'd taken her own leap of faith. 'I can't,' I said.

'You must.'

Blythe walked us closer to the fire, the heat coming over me in waves, making it difficult to breathe. A scrape of the lungs.

'Jump,' she said, and I knew I had no choice, that if I refused, something would be closed off to me for ever. I would have to leave Breach House, leave Hazel.

I squared unsteadily before the bonfire, so ferocious I couldn't see beyond it. Everything else drained away, leaving only the heat and light and the brick of my heart rising up inside me.

I jumped, I must have. Closed my eyes and opened them to find myself on the other side, my nostrils burning from the smoke.

I looked down at myself and realised the sleeve of my shirt had caught fire, cheap nylon melting against my skin. I cried out, shaking my arm as if I could fling the flames off, but they continued to lick higher, spreading up my shoulder. Before I understood what was happening, the other women were dog-piling me, smothering the flames with their bodies. They wrapped themselves around me – a comforting, brilliant weight – and told me what a good job I'd done, their laughter tangling into one loud sound.

Somewhere in the scrum I could feel Hazel, her hand seeking mine, squeezing its approval into me.

2018

They wanted to know everything about us. Scrambling through court documents and police reports, desperate to throw light on to the mystery of Breach House. What was our favourite thing to eat for breakfast? Did we pile into the shower together like otters, scrubbing the dirt from each other's necks? What kind of protection did we use during our periods – pads or tampons, or did we use nothing at all? Simply let the blood soak into our underwear, sticky-thighed and feral. That was how they liked to imagine us best. Unhinged from societal norms, obscene in our habits. It made them feel better. To think of us as something animal, a different species to their own mothers and daughters, who could never do the things we had done. They wanted to believe we were born this way, rather than made.

Mingled with their repulsion, of course, was desire. Scouring the online forums, it became difficult to know where one emotion ended and the other began. Perhaps it was a spectrum, or a cake: something you could dip your fingers into. They wrote fan fiction about us, self-insert stories where the author imagined what it would be like to live at Breach House, reams of words dedicated to eating with us, sharing meals around the dining table, which was always described as being round, even though it had been rectangular in real life. I suppose they wanted to imagine us as being able to see one another. Many of the stories featured janky sex scenes, piles of mouths and fingers, where we all came at the same time. Occasionally a man appeared, infiltrating the farm in the hopes of saving a relative and ending up somehow seducing one or more of us. We were always submissive in these scenes, as if grateful for having something terrible fucked out of us.

I moved to the city after the events of Breach House, craving anonymity. Eventually I found work writing instruction manuals for a large furniture company, an anonymous job that allowed me to hide in a cubicle eight hours a day. I came to appreciate the concision it required, rendering the complicated diagrams into instructions that anyone could understand. My new colleagues were friendly, asking reasonable questions about where I'd lived before moving to the city, if I was single. I avoided them as best I could, until eventually they stopped inviting me to lunch and after-work drinks. It was better that way, I told myself.

Distraction as shelter, something to hide behind. I filled every hour of my day, an exhausting rotation of work and sleep, and took myself on long walks, disappearing into the city. I visited landmarks I'd only ever read about or seen in historical documentaries, a pilgrimage of dour-faced statues or else buildings that were made of too much glass, but I couldn't seem to find the significance in them, the glamour which drew herds of tourists every day. I listened to my once-favourite musicians sing about budding cherry blossom, muddy riverbanks, beer gardens, but their lyrics elicited nothing in me, plucked no emotional chord. After Breach House, I was immovable. In a moment of hysteria, I enrolled myself on a cookery course and learned how to make pad thai, dousing the noodles with so much lime and tamarind my mouth shrank, made it difficult to talk. The man who taught the course said I was too sloppy with the knife and swapped it out for a smaller one, something I was less likely to chop a finger off with. He was only trying to be kind, but I was easily spooked, convinced he'd seen through my disguise. My name was not mentioned in the papers and yet I searched everyone's faces for a sign of recognition, expecting someone to point at me in the street and say, *I know you.*

Days smeared into months and finally produced a year, a full three hundred and sixty-five days since I'd left Breach House. Nothing became easier, but the pain lost its edges, settled into a bruise you sometimes forgot was there until accidentally knocking it against something. Days passed where I didn't think about the farm, could almost convince myself that it had happened to someone else – or even better, hadn't happened at all. But other people were not as quick to forget. Like a child standing over an anthill, they poked and prodded, their curiosity unwavering. Their fascination found me in the most random places; on comedy panel shows, jokes about lesbian cults; an elderly couple gossiping in the café around the corner from where I lived; on the radio.

I'd done my best to avoid the aftermath of what had happened, but the facts found me anyway. How first responders hadn't been prepared for the state the body was in – torn open and gaping – and then about Blythe. The audience she amassed during the trial, people who wanted to see for themselves the woman who'd plagued their televisions for so long, wanting to hate her just as much as they wanted to be noticed by her, to fall under her purview. Her voice, which was loud and clear and filled the room. And the women. Even after learning about Breach House – or perhaps because of it – they came to see her. Disillusioned teenagers and wives trapped in unhappy marriages. Women who needed something they felt they couldn't get elsewhere. They dressed themselves in denim cut-offs and dyed vests, their scalps shorn smooth, emulating what little they knew of us, and stared shyly into the camera, their little puckered mouths. Trying to communicate a multitude of feelings. These were the ones I felt sorry for the most.

If I expected Blythe going to prison would neuter the pull she held over others, or dampen their interest in Breach House, I was wrong. People wrote to her. Declarations of love and devotion, appeals for direction. Should I marry this man? What would you do if you were me? It was reported in one paper that Blythe received so many letters that prison wardens had to keep a separate area to process them all. She wrote back. Of course she did, couldn't help herself. Eager for this second chance, a new flock to lead. She filled her days with letters, her writing swooped and narrow, like a series of fishing hooks on the page. Her words were written in a way that felt ripe with meaning. On message boards and forums, people spent hours dissecting her replies, intuiting them like birth charts or Tarot cards, something with infinite possibility. They prescribed them to every aspect of their lives, found permission in the most abstract sentences.

In one letter, she wrote: *Death is love.* The words began cropping up like mushrooms, sprouting where you least expected them. On a person's T-shirt, on social media. Black-and-white portraits of a sunset with the words transposed over it. It became a mantra for rebellious teenagers, words to throw back at their parents and teachers. *Death is love.* Once, at a concert, I saw the words tattooed on a girl's arm. I'd come to love the spotlights haloing the stage, floor sticky with alcohol, rooting you in place. A voice singing into a microphone, bodies everywhere, the rhythm charging straight through our bones. It was an obliteration. I screamed until I went hoarse and then I went to the bar for some water. While I was waiting to be served, the girl reached across to grab a napkin, revealing the words on her arm, inked into permanence. *Death is love.* I tried to swallow but my throat had suddenly closed up, made it difficult to breathe. A noise came out of me, somewhere between a gasp and a cower. She looked at me, asked me if I was all right. The vein in her arm snaking under the word *love*, raising it slightly. It was easy to believe I knew her. There was something familiar about the slow smile she gave me, her eyebrow arching as if she carried a secret. I could picture her at Breach House, leaping over the bonfire, one of us.

PART TWO:

SUMMER

12

2008

Breach House was its own ecosystem, removed from the malfunctioning world of indecision and patriarchy. On its land you felt sheltered, guarded against the reasons that brought you there in the first place, briar and holly and gorse forming an antlered barrier against outsiders. It had everything we needed to sustain a private life: the nearby stream that was warm enough to swim in, the orchard, the year-round allotment that continually spilled out sweet bell peppers and courgettes, lentils and turmeric, which we cooked down into daal. It was tucked tightly into the downs, invisible unless you were looking for it. Nobody seemed to know the farm's history, but it was easy enough to imagine men chopping down trees to lay its foundations, bent on survival and seclusion. The same rejection of society threaded through their veins. It must have been that same thread that first tugged at Blythe, although as my days at Breach House turned to weeks, I began to wonder whether she'd had the idea for her new society long before coming to the farm. Or if it was the rough landscape that had spoken to her, planted the idea in her head as she walked barefoot through its fields.

Yes, we came to Breach House to escape society, but there

were times when it couldn't be avoided, like trading in the farm shop or local markets. Hexagonal jars of honey into which we dipped lollipop sticks and offered as samples to customers. The other farmers treated us with hostility, muttering words like dykes and freaks and whackos between themselves, warning their children not to come near. If it were a hundred years ago, they would have shunted us into institutions, claiming hysteria, or else named us as witches. Tied stones around our ankles and pushed us into the nearest body of water. Even so, they found unending excuses to walk past us in their wax jackets and boots, their noses cherried with burst capillaries – desperate to know more about us, their curiosity only fuelling their distrust. Blaming us for the longing they felt. We had crocodile smiles for each of them, sharp flashes of teeth that made them blink and then look away.

The women were no better, but at least they found ways to make use of us. Paying us to work in their gardens, where we trimmed their hedges and laid fresh bark down on their plant beds. There was a sense of pageantry about it, being paraded around their homes for everyone to see. Often we would be working in one of their gardens, only to turn around and find they'd invited their friends over for an impromptu game of solitaire in the garden, their gazes licking over our bare arms and the ropes of muscle underneath. Or if not pageantry, then subjugation: like training a group of bears to tap-dance. It went both ways. Blythe enjoyed advertising the women of Breach House, sending us into the homes of people who gossiped about us and yet couldn't seem to leave us alone. She wanted them to see what she had achieved, the loyalty and the obedience. And sometimes there were women who wanted to learn more about Breach House, earnest in their interest. Either way, it was an opportunity to get more money out of them.

Hazel and the others didn't mind the labour. Rather, they seemed to enjoy the attention, talking loudly among themselves, tying their vests into knots below their bras and exposing tanned flanks of midriff. Knowing just how much to tantalise, to provoke. I went where I was told, still too anxious to do anything other than obey. Mostly I just wanted to be wherever Hazel was.

It had been almost a month since I'd moved into Breach House, my skin still singed after the events of Beltane. I'd passed Blythe's literal leap of faith, proven something of myself. The news didn't come from her but rather Sarah, who mopped my burns the morning after and said I should think about what I wanted to bring with me. She explained there was no room in the farmhouse where she, Blythe, Molly, Ambika and Hazel slept, so I would move into the coach house with the others.

It was a small building which smelled as if it had contained horses at one point, a row of rusted nails along one wall where their saddles might have hung. There was only room for several beds and an electric heater, which we shared between us. Because of the limited space, I could only bring what was practical, or useful, with me – sentimentality an extravagance I could no longer afford. I packed the clothes I didn't mind getting dirty and a few books and took the rest to the nearest cash exchange. It surprised me, how easy it was to part with everything. Understanding that it was all slack that could be cut away. I emptied what was left in my bank account and gave it to Blythe. I no longer needed it.

I would pay for my living at Breach House with work, find currency in the ground.

At first I thought it would feel claustrophobic sleeping in the coach house with so many other women, but I felt much happier there than in my childhood bedroom. It didn't matter that I no longer had any privacy: I was glad to be in the thick of it.

Some nights the women would go around sharing stories about their past lives, their confessions veined with trauma – but also with pride. Lucy, who slept directly next to me, revealed that she'd joined the commune after suffering a miscarriage and needed a place to recover. And then there was Tanya, a shy woman in her fifties who'd bounced around women's refuges and homeless shelters all her life, and only now felt at home. Or Moira, who said very little during the day but screamed in her sleep. My own pain, in comparison, felt trivial. Whenever the conversation made its way round to me, I was careful to bury the worst of it deep down, or else say nothing at all.

When I told Nessa I was moving to Breach House, she was pleased and then worried. Wouldn't it be difficult for me living in the middle of nowhere if I couldn't drive? How would I get to work? I patiently explained to her that I'd quit my job and so it wouldn't be a problem. In truth, I felt as if I'd already moved on from my old life. I couldn't remember the last time I'd even thought about Nathan. But there was no point in trying to explain all of that to Nessa.

'Can I come and see it at least?' she asked me. 'Just to make sure they're not taking the piss. Or at least try to get in touch with Helen's sister again. I mean, how much do you even know about these people, Iris?'

'It's fine,' I told her. 'You don't need to worry.' Her doubt was an accelerant, proof that she didn't think I was capable of doing something like this, and therefore all the more reason to do it. In the end, all I really told her was the following: that I would be living with a group of women, and that it would be good for me.

I told my mother even less. I explained to her that I was moving out to stay with some friends, that I would try and visit her as often as I could. She remained stoic while I explained the situation, silent up until the last moment when I was on her doorstep and she said, 'Maybe this is all for the best.'

*

Pollen clustered in the back of my throat, threatening a sneeze. A few of us had been sent to another garden, a woman who said she needed her hedges cutting back. They looked pristine to me, but I chopped at the laurel anyway, Pearl and Hazel gathering the cuttings into a pile. Molly and Ambika were on the other side of the garden cleaning out the gutters with broom handles, leaves and lichen crumbling on to the patio below. I'd learned there was no point in trying to eavesdrop on them: their language was their own, a lexicon of knowing smiles and nods, indecipherable to other people. Living in a women's commune, relationships were inevitable, or flings, or the occasional messing around. Blythe said nothing was prohibited, that she had no interest in controlling our love lives. It would only become a problem if the relationship caused wider issues for the farm. Love triangles that ended in personal grudges, bad break-ups. Anything that could disrupt the normal flow of things. Women who couldn't control themselves were known to be excommunicated, sent from Breach House without a backwards glance.

In my time at Breach House, I'd only witnessed a couple of serious disputes. Not spats, which were common and occurred several times a day – women squabbling over hand cream, hogging the only bathroom on the farm – but something harsher and enduring, that pulled the other women in, made them pick sides. A couple of weeks ago there had been a theft. Molly had stormed into the kitchen and told us her watch had been stolen. She said she knew who had taken it, a woman named Patty who didn't live on the farm but sometimes stayed over when it was too late to drive home. The narrow lanes could be treacherous at night. Molly said Patty had been looking at her watch when they were chopping firewood earlier that afternoon, quick-flint glances down at her wrist when she thought Molly wasn't paying attention. It wasn't an expensive watch, Molly explained, but that wasn't the point. It was hers, and it had been taken, thieving bitch. Are you sure you haven't misplaced it? Ambika asked, smiling to make it seem casual, the only one of us who knew how to reckon with Molly's temper. Yes, Molly said. I'm sure.

Later that day I was helping Hazel feed the pigs when we heard a noise coming from the allotment: a pulping sound. Hazel looked at me and shrugged, led us outside to go and see. When we got there, we found Molly standing over Patty, who was curled on the ground, one arm thrown protectively over her head. There was an unmistakable crunch of cartilage as Molly's fist came down, cornicing Patty's nose into uneven ridging. Blood shot from her nostrils. The smell was in the air, mineral and sweet. A crowd had gathered, but nobody intervened, until Sarah arrived and pushed her way to the front. By then Patty had gone quiet, Molly too, so all you could hear was the meaty sound of fist on skin.

Molly obeyed when Sarah told her to stop. I'd learned there was a strict hierarchy on the farm, the women who lived permanently at Breach House presiding over those who didn't, Sarah presiding over us all. At the top of the food chain was Blythe, our alpha, whose words we would have transcribed on to stone if we'd had chisels sharp enough. Sarah separated the women and told us to get back to our chores, that was enough rubbernecking. Patty kept making wet noises, blood and saliva working its way down her face in a streaked rivulet. She looked around at us – pitiful thing – as if we might say something, jump to her defence. But we were brittle creatures, our loyalty to Blythe, not each other.

When Blythe heard about what had happened, she told Patty to return the watch or leave Breach House for ever. There was no discussion about whether there might have been a mistake or miscommunication. Ultimately it didn't matter who was to blame, so long as we obeyed Blythe. Her word was final. Not even Patty argued, although you could see on her face – underneath the crust of blood – that she was angry, wanted to speak her mind.

She was gone the next day.

A week later Ambika found Molly's watch buried between the sofa cushions, but by then we had all forgotten what had happened and merely shrugged our indifference.

'I need to take a break,' I said, putting down the garden shears. I wasn't as fit as the other women, my body soft in comparison to theirs. 'Do you know where the bathroom is?'

Hazel shook her head. 'You can ask, but be prepared for her to tell you it's having work done.'

'What do you mean?' I asked.

'They don't like it when we go inside their homes,' Pearl clarified, tugging on her ponytail. 'They're fine with us doing their manual labour, but it doesn't change the fact they think we're going to steal their stuff or something.'

Hazel smirked. 'I dare you to take something from the bathroom, if she lets you in.'

'Oh my god, yes,' Pearl said. 'Steal some toilet paper, we're always running out.'

I smiled, unsure if they were being serious. 'No,' Hazel said. 'It should be something smaller that nobody would notice. Something in the bathroom cabinet.'

They were pushing me towards the woman before I could say anything, their breathy laughter in my ear. The woman was sitting on the patio, sipping her gin and tonic, condensation slipping down the neck of the glass and pooling moisture into her fist. I realised she hadn't offered us anything to drink since we'd arrived, despite the growing heat.

I angled my body so my shadow fell over her. She tried to contain her startle, pretending to readjust her sunglasses, her mouth which gaped like a fish. 'I need to use the toilet,' I told her.

Something about the way she looked at me, her eyes quickly glancing down at my groin, made me think she was disappointed. That I was normal after all, with the same bodily functions as her, and not one of the fey creatures rumour had transformed us into.

She set her glass down on the table. Cast about for something to wipe her hand with, the rings on her third and fourth finger clacking together as she shook it, and in the end settled for the cushion of her seat. She looked back at me. 'Yes, all right. You can use the downstairs loo. It's just through the kitchen, on your right.'

I went to go inside, but then she shot up from her seat and followed me. 'Wait,' she said. 'Let me show you.'

Inside, the kitchen was large and warm, last night's meal hanging stale in the air: something metallic, like mince. The smell made me uncomfortable, revealed more about this woman than I cared to know. How she must have stood behind the stove breaking the mince apart in the pan, hot fat spattering her wrists. The fresh herbs that went into the sauce, rosemary and oregano and – yes, there – lemon thyme. As she raised one hand to point at the bathroom door I imagined I could still smell the green on her fingertips, bright and sharp. 'Just through there,' she said. Her mouth flapped as if she might say something more, ask a question. I waited, but she corrected herself with a quick smile and went back outside.

After using the bathroom at Breach House, it felt strange sitting on the toilet in peace. I'd got used to other women barging in, looking for a spare hair band or else unable to wait for the shower, different textures and colours of hair clogging the drain, difficult to unravel. There were no locks on any of the doors and so there was a constant flux of bodies, a rotation of impatient women. At first it had felt impossible to acclimatise to, knowing that nothing I did was truly private, that eyes were always upon me.

But then my doubt scabbed over into acceptance, and then welcoming. Wasn't this why I had come to Breach House in the first place? For total immersion, dissemination of the self. If I wanted to make a success of things, I'd have to give myself over completely. Suddenly it didn't seem so bad, to be able to reach out a hand, knowing someone would be there to take it. The toilet seat which was perpetually warm from another woman's backside.

When I was finished, I looked inside the bathroom cabinet but couldn't bring myself to take anything, not the multiple bottles of antacids or the wrinkled tube of steroid cream.

There was a group of men outside when I returned. One of them seemed to be the woman's son, bending at the waist and allowing her to kiss him on the cheek. The way she smiled at him, such indulgence. The others must have been his friends, interchangeable in their jeans and hoodies, their hair slicked back with so much gel it looked as if they'd just stepped out of the rain. Their eyes on Hazel, Molly, Ambika and Pearl, who pretended not to see them, though I noticed Hazel square her shoulders, pushing out her chest. Turning just so to reveal the best angles of herself. She was a creature who enjoyed being looked at.

I hovered in the doorway of the conservatory, a tightness growing in my chest that I could not name, did not want to. 'We've come straight from work,' the son explained to his mother, wiping sweat from his brow. Muscle and musk, the smell of him reaching across the garden to me. 'Got any beers in the fridge?'

The woman stood. 'Sit down, I'll bring them.' As she walked past me, the woman furrowed her brow, weighing up whether to leave her son and his friends alone with us, not because of what they might do to us, I knew, but because of what we might do to them. Eventually her maternal instinct seemed to win out, and she muttered something under her breath as she went inside the house.

'You've made a difference.' The son gestured to the laurel.

'It was beginning to look a mess. My mum's never been good at any of that stuff.'

'It's not that hard,' Hazel said.

He smiled. 'Still. I like how it looks.'

Names were passed around. He was Scott, his friends something bland like Matthew or Gareth or Anthony. Pearl did most of the talking, which they seemed to like, sweet and amicable as she was. 'Iris,' she said, beckoning me with one hand. 'Come and say hello.'

I felt their eyes on me as I crossed the garden, an unpicking. Noticed in my periphery two of the men exchanging glances, some private information communicated. I went and stood next to Hazel, hoping that she might provide reassurance, whisper something only I could hear, but she remained implacable as if she hadn't noticed me at all.

Molly and Ambika held on to each other, discomfort mirrored in their faces. Ambika shifting her weight from one foot to the other, as if preparing to run. Different to Pearl, who bathed in the attention like milk, her voice rising an octave higher so it sounded infantile. The group of men laughed and asked things like were we meat eaters, did we like meat – thinly veiled innuendos they thought were clever. Eyes roving over us, and Pearl's simpering filling the garden.

'Aren't you ever scared, though?' Scott asked. 'Living all the way out there. I mean, what would you do if something happened?'

'Like what?' Ambika asked.

He shrugged, only half serious. 'I don't know. What if one of you fell down the stairs and bumped your head?'

Hazel snorted. 'We have a car. We're not stranded.'

The inclination of his head a concession. 'Well, sure. But

how far are you from the hospital? What, fifteen, twenty miles? And on those country lanes too. Enough time for a person to suffocate or bleed out.'

'We can look after ourselves,' Molly said.

Scott held his hands up in a placating gesture, and then looked at me. His eyes were cut glass, too pale to be blue. They held me in place. 'What do you think? Wouldn't it be nice knowing you have someone on the outside looking out for you? We could all be friends.'

I smiled, wary. Unable to shake the feeling that he was mocking me somehow, that they all were.

'She's new,' Hazel said before I could say anything, taking a step forward to obstruct me. 'She doesn't know anything.'

13

When we returned to Breach House the five of us separated without a word, an unspoken agreement to part ways. The drive back had been a quiet one, punctuated only once by Pearl cracking a joke to lighten the mood. 'Did you see the one with the hat? I'm pretty sure he had a boner the whole time we were there.' She looked around at us, but Molly shook her head, knuckles white on the wheel. I glanced at Hazel, tried to communicate my confusion with a look, but she either didn't notice or pretended not to see. We had only talked briefly with the men and yet there was a definite sense of indignity about the whole thing, as if we'd betrayed ourselves in some way. An aftermath of dropped gazes and nervous laughter.

There was no concrete rule about socialising with men away from Breach House, only that they weren't allowed on the farm. Plenty of women went home at the end of the day to their families, children who expected to be fed. I couldn't imagine that kind of dissection, the splitting of self. How were they able to go from dancing around bonfires to cooking fish fingers and doing the ironing? It had taken a severance for me to join Breach House, a shedding of my mother and Nessa. It was the only way that made sense to me: emptying my body of one life and filling it with another. Was that why speaking to those men had felt like a disloyalty? Because they belonged to an old world, not this new one which I'd fought tooth and nail for.

It must have been close to three o'clock and the sun was bearing down. I was desperate for a shower. To wash the sweat off me, scrub at my skin with the old loofah that smelled of mould and was claggy with other women's skin cells. I went inside the farmhouse, pausing in the hallway to listen for the rodent scuffling of the women, but they must have all been out in the allotment. I moved slowly down the corridor, the first time I'd been in the house alone. There were details I'd never noticed before: one section of the skirting board torn away to reveal chipped plaster underneath, a framed painting of the downs. Etched into the doorway of the living room were faint traces of ink where Sarah had charted the growth of her children, one taller than the other. It was a detail that seemed fabricated, unreal. The kind of thing you only saw in straight-to-television movies. It was difficult to imagine Sarah being so sentimental: she enjoyed feeding us, but there was a practicality to her cooking, the binary change of state from empty to full. I stroked a finger along the lines. Daniel, age 6, 112 centimetres. Callum, age 4, 102 centimetres.

As I went to go upstairs there was the sound of someone clearing their throat, a beckoning. I followed it into the kitchen. Blythe was sat at the table drinking hot chamomile, the mulchy smell of it drifting towards me. I watched as she put the cup down and blew her nose, hawking phlegm on to the tissue next to her hand. A yellow-green wad of it, obscene. 'Kettle's still hot,' she told me. 'Why don't you join me?'

I'd been expecting Blythe to come and find me those first few days after moving to the farm, to seek me out as she'd done on Beltane, and was disappointed when she did not. I didn't know where she went or what she was thinking, only that – according to the other women – her absences were normal and I should get used to them. Sometimes she was gone for days, long walks in the woods that stretched on into the week and left us with a sense of displacement. Or else she worked in the allotment, hefting rubber tubs of compost like it was nothing, the muscles in her arms bunches of iron. She was vocal in her work, grunting as she ploughed her shovel into the earth, her almost-carnal sounds echoing across the farm. I knew she had no reason to impress me and yet it was impossible not to think of her as an unrivalled force. I wondered if my awe of her would ever fade, if I'd eventually come to think of her as just another woman; thought it unlikely.

Tea was the last thing I wanted, but I went over to the stove and poured myself a cup. She gestured for me to sit opposite. I did that, too. 'How was it today?' she asked.

'It was fine,' I replied. 'We trimmed the hedges, and the gutters needed cleaning out.'

Blythe nodded, a slow levering of her head. 'Gone a long time just for that,' she said.

The urge to lie. To make something up, an obstacle that explained why we were late: traffic or a dead animal in the road. It happened more often than you'd think. A couple of weeks ago we'd been driving back from a supply run when we'd driven past a beached cow, escaped from one of the farmer's fields, flies swarming across its eyes.

'The woman's son and his friends came over,' I told Blythe, holding the cup of tea very tightly so the pads of my fingers began to burn. 'They started talking to us. We must have lost track of time.'

Without Hazel and the others to bolster my story, the events suddenly felt like my own, as if I'd orchestrated the entire thing. I couldn't help but feel as if I'd been shanghaied, willingly tricked into entering the house alone, like they knew Blythe would be waiting. They were tricksy women.

'And what did they have to say?' Blythe asked. Smiling so that it seemed like a harmless question, an unloaded gun.

'Not a lot,' I told her. 'They weren't amazing conversationalists.'

'They didn't ask about the farm?'

I shook my head but sensed my mistake immediately. She knew I was lying. I rubbed the skin above my eyebrow until it chafed, grateful for the momentary distraction. 'They did, but we didn't tell them anything. We talked long enough to be polite, and then we left. We didn't want the woman to think we were being rude and try to get out of paying us.'

'Listen,' she said. 'The beauty of this place is that we can be alone. We have time to think up here, out of the way as we are.' She fiddled with the tissue she'd spat into, eyed the globule of phlegm. 'I do most of my thinking in the morning, when it's quiet. When everyone's still asleep and I can be alone with my thoughts. Remember why I built this place. You remember when I told you the women who come here are running away from something?'

I nodded.

'Well, it's none of my business what that something is. Poverty or violence or dead daddies' – she glanced at me – 'but it's my job to keep you safe, to preserve what we're doing here. Wouldn't you agree with that?'

Yes, I said, I would.

Blythe nodded again. 'That means there are rules, things we

must abide by. We're not always going to agree on everything, and if you have a problem with how I run things then you can tell me. But listen. We cannot let the outside world in. Women are treated like dogs in the outside world. Like we're a different species altogether, something dangerous. We earn less, we are given less, we are raped and murdered on a daily basis. I know all about it. So do you. We grow up being told what to wear and how to act, and even if we do all those things we're still raped and murdered. But here, here we can control our circumstances, live without that kind of judgement. I know it's not perfect. We fight and argue and treat each other like shit. But it's *ours*. It's worth preserving.'

She reached across the table and for a moment I thought she meant to hit me. I felt myself flinch, bracing for the cannonball of her hand. She must have sensed my fear, the corners of her mouth tensing in what might have been a smile. At the last moment her hand softened as she reached into my hair and plucked out a laurel leaf. Held it up to the light to reveal its arteries. 'We owe it to each other not to let any of that old world back in.'

*

A few days later, we were sat up on the bank, silt clinging to our wet legs. The stream was an offshoot of the Stour, winding itself through the woods like a silver ribbon and occasionally sparkling with minnow. The first time Hazel brought me, I saw a newt perched on a rock – not yet fully formed, so that it looked like a cross between a frog and some kind of slug. Sometimes we tied scraps of hessian around our feet to protect them, wading out into the water and feeling along the waterbed for whelks and other morsels.

We'd been given the afternoon off to celebrate Molly's birthday, and she wouldn't let us forget it. Prompting us to shower her with compliments, offering her cheek for us to kiss. I was surprised by the other women's indulgence, how they ferried cups of tea back and forth to her, made little gifts of things they'd cadged from the local charity shop. Even Blythe was doting, ordering us to stop work and follow her into the woods, where Sarah had prepared lunch on the bank – a children's picnic, for grown women. Sandwiches cut into little triangles, biscuits iced with smiley faces. We sat in a circle and ate, and afterwards stripped down to our underwear and waded out into the cool, clean water.

I was surprised by how deep it went, eating me up to the thigh, the groin, my waist. Hazel spun around to face me, my vision bleached by sunlight so I could only make out the rough topography of her face. A dark hole which I guessed was her mouth. 'Come on,' she said, gesturing for me to take her hand. 'Come all the way in.'

I flinched as Molly launched herself into the water, sending up a spray, her screams filling the woods.

'I'm not the strongest swimmer,' I told Hazel. 'I have zero coordination.'

'You can hold on to me,' she said. 'Don't be a baby, come here.'

I grabbed on to her and felt the silt beneath my feet give way: a lightness, almost euphoric. I laughed as she twirled us in a circle. 'I saw an eel here once,' she said.

'Why would you tell me that?' I kicked my legs, expecting to feel its body slide against me, oily and muscled. Hazel laughed, throwing her head back, revealing the lacteal glow of her teeth. She wrapped her arms around me – to protect me or prevent me from leaving, I wasn't certain.

After a while my body eased up and I sank into Hazel's grip, the soft damp of her skin. Behind us, Blythe and Sarah were still sat on the bank, deep in conversation. Blythe had rolled the cuffs of her trousers up, revealing the thick trunks of her legs. Red marks latticed the skin, as if she'd carved a direct path here through the thornbushes. I imagined them callousing into scars, creating a barrier of tissue, just like her hands, which were tough and strong: I'd once seen her retrieve a baking tray from the oven without using a tea towel. How could you not be in awe of someone like that?

The other women took turns tossing Molly into the air, their hands netting under her foot to create a launchpad. It soon became a competition of who could throw her the highest, the fastest, who could make her scream with genuine fright. I half expected Blythe or Sarah to say something, tell them to be quiet, but the day seemed to carry some of Beltane's magic, where anything was permissible. Even when Molly accidentally splashed the bank, catching Blythe, she merely wiped her face and smiled.

I held on to Hazel tighter, our glide through the water making me feel weightless, unbound.

'Who was your first boyfriend?'

Her question was so unexpected I thought I'd misheard.

'What?' I asked. 'Why are you asking me that now?'

She shrugged, water rolling off her shoulders. 'The thought occurred to me and I was curious, so I asked. You don't have to answer if you don't want to.'

I shook my head but knew better than to deny her.

My history of dating was short and panicked. When I

was eleven my father told me men only wanted to marry virgins, speaking the words so confidently I had no choice but to believe him. I began to think of my virginity as a pearl inside me, something small and lustrous that needed preserving. When I started secondary school my conviction only grew stronger. Girls in my class recounted their transactional encounters with boys, blowjobs in the toilets that were spoken about like self-inflicted wounds, something dangerous but which still carried a mark of pride. I watched as they changed, an alchemical shift from girl to something other – not quite women, not yet. Their soft skin several shades too-orange with foundation, skirts rolled up at the waist. It was difficult to believe their illicit forays didn't have something to do with their transformation, and explained why I had remained the same, a shapeless child sweating in my school shirts. The cotton bras which my mother still bought from the junior section of Marks and Spencer.

When I turned fourteen, I made eye contact with a boy named Lewis Callaghan. He sent his interest through the playground grapevine, so that I knew he was going to ask me out days before he actually did. He was too tall for me. Little did I know that would be a recurring theme in my future relationships, tall men who had to bend at the waist to hear what I was saying. We dated for three weeks before he asked to have sex with me. My father's words ricocheted in the back of my head, that men only wanted to marry virgins, and so I viewed Lewis's request as a kind of test, something I had to withstand in order to be considered good, a girl worth keeping. I kept telling him *maybe* every time he asked, all while secretly enjoying the attention I received from the other schoolgirls, who knew what was happening and offered me guidance, earnest advice about what sort of underwear to buy and how to pluck my eyebrows.

Eventually Lewis gave up on trying to have sex with me and started going out with another girl. When my father found out, he rubbed the skin above my shoulder – what was meant to be a comforting gesture but which always hurt a little – and said, 'Be careful with the next one, sweetheart. You don't want to get a reputation for being frigid.'

Hazel asked me to tell her the story of Lewis three times, so she could get it right in her head. 'Were you upset when he dumped you?' she finally asked.

'Not really,' I said. 'His breath smelled like Monster Munch. And he always kept his eyes open when we kissed.'

'Did he have nice eyes at least?'

I tried to remember them. 'They were blue, I think.'

'I once had a boyfriend who liked to choke me. He said it was for my benefit, that it was meant to feel good that way, but he kept doing it even when I asked him not to.'

'That's horrible,' I said. 'Is that when you came here?' She looked at me and I felt myself redden with the crudeness of my question. I still knew so little about her, was increasingly desperate to learn even the slightest morsel, something she hadn't told anyone else, not even Blythe. Our relationship was still weighted unevenly, with her knowing so much about me while she remained shrouded, a ghost.

She lifted a shoulder. 'It was one of the reasons, I guess.'

*

Gradually, we became aware something was wrong. Not because of any particular sound – but a lack of it. Molly had been tossed into the air by one of the women, but this time she didn't surface. We watched, waiting for her to reappear and hurl a clod of wet mud at us, laugh at the nasty trick she'd played. It was her birthday, and so we couldn't be mad. But she remained under the water, the seconds spilling over, all of us watching, until Ambika screamed and we knew something bad had truly happened.

'Oh fuck,' Hazel said, letting go of me. 'Somebody grab her.'

'I can't see her,' Ambika kept saying. 'I can't see where she went.'

Afterwards, I would think about how unprepared we were. How none of us knew what to do, staring at one another as if a solution would magically present itself.

And then Blythe was striding towards the water, cutting a clean line through it, her mouth drummed into a tight seam. She dived underwater, the rest of us inconsolable now, crying like children. When she finally reappeared, she had Molly in tow, whose head bobbed limply up and down.

We followed Blythe on to the bank, where she laid Molly down. Her eyes were closed and she wasn't moving. Beside me, Hazel's breathing quickened. I glanced at her, but she didn't seem afraid or upset – rather, there was a freneticism about her, something that bordered on excitement.

It took what felt like several minutes for Blythe to beat life back into Molly, pounding the water from her lungs – and then she was sitting up and spluttering, and saying thank you, and laughing like what had just happened was all part of a game.

'I hit my head on something,' she explained, reaching into her hair and showing us the red. 'I didn't even feel it. I didn't even know what had happened.'

*

It was all we could talk about for the rest of the day, Molly's near-death experience eclipsing her birthday, which she didn't seem to mind. In granular detail, we relived the moment Blythe had charged into the water after her, punched life back into her lungs. Even Sarah couldn't help joining in, wetting our mouths with cups of tea so we wouldn't grow hoarse and stop. We spoke about the event as if it proved something essential about Blythe, like what she had done went beyond quick thinking and good luck.

'My cousin drowned in a swimming pool when we were kids,' Pearl told us. 'She was under the water for less than a minute, but she still died. Molly was under way longer than that.'

'Do you remember anything?' Ambika asked Molly. 'Did you feel anything when Blythe brought you back?'

Molly took her time formulating an answer, until she was certain we were all looking at her. 'I felt a rush of warmth, and when I opened my eyes, it was as if this light were shining all around her. Like a halo.'

No one laughed when she said it. Instead the women nodded, as if they'd shared the same vision. Their adulation was infectious. Already my mind had gilded the memory of Blythe, causing her to loom even larger than in real life, the water cleaving to make way for her, time elasticating so that it felt as if Molly had been under for minutes, not seconds. When I thought about it now, I could have sworn Blythe had been muttering something under her breath. Easy to believe it had been an incantation, words drawn from somewhere deep and breathed into Molly.

'You okay?' Hazel asked, watching me closely. The others had gone and the kitchen felt cooler without them.

'Yes,' I told her, and found that I meant it. She stared at me a moment and then looked away, satisfied.

More than anything, how good it felt to be part of something so unbelievable, that defied all logic and sense.

14

When I was younger, my mother would plan her week around her horoscope. Careful not to walk under scaffolding if it warned her about an upcoming health scare, or putting on lipstick if someone new was about to enter her life. She enjoyed living like this. There is a comfort, I suppose, in believing your life has been mapped out. That all your beginnings and endings already exist inside you.

The longer I spent at Breach House, though, the more I became convinced that the truth lay further down, in the ground. Dirt told no lies. It contained both the cause and the effect. When I pricked my thumb on a thorn, I used rosemary oil to disinfect the wound. Dock leaves grew next to the nettles that stung me when I walked through the woods. There was a candour in the earth that, after years of scrabbling for purpose, I found calming. Hazel said the earth was the only thing that gave out what you put into it, and that felt true, too. Every evening when we sat down to eat I was amazed by the bounty the allotment provided, heaped plates of tomato and chicory, beetroots pulled from the ground that very morning, specks of dirt still clinging to their skin. We were being rewarded for our work and sought guidance from no one but ourselves.

One morning, I rose early and crept outside, careful not to

wake anyone. The farm was a different place just after dawn, signs of reclamation everywhere. The badgers who came and shat outside our windows, cabbages chewed to their root by snails. The fog which unfurled like a pelt across the ground, obscuring the farmland beyond. It felt as if we were only ever a hair's breadth away from being overrun completely, a miracle to wake up each day unscathed. As I headed towards the woods, I became convinced I was being watched. Not by the other women, but by the animals which seemed to lurk just out of sight, the penny-shine of their eyes glinting between the trees before slinking back into darkness.

I stopped in front of the trees and stood very still, waiting. If I was lucky I would hear it, the murmur of a conversation being spoken miles away. Hazel was right: sound worked differently on the farm. No secret could be kept from us. We heard housewives arguing, affairs being consummated, children playing. Depending on which way the wind was blowing, sometimes we could even hear screams from the theme park miles away, whips of frenzied sound. I listened to remind myself there was a world out there and that we were safely hidden away from it.

*

After breakfast, I scraped the leftovers into the slop bucket for the pigs. The smell was terrible. Sarah promised me I would get used to it, but she was biased. She'd known the pigs far longer than me, and loved them more than I ever could. Talking to them when she thought no one could hear, scratching their fat bottoms until they squealed. One of them had a tooth that had grown so long it hung out of its mouth like a cigarette, which Sarah sometimes tugged fondly.

I worked until lunch weeding the allotment, a loamy smell in the back of my throat from the raspberries which shone sweetly pink. Later, we would gather them into paper punnets and take them into the village to sell. Mothers liked to buy them for their children, who gorged until their tongues turned bright red, their chubby little hands grasping for more.

Despite my promise to visit, I hadn't seen or spoken to my mother since moving to Breach House. There was no way of knowing if she'd tried to contact me: I'd got rid of my phone. Occasionally and out of nowhere I would remember something about her, an obscure detail dredged up from my childhood. How she used to sit me in the bath and conjure stories from the tiles on the wall. They had pictures of cottages on them, with garden paths leading from one house to the next, and I'd beg her to keep going until the water turned cold. Or later, right before the death of my father, making a weeknight tradition of pizza and bad movies. How she would order extra olives for me even though it spoiled the taste for her, making little piles of them on the side of her plate.

After I'd finished in the allotment, I went inside and closed the door to the living room. I knew the landline was still connected because occasionally the phone would ring, women like me who'd heard about Breach House and wanted to know more. There was something uncanny about being on the other end of those calls, like gazing through a portal and witnessing an earlier version of myself. I perched on the end of the sofa and began dialling, hung up, dialled again.

She answered on the third ring, sounding out of breath like she'd just come from upstairs. 'Hello?'

'It's me,' I said.

Without delay, she replied: 'The boiler's been broken for two days now.'

I fidgeted with the fabric of the sofa, unpicking its threads. 'You don't need the heating,' I told her. 'It's boiling out.'

I could almost hear her rolling her eyes. 'I know that, but I need hot water for my baths. You know my joints ache unless I'm able to soak them. I've been hobbling around since Tuesday.'

I thought about hanging up. The truth was I didn't particularly care about my mother's joints or what state her appliances were in. That's not to say I was callous – I'd just been hoping for something different.

'There's a sticker for the number you need to call on the boiler,' I told her. 'Don't try and repair it yourself, you'll make things worse.'

There was a scuffling sound on the other end of the line. I pictured her carrying the phone into the kitchen, putting the kettle on. 'I bumped into Nessa the other day,' she told me. 'She mentioned she hasn't seen you since you moved.'

'I've been busy,' I replied. 'It's not as easy for me to get around any more, where I am.'

I heard her sniff. 'You left some things in your room. I wasn't sure what to do with them so I put them in the garage. I can't guarantee they won't get damp though, we've always had a problem with damp in there.'

'It's fine. I won't need anything.'

I waited to see if she would say something else, a plumbing for information. I wanted her to be concerned, I realised. I wanted my mother to ask me if I was all right. She hadn't asked me that in years. Even when I told her about my break-up with Nathan, the only thing she wanted to know was whether I'd done something to upset him. I'd joined Breach House to do something monumental with my life, but if I was being truthful with myself, I'd also joined to get a rise out of the ones I'd left behind. I wanted my absence to be grieved. I wanted to be missed.

'What have you been up to?' I asked when my mother didn't say anything.

She cleared her throat. There was more scuffling. 'Well, actually, I've been thinking about taking a leaf out of your book and going on holiday. Somewhere with impressive vistas. I want to feel like I'm in a James Bond film.'

I imagined my mother in a different country, struggling to order sparkling water in a foreign language. She would be the sort of person who'd interrupt a couple's romantic dinner by asking to sit with them, thinking they'd recount the anecdote fondly to their friends back home – the interesting older woman who'd instilled her wisdom, and not as the spinster who'd spoiled their evening.

'When are you going?' I asked. I thought I heard the floorboards creak outside the corridor, but when nobody came in I assumed it must have been the heat causing the wood to expand.

'Nothing's been decided yet,' she said. 'But I was thinking in a month or so. Helen next door says she'll look after James while I'm gone.'

'It sounds like you've given it some thought,' I told her.

'A change of scenery,' she said, wistful. 'You've inspired me.'

I looked down and saw that I'd almost shredded the fabric on the arm of the sofa. My fingers felt sore. 'Mum,' I said. 'Do you ever think about what happened with Dad? Not the accident, I mean, but before.'

Silence. It wasn't the first time I'd asked the question and I didn't expect her to answer. But then she made the smallest sound in her throat, as if trying to dislodge something. 'Yes, sweetheart. I think about it all the time.'

'Do you ever blame yourself?'

The sound of hot water being poured, a gush of steam. 'Do you?' she asked. I pondered the phrasing of her question, whether she was asking if I blamed her, or myself.

'I don't know,' I told her, a familiar flush of anger and blame and something that felt remarkably like guilt. 'I think your trip sounds perfect,' I said, my voice sticky as I struggled to take a breath. 'I think you're going to have a wonderful time.'

After I'd said goodbye and hung up, I went to open the door but then stopped myself. I couldn't say why but I was certain there was somebody on the other side of the door, listening. I pressed my ear to the wood but couldn't hear anything. It might have been Molly trying to scare me, or Pearl playing one of her tricks, but I didn't think so.

I called out to whoever might be there, but there was no reply.

15

We were too old for hide and seek but I soon learned it was the women's favourite pastime, and that a game could begin at any moment. During breakfast, a woman might bang her spoon down on the table and scream, *Hide!* Or in the middle of the night, a hand would rap against the window and you'd jolt from sleep already counting. Then it was a case of finding somewhere to hide. Nowhere was off limits except for Blythe's room.

The first few times, I ran into the woods. Ducked behind a fallen branch and waited. However, I soon learned that the woods held no allegiance to me, that I could be found too easily, the women knowing the land far better than I did. Most times I wouldn't even hear them: they'd simply wrap a hand around my mouth or push me down, and that would be that.

I learned to hide in the places no one thought to look, cramming myself into the airing cupboard or the gap behind the television we never watched. I found that my body could be mangled into the perfect shape for these narrow spaces, elbows stuffed into ribcage, nose touching kneecap. Sometimes a whole hour would pass before anyone found me. It was important to live in a state of readiness, balanced on the balls of my feet. Ready at a moment's notice to run.

I was hanging my laundry out to dry when the next game began, a group of women bursting from the house, screaming. I ran inside the house, leaving my sheets to moulder in the dirt. The kitchen was empty and I pressed myself against the counters, skirted towards the walk-in pantry. I found that if I exhaled all the breath from my lungs, I could fit behind the wall of spice jars. There was a small window in the pantry overlooking the driveway. I watched as Lucy, the woman I slept next to in the coach house, crawled underneath the car, scrambling on her hands and knees. She looked uncomfortable, gravel imprinting her forearms like soft clay. She tried turning on to her side but the space was too narrow, and I watched as she began to panic, floundering until she was pinned by the exhaust, her legs kicking uselessly. The sound of her struggle drew attention, and soon Molly appeared from around the side of the house with her arms outstretched, loping towards the car. The two women tousled for a violent moment before Molly dragged Lucy from underneath the car, shrieking.

The pantry door opened. I remained very still as Pearl edged her way inside. 'Shit,' she said, noticing me. 'Can I hide in here with you?'

'I don't think we can both fit.' But she'd already followed me into the negative space, our shoulders knocking together. She slipped an arm around my back to make more room and I could tell she hadn't washed yet, the spice of her catching in the back of my throat.

She squirmed, impatient. 'I used to hide behind the stage during lunchtimes at school. I hated the playground.' I pictured Pearl as a pupil, knew that we would not have been friends. Not because of our differences, but because of our similarities. There was a molecule in each of us that made us defer to others. I saw it in the way Pearl tried so hard with the other women, always striving to make them laugh and notice her. I suspected it was a large part of why she'd wanted to talk to those men, to provoke a reaction. She was weaker than the other women. If we'd been in school together, I would have avoided her to prevent other students from noticing my own weakness – it was terrible, but true. Hazel, on the other hand, struck me as someone who'd dipped in and out of social circles on a whim, the kind of girl who was invited to every party and went to none. Her desirability only increased by her indifference. We would not have been friends either.

Pearl readjusted, the movement causing the shelf to sway. We held our breath, bracing ourselves for the jars to topple and smash. 'Nobody ever looked for me behind those big velvet curtains,' she continued. 'I was quiet as a mouse.' I felt something tickle along the back of my neck and cried out, but it was only Pearl, running her fingers along my skin. She laughed, a flash of gum and yellow teeth. 'You're so gullible.'

'If you keep making noise, you can go and hide somewhere else,' I told her, surprised by my own anger. The temptation to shove her out the way.

She made a watery noise. 'All right, jeez. I'm sorry, I was only joking. I'm being quiet now.'

Guilty, I wound my arms further in so they pressed against my ribcage, a concession of space. She smiled, tucked in closer.

After a while Pearl complained of being hungry and opened one of the jars of apricots on the shelf. She drank the syrup noisily, the silvery liquid pooling at the corners of her mouth. When she offered the jar to me I popped one of the fruits in my mouth whole and chewed slowly, letting it break down to paste between my teeth. There was a fuzziness to the apricot which reminded me of a cat's tongue, surprisingly dry. Occasionally we heard the scurry of footsteps outside the pantry and fell still, our breath the only thing passing between us. Pearl seemed perpetually on the brink of laughter and I clamped a hand around her mouth, feeling the tacky residue of apricots on my palm.

I was so preoccupied with keeping her quiet that at first I didn't notice it, the gathering fire-crackle of tyres on gravel. I looked out the window and saw a silver car easing down the driveway. It stopped outside the house and cut the engine. The sun shone on the passenger window, obscuring what was on the other side. I felt Pearl tense next to me, her sticky fingers pressed against my shoulder.

It wasn't unusual to see other cars. Women regularly came and went. But I could see on Pearl's face that something was different. The way she tugged at her bottom lip, skittish. 'What?' I asked.

She scrambled out of our hiding space, the game forgotten. 'It's nothing,' she said. 'Stay here, I'll go and see.'

I waited two minutes before following. Out in the hallway the other women seeped from the crevices of the house, crawling from their hiding places. Underneath the table, behind the sofa. One woman unfurled herself from the hollow bench in the hallway, nothing but a tangle of limbs. The air jumped with their apprehension. Hazel appeared and instinct drove me to her, my interest quickening to panic although I couldn't say why. She touched my shoulder softly; so unlike her to offer comfort.

We flocked outside. Pearl was already on the driveway, waving her hands and saying something.

The car doors opened and two men got out. There was something uncanny about it, like seeing a dog walk on its hind legs. They shouldn't have been here. It was a physical sensation, acid percolating in my stomach, working its way up to my tongue as if to spew a warning: *Leave this place.* Their boots on the gravel were obnoxiously loud, grinding as they came towards us. One was taller than the other and they looked related, a duplication of crooked brows and too-large mouths, the way they both favoured their left leg when they walked. Hazel was rigid beside me – all the women were. It was different from when we'd spoken to the men in the village; that had at least been our choice. This was an invasion.

'Do you know them?' I asked.

Hazel wet her lips. 'They're Sarah's boys.'

A flash of recognition. Daniel and Callum, their heights recorded on the living-room wall. Only boys then, relics of their childhood scattered across the house. Plastic cups and plates with faded cartoon characters on them, a small child's raincoat buried at the back of the downstairs cupboard. When I'd first come to Breach House the women told me Blythe had rescued Sarah from an illness, that she'd saved her life, and in return Sarah had given her the farm. It didn't occur to me until now that she may have evicted her own children in order to help execute Blythe's vision.

The taller of the men – Daniel, if the brothers had continued to grow at an exponential rate – veered slightly to the right, approaching the wall of the farmhouse. He ran a hand along one of the windows, checking for signs of rot. I resented his suspicion, the implication that we were unable to look after the house ourselves. That we were not good women. He continued his inspection, unscrewing the light fixtures to see if the bulbs had blown, pulling a handful of weeds from the plant bed by the front door. He struck me as a man who bought his clothes in bulk, who would find a pair of trousers he liked and wear that style for ever.

Finally, he looked up at us. 'Where is my mother?' The women remained silent, chewing the dry skin off their lips. 'I tried calling,' he continued. 'But nobody answered.'

'You're not allowed here,' Molly said, all petulance and gloat. 'You have to go. This is sacred ground, for women. You are trespassing, you are defiling.' She would have sounded hysterical, if not for the indignity which was growing inside me, inside us all.

'I have just as much right to be here as you,' he replied. And then, sensing he wouldn't get much further if he carried on like that, added, 'Please. I have something to give my mother. I'll give it to her and then we'll go.' Clever man, trying to placate us. But we weren't so easily fooled.

Molly shook her head. She had something in her hand, was playing with it. 'You can give it to one of us and we'll decide if she needs it.'

The sun was a heavy fruit in the sky, its heat a nagging presence that made it difficult to move or think. My body felt salted, sucked of moisture. I kept forgetting to drink. There were sockets in the earth, holes where women had begun planting spinach and radishes and abandoned their task, drawn to the sound of Sarah's sons. A wheelbarrow full of plants was rapidly withering, their roots petrified and crisp. Daniel swiped a hand across his forehead, brushed the moisture off on his jeans. 'Be reasonable. I want to talk to my mother, and then I'll go. This is insane.'

'This is insane,' Pearl parroted, gleeful. I saw Molly whisper something to Ambika, who took off towards the allotment.

The other son, Callum, slammed the car door shut. I had forgotten about him until now and jumped at the sound. 'Let's go,' he said to Daniel. 'We can come back another time.' I could see Sarah in the shape of his jaw, the way he blinked harshly every now and again. I imagined him as a boy, eating from his colourful plastic plate, squeezing fistfuls of chopped cucumber on to the floor. Sarah taking him into the barn to look at the pigs, how he must have loved to hold the silken folds of their ears.

'We'll leave after we've talked to our mother.'

It was a fair request. Both of Sarah's sons, from what I could tell, were reasonable men. I didn't fear them the same way I'd feared the village men, who'd been hungry in their attention of us; demanding. They just wanted to see their mother. That was rational, wasn't it? We could permit them that, surely. And yet. Indignity washed over me, the certitude that they mustn't come any closer. This was our land now. We had suffered to get here and now they were threatening to spoil what we had created. With each step they took it felt as if something was being taken away from us. The other women seemed to sense it too, growing restless. We looked around at one another for reassurance, but what could we do? What could we say that would make them leave?

Callum came around the side of the car, giving us a wide berth. He had a softer face than his brother, watery eyes that reminded me of a cocker spaniel. On his left hand he wore a wedding ring. I wondered if Sarah had gone to the ceremony, doubted it. How did he explain his mother's absence to his wife? Did he say she was mentally ill? Or perhaps he invented a new life for her, a villa in the Canary Islands, somewhere flat and open where her lungs could bolster themselves on fresh coastal air. I'd never considered that the women of Breach House could be considered a source of shame for their families. Up until now I'd only ever thought of us as trailblazers. But seeing the hurt on Sarah's sons' faces was disconcerting.

'You can go inside if you want to,' Hazel said to me as the men continued their inspection of the house. 'You don't have to be here for this.' I told her I didn't mind, that I wanted to stay. It seemed important, just then, that I remained a part of the group. She shrugged but seemed pleased. 'Okay then.'

A few minutes later Ambika returned with Blythe and Sarah. They were filthy, must have been foraging in the woods, their pockets bulging with wild garlic and mushrooms. Blythe was barefoot, looking first at us and then at Daniel and Callum. If she was angry, she didn't show it, a slight movement on her face the only evidence she'd noticed them at all. Her arrival altered the dynamic on the farm, a subtle shift as the other women stopped fidgeting, waiting for their next instruction. I was reminded of the first time James had seen the neighbour's cat in my mother's garden, the alertness of encountering a new species without knowing whether it was a threat, an allowance of territory that could only ever be temporary. Sarah came forward and asked what Daniel and Callum were doing here. The brothers glanced at each other, unsure of what to say under Blythe's watchful scrutiny. Eventually Daniel reached into his bag and held out something to Sarah. Soft words were passed between them.

I strained to listen but could only make out disconnected syllables, hand gestures that seemed to communicate concern and dismissal in equal measure. All the while Blythe remained stalwart, no attempt made to interfere in Sarah's conversation with her children. She didn't need to, was confident in our dedication to her.

Finally, a decision was reached and the men began to back away. Sarah returned to Blythe's side, holding whatever it was Daniel had given her.

'Don't come here again,' Blythe told them. 'If you come here again, I can't promise what will happen to you.'

Daniel and Callum got back in the car. As they began reversing down the driveway there was a blur of motion followed by the shattering of glass. I looked over to see Molly with her hand splayed open, whatever she'd been holding a minute ago now gone. She let out a whoop of laughter, began pointing at the car's broken headlight. 'I got him,' she shouted. 'Look, I got him.'

We looked from the car – now ground to a halt, Daniel behind the wheel pie-faced and blinking – to Blythe. How she smiled, approval glinting from between her teeth. Not just approval, but permission.

One by one, the other women began picking up stones from the driveway. Lucy and Pearl and Ambika, even shy Tanya, who let out a scream as she aimed hers at Daniel's head. I watched as Hazel hefted a jagged piece of slate, the tip sharp enough to slice, and in one clean movement hurled it at the car. A metallic sound as it hit the bonnet and bounced off.

It quickly became a competition, who could cause the most damage. A rain of stone and gravel as the women aimed for the car's headlights, mirrors, windshield. At some point I looked down and saw that I was holding a rock. Someone must have given it to me, or perhaps I'd bent down and picked it up, I couldn't remember. I wasn't a violent sort of person and yet I was seized by the sudden urge to do damage, to reclaim our land from Sarah's sons. I wanted to join in. It looked *fun*.

I threw without really looking and was surprised when I heard the windshield fracture. Hazel was next to me, laughing loudly, wrapping an arm around me and guiding us backwards as the car finally began to move. For a moment I thought Daniel would get out, wondered what the women would do to him if he did. Wanting – for just a moment – to see them devour him. But then the car was reversing, peeling back down the driveway, out of range of our onslaught, although we continued throwing rocks well after the car had vanished from our sight, until the sound of the engine had faded into nothing.

*

Later that evening Hazel took my hand and led me upstairs. There was only one bathroom on the farm and it was shared between all of us, a constant stream of breasts and thighs fighting for the remaining hot water. All the fittings were seventies avocado, even the pipes, which had been painted green to match. The tiles had pictures of kingfishers on them. On the floor, tufts of hair swept across like tumbleweed. Hazel closed the door behind us and wedged the laundry hamper in front of it, the lock having been removed some time ago. She gestured for me to perch on the toilet seat and ran a bath.

Steam filled the room, revealing messages on the cabinet mirror drawn by the other women. Smiley faces and declarations of love, the word 'whore', which meant very little in a place like this. I looked down at my feet and saw the brittle crescents of someone else's toenails. 'They're pigs,' Hazel said, resting her backside against the bath so we faced each other. She brushed the clippings away with her foot. 'It's like living with my sister, but worse.'

'You have a sister?'

'Yes, I have a younger sister.'

I considered this, recalculating my ever-changing image of her. 'What's she like?' The pounding rush of water: I had to listen carefully to hear her next words.

'She likes banoffee pie and gymnastics. She broke both of her legs in a trampoline competition when she was twelve and I had to wheel her around school for weeks afterwards.'

'I think I'd have liked having a sister,' I said.

'Everyone who doesn't have one says that,' Hazel replied. I wanted to ask where Hazel's sister was now, if she was waiting for her to come back. What happened in a home that led one sister to a place like this, but not the other? Hazel ran her hand under the tap to check the water temperature, adjusted it. 'Are you upset about today?' she asked.

'No,' I said, but it came out all wrong, the word puckered and petulant. The excitement of our earlier violence had drained from my body, leaving behind a chalky residue. I'd be lying if I said I hadn't enjoyed scaring Sarah's sons – that the rock in my hand hadn't felt like power – but now that it was over, I felt mean, and tired.

After we'd chased them away, Blythe had peeled Sarah's hands apart to see what she'd been given. It was a pink cosmetic bag, the kind of thing you might find discounted at a chemist. I'd glimpsed boxes of medication inside. Blythe didn't say anything, but I could tell some order had been issued by the way Sarah bobbed her head, made her way back inside the farmhouse without looking at any of us. Later, I'd gone to wash my hands at the kitchen sink and looked down to find the half-melted residue of a capsule lodged in the drain. When I pulled Pearl aside and asked if anything like that had happened before, she smiled at me and shrugged as if she'd already forgotten the whole thing. We didn't eat dinner that night. Blythe's mood had shifted by then, grown dark. It wasn't so much the fact they'd been men, I thought, that angered her, but the medication they'd given to Sarah. The idea that there existed a solution that was not her.

'You have to understand,' Hazel went on. 'Those people, they don't mean anything. They don't know what's best for us. And if they did, they wouldn't want it for us anyway.'

I found myself needing, very badly, to believe Hazel. And maybe she was right. How could people like Sarah's sons know what was best for us? We had spent our entire lives having things prised out of our hands by men like them. Men who wrapped their arms around us and squeezed until we couldn't breathe, and told us to be thankful that we were being held at all.

When the bath was almost full, Hazel turned off the taps. 'You go first,' she told me, standing up. I waited to see if she would turn around. When she didn't, I undressed quickly and got into the bath. She took up my place on the edge of the toilet seat, began to pick under her nails. The water was hot and delicious, eating me up to the neck. I leaned back to soak my hair, submerging myself until only my nose poked out. Underwater, the language of the house intensified. I could hear the other women's footsteps below me, muffled and deep as if I had returned to the womb. When I finally came back up, Hazel was in the middle of saying something.

'What?' I asked.

'I said, do you want me to wash your hair?'

'Okay.'

She dug around under the sink, found an old cup to fill with water. Her other hand gently tugging on my hair, guiding my head back. Her nails were long, and when she began lathering shampoo on to my scalp it stung a little. I didn't say anything, not wanting to ruin the moment. There was no way of knowing when she would next touch me like this, power in her fickleness. Some people were just like that, able to wield their affection like a weapon.

'You have nice hair,' Hazel said, her voice close to my ear.

'Thank you,' I replied, disbelieving. 'So do you. It was one of the first things I noticed about you, when I first saw you up on the downs.'

Hazel's hands faltered. Only for a moment, her fingers tight on my scalp. Long enough to make me worry. But then she carried on shampooing my hair. 'You're sweet,' she said softly.

The water soon grew tepid. My fingers became doughy, boneless. I imagined myself slipping down the plughole, disappearing into the pipes of the house. There was a layer of dirt floating on top of the water and I peered down at my body with faint disgust. Went to get up, but then Hazel was forcing my head under the water, rinsing the soap away.

16

After the appearance of Sarah's children, my dreams became unstable. I dreamt in lurid colour, the recurring beam of a headlight cutting through the window and carving a laser-bright trail across the room, setting fire to my bedsheets. Foxes and owls duplicated in size and roamed the farm's perimeter, a wild rumpus with their eyes like yellow dinner plates. One night I dreamt my father was standing outside my window. He was wearing glasses, which was unusual because he'd usually worn contacts, said it made him look younger. Light bounced off the lenses, obscuring his eyes. In the dream I opened the window, a wash of cool air rising to greet me. My father was holding something in his hand. A present, wrapped in childish paper. I knew it wasn't meant for me and the certainty of this was sickening. *Why?* I wanted to ask, but my mouth would not move in the way I wanted it to, kept flapping open and closed. *Why did you do it?*

It didn't escape my notice that all my dreams took place at Breach House now. Even my subconscious recognised my tether to the place, as if I could no longer exist outside of it.

*

There were physical changes too, a gradual transfiguration that I noticed in fits and starts. Carting the wheelbarrow up the compost heap and realising it no longer stripped the breath from me, the new muscle in my arms making easy work of it. My fingernails became blunt, I went up two dress sizes. There was an intensity to mealtimes, the other women squabbling over the final scraps on a plate, their gums rimed with second and third helpings. My skin hardened from the heat, layers of it peeling away under the sun to reveal something coarser underneath, like a pelt. Mosquitoes laid their eggs in the stream and came to us at night already fat on the blood of other animals, stippling our wrists and ankles with bites. I spent hours scratching myself, nails digging into skin until there was a rupturing, followed by a spurt of red. Eventually the bites crusted into scars, formed a braille across my body which I compulsively felt the need to stroke over and over again.

Blythe noticed the changes happening to my body too and rewarded them with her attention. Passing me in the corridor and resting a hand, briefly, on my shoulder. Gifting me a spare pair of gloves. Once, at breakfast, she made another woman move down the table so I could sit next to her and spent the entire time asking my opinion about various matters: did I think one of the pig's eyes looked inflamed? Would planting extra marigolds in the allotment keep the rabbits away? I tried my best to be helpful, imbuing my voice with a confidence I didn't always feel. I wanted her to think of me as useful, a boon. That desire only increased the more I got to know her.

I'd soon learned after joining Breach House that Blythe's temper was constantly in flux. A good mood should be taken advantage of when it came, but it was just as important to know when to make yourself scarce. Her anger was a wild dog, could snap without warning. It needed something to latch on to and inevitably that meant us. One day Ambika forgot to close the freezer door and everything inside defrosted, casseroles leaking rancid from their Tupperware and stinking up the entire house. When she realised what had happened, Ambika sat on the floor and cried. Molly, who'd helped raise three of her siblings and therefore always seemed prepared for some low-level disaster, rolled her sleeves up and began to clean the mess away. But when Blythe saw what had happened, she accused us of being wasteful, stupid women. For the next two days she took away our toilet paper, an infantile punishment that was surprisingly cruel, made us feel incapable. I learned from that point onwards to be vigilant, to behave as if Blythe was always standing behind me, watching.

*

One day we decided to cut our hair into matching pixie cuts to keep the heat off our necks. It had originally been Ambika's idea after she'd grown bored of listening to Molly complain, although once we saw how it looked, we all begged Ambika to do ours. It suited some more than others and didn't suit me at all. My mother told me my ears were too long for my face, joked that the doctor must have grabbed on to them when they pulled me out of her, causing them to stretch. But it was the kind of thing I felt I couldn't say no to, especially once I saw the other women in their matching looks.

We were upstairs in Molly and Ambika's room. It was slightly larger than Hazel's, and less austere, covered in the kind of clutter you'd expect from a long-term relationship. Piles of clothes on top of an armchair, multiple glasses of stale water on the bedside table. I caught a glimpse of someone's dirty underwear discarded underneath the bed and quickly looked away.

When she was done, Ambika blew the shed hair from my shoulders and held up a mirror. She asked me if I liked it and of course I told her yes.

As I went to go back downstairs, there was the sound of someone whistling. I looked and saw Hazel watching me from her bedroom, the door pared back just far enough to show a sliver of her face. She was sat cross-legged on top of her bed.

'Come here,' she told me.

I went into her room and closed the door behind me, blocking off outside noise. It was easy to believe, when it was just the two of us, that we existed inside a vacuum. Or else we'd sunk to the bottom of the ocean where no one could find us – a feeling of muteness, of isolation.

I approached the bed slowly, the grain of the floorboards uncomfortable on my bare feet. Hazel had brought the kitchen radio upstairs, which I didn't think was allowed. She'd tuned into a station playing classic rock anthems, the kind of thing my father would have listened to in the car.

'During the seventies when he was doing a lot of cocaine, David Bowie said he lived off a diet of milk and peppers,' I said, offering the fact up like currency and immediately feeling foolish for it. Hazel raised an eyebrow, unimpressed. She had a notebook in her lap and was jotting something down, the ebb and flow of her handwriting momentarily distracting me. 'Is that your diary?' I asked.

'Do you really think I'd keep a diary?' she replied. I noticed now she held her pen a strange way, hand curled over the page, effectively writing the words upside down. 'These other bitches can't keep their hands to themselves. The only way to keep something private is to keep it private.' She tapped on the side of her head.

I took another couple of steps forward until my leg touched the bed. When she didn't react, I perched on the mattress. 'You don't trust the other women?'

She pulled a face. 'It's not about trust. But no, I don't trust them.' She closed the notebook and leaned back against the headboard. 'Are you telling me if the chance presented itself, you wouldn't read my diary?' It seemed absurd to try and lie to her. Luckily, I didn't have to. 'I mean, I'd read yours, if you had one. That's just obvious.'

'I'm not sure what you'd be expecting to find,' I told her. 'You know everything about me already.'

She narrowed her eyes. 'You can't know everything about someone. But, I know enough about you. I know the important things, otherwise I wouldn't have brought you here.'

I was a moth, drawn to an inexplicable flame. 'Like what?' I asked.

There was an eruption of laughter outside the room, more women come to be shorn. I shifted on the bed, reminding Hazel I was there.

'Most of the women here want to be looked after. They don't want to make decisions that might end up hurting them, so that's why they look to Blythe – for direction. It comforts them to know they're safe here. But I don't think you're looking for safety.'

I wondered if that were true. I wanted to believe Hazel knew me better than I knew myself, took comfort in being perceived so deeply, but there was a part of me that felt no different from the other women. It was difficult to know, sometimes, how I felt.

I waited to see if Hazel would say something more, but she'd gone back to writing in her notebook, the tip of her tongue peeking from the corner of her mouth.

'I guess you learned through trial and error about keeping a diary,' I said instead. She shook her head, a question. 'Diaries seem like the perfect leverage when you have a sister.'

'Oh,' she said. 'Yeah.'

Her hair fell across her face in a sheet. She was the only one of us who hadn't wanted to cut her hair. I was quietly relieved. Not only because I loved the length of her hair as it was, but because it reaffirmed to me that Hazel was different from the others.

As if sensing my thoughts, she asked: 'Are you happy with it?'

I touched my hair. 'It's different.'

'Come here,' she said, and again I obeyed, shuffling forward until our kneecaps knocked together. She leaned in, her breath milk-sweet against my cheek, and dusted the fringe from my forehead. Adjusting strands of my hair in a particular way until I felt it sit differently against my scalp, more comfortable than before. It continued like this, the careful give and take of touch, her fingers never making contact with my skin long enough for me to memorise the sensation of them. It occurred to me that I had been living with Hazel for months now and still lacked crucial information about her, the kind of things I'd learned about Nathan without really meaning to. For instance, I didn't know whether she flossed or if she preferred to sleep on a particular side of the bed. Did she have a favourite fruit? I should have paid closer attention to her writing: I hadn't noticed whether she was left- or right-handed.

Her hand travelled from my head to my jaw, a slow trace of skin and muscle. Electricity jumped between us, a quick shock of static that almost made me recoil. But the rarity of the moment – Hazel's affection – stayed me. She was cool even though it must have been close to twenty-five degrees in her bedroom. The heat didn't seem to affect her as it did everyone else. Even Blythe suffered during the day, complaining of her thighs chafing, but Hazel continued to be the exception, could spend all day in the sun without burning.

We had to get back to the allotment soon. If I thought work would ease up in the summer, I'd been wrong; we drove into the village almost every day now to sell our produce before it spoiled in the heat. But I didn't want to leave and ruin the moment, whatever it meant. 'There,' she said, admiring her work. 'That looks more like you now. Do you want to see?'

I nodded, and she climbed off the bed, went and found a hand mirror in one of her drawers. She held it up to me. The hairstyle still didn't suit me but she had done something new to it, softened it so I didn't look so severe. 'I like it,' I said, and found that I was telling the truth. 'I think it will look better when it grows out a bit, to cover my ears.'

'No,' she said. 'That's the bit I like most.'

'They're too long for my face,' I said, my voice slipping into a whisper.

Hazel shook her head. 'This is exactly how you're meant to look.'

I would have been angry with her if I'd had the capacity for it. She reminded me of Blythe, her intentions so unknowable. Being with her was like standing in a room with all the lights off, blundering around and hoping you didn't knock anything over. I often had no idea what she wanted from me. She'd been the one to bring me to Breach House and yet sometimes I got the feeling she didn't want me there at all. She would snap at me or ignore me altogether, and I would feel the need to overanalyse everything I'd said or done. She didn't like hearing about my life before Breach House and yet it was the only thing she ever wanted to talk about. Endless questions about Nathan, whether I wished we were still together and if I missed him. She was jealous, I understood, and yet there was something stopping her from coming to the same realisation.

Lately I'd begun to fantasise about making a small incision in her skin. Imagined the task being near-impossible, the scalpel struggling to cut through her. When I was finally able to, I'd stick my finger inside the gap and open it wider. Just to see – to know – what was hiding underneath.

17

The next day I accompanied Hazel, Molly and Pearl into the village, lugging crates of cherries and raspberries between us. The market wasn't on so we found a shaded spot next to a bus shelter and draped a pink gingham cloth across the ground, displayed the punnets of fruit like exotic wares. The summer holidays had begun a few days earlier and teenagers were out in full force, groups of them in their oversized shirts and trainers, talking too loudly and looking for something to impress each other with. They circled us, trying to be clever, daring one another to say something, to steal one of the punnets. A boy, no older than fifteen, pushed a girl forward and said, 'Can she join you lot? She's grade-A butch.'

Bravado. I saw the whites of their eyes as they came close, the twitch of muscle in their necks as they willed themselves to keep on grinning. It was clear they were afraid of us. Good, I thought.

Maybe it was the heat, but I gradually sensed a change in the village's atmosphere. Everyone seemed agitated, reluctant to part with their money. 'This is pointless,' Hazel complained, swatting an insect against her neck. 'We should just go back, we're not selling anything.'

'No,' Molly said. 'Let's wait it out a while longer. Unless you want to be the one to tell Blythe we came back empty-handed.'

Hazel swore but conceded, kicked at the pavement.

I sifted a hand through my hair, glanced at the others and wondered: was it the uniformity that frightened the villagers? Before, we'd looked similar with our dirt-stained hands and clothing, but there'd been enough physical permutations to differentiate us. Now, except for Hazel, we were all identical in our new haircuts. I didn't know how to feel about that. I'd been working towards cementing myself as one of the women of Breach House for some time now and grooming myself to look like them had felt like an important step. But there was something disarming about the way people looked at us now, as if unable to make out our individual faces.

Pearl said she needed the toilet and went to go and find one. I made myself busy while Hazel and Molly continued to bicker, wandered down the street with one of the cherry punnets and an empty cup. Offering a taste to anyone who made eye contact with me. Most people chewed the cherry slowly, careful not to snap a tooth, and spat the pit out into the empty cup. But some would miss and spit it on to my arm or wrist and walk off without apologising. By the time the punnet was empty, my skin was mottled with juice and saliva.

I walked further on, into a narrow alleyway between two buildings. It was a relief to be out of direct sunlight – a relief to be on my own, if I was honest, although I felt bad for thinking it. But there was only so much squabbling and the sound of other women's breath and gas that I could take. Humans weren't made to be on their own, but they weren't made to be in constant contact with one another either.

By the time I headed back, Pearl had also returned, with a group of men in tow. I recognised them as the same ones from a few weeks before – Scott and his friends.

Pearl was talking excitedly with Scott, laughing louder than was necessary. She held a punnet of raspberries up to him, crushed one in her fist so the juice dripped down her wrist. He smiled and handed over some money but didn't take the fruit.

I'd seen Scott a few times on various trips into the village but hadn't thought much about it. He and his friends hadn't tried talking to us again, although it was clear they wanted to. Their gazes burrowing, trying to get the shape of us. After what had happened with Sarah's sons, I felt even more uncomfortable around them, kept looking over my shoulder as if Blythe might suddenly appear. The thought of men in general made me uncomfortable now. I realised I'd begun to think of them as something wholly separate to me, a feeling of betrayal when I thought about my father or Nathan, as if living at Breach House meant there was no longer space for them in my head.

Pearl said something to make Scott laugh. They were leaned in close so I wasn't able to catch the flow of their conversation, although I saw Scott nod and relay something to his friends.

'She's embarrassing,' Hazel said, scratching a layer of dead skin from her shoulder. 'I'm embarrassed for her.'

'What did they want?' Molly asked when Pearl finally came back.

She shrugged. 'Nothing. I was just being polite.' Laughing when we didn't reply, like it was all some kind of game. 'Relax, ladies. You'll get wrinkles.'

Eventually the heat won out. Fruit beginning to moulder in their crates, a fermented reek that made you light-headed when you got too close. What cherries were left turned jammy, the stones falling out of them already dark with rot. We were sun-scorched, our noses and ears painful to the touch. Molly was the last to give in but nodded when we said it was time to pack up.

Hazel insisted on driving back to the farm and we felt her impatience in the hydraulics. The way she steered the car around blind corners recklessly, narrowly avoiding oncoming cars, which sounded their horns in fury. I began to feel so nauseous I rolled the window down and pressed my tongue against the roof of my mouth, willing myself not to be sick.

Other things I noticed along the way: the wind lashing against my face. Pearl fiddling with the radio until she landed on some wretched pop song, nobody bothering to stop her. The fungus gnats which somehow always managed to get in, which we crushed to pulp against the dashboard. Dog walkers. The road gradually sloping downhill, enveloping us in tree-shade. Hazel, Hazel, Hazel.

*

Blythe was going on another one of her trips to meet with a woman who was interested in the farm. There was talk of an investment, although who could say what that really meant. According to the others, the woman had received a small fortune from a wrongful-death lawsuit after her mother was crushed in the warehouse where she worked. Now, grieving, she was searching for a way to put the money to good use. Of course, this might have been the kind of story that got bent out of shape on its way along the grapevine, so that by the time it reached me, it seemed too sensational to be anything other than true. Molly claimed she'd met the woman once and that she wore a watch worth over two thousand pounds. That, more than anything, seemed to confirm the story we'd been told.

Blythe said she would be gone a couple of days and that Sarah was coming with her, to help with administration. This surprised us. Usually when Blythe left on one of her errands Sarah became leader *de jure*, mother hen. With her gone as well, it would be the first time we'd been left by ourselves. Realisation dawned quietly on the women, who didn't discuss this new development but rather communicated their surprise by exchanging fleeting glances; curious quirks of their mouths.

I didn't know it at the time, but we'd gone exactly four weeks without rain on the morning Blythe and Sarah left. The heat was getting to us. Our skin kept breaking out in rashes of pimples that speckled across our foreheads and chins and which we couldn't help but pick at. My scalp came away in thick flakes. Everyone on the farm had the same tight look about them, as if their flesh pressed too close to their skin. We were more lacklustre than we should have been, the onslaught of the day stifling our reactions as Blythe and Sarah disappeared down the driveway.

Blythe hadn't left us with any instruction other than to keep the crops watered.

*

At lunch we gathered in the kitchen, peering around at one another. There were fewer of us than usual, the women who didn't live on the farm drifting back to their own homes after a few hours, as if they didn't see the point of remaining without Blythe.

We formed an assembly line and began making something

to eat. I drained a large bowl of butterbeans which had been soaking overnight and emptied them into a saucepan to boil, cooked them down into some kind of stew. Pearl chopped cucumber until someone told her to stop. We served everything on matching plates because that was what grown-ups did. Despite the irregularity of the situation, a frisson of excitement passed through the kitchen. Afterwards, someone suggested we watch a movie. We scratched our chins and said nothing. Despite knowing there was a television in the living room, for some reason we'd never thought to turn it on. I suppose because Blythe had never mentioned it, we assumed it was off limits.

'I doubt we get reception out here,' Molly said, which seemed to put an end to the discussion.

'I saw some VHS tapes on one of the shelves,' Ambika said. 'We could watch one of those.'

Pearl rolled her eyes. 'They're movies for babies.'

Molly said that meant they'd be perfect for Pearl, who stuck out her tongue and called Molly a slut.

We left our plates on the table and walked across the hallway to the living room. The curtains were drawn to keep the heat out, but spots of light shone through, casting a patina over the sofa, the stacks of old magazines I'd never seen touched. The television looked like it came from the eighties, set into a wooden cabinet with a dial on the front that made me think of bank vaults and robbers. A thick layer of dust coated the screen. We hovered, not wanting to be the first to sit down. It was still the middle of the day: we should have been working.

'Oh, fine,' Hazel said, going over to the bookshelf where the tapes were kept. Spaghetti westerns and Disney films,

The Little Mermaid smiling at us through a layer of grime. I tried not to think of the room as a crypt, the remnants of Sarah's previous life lingering in the corner like ghosts. Still. It was easy to imagine a family tradition, Saturday nights when Sarah would gather her children and husband, a man I imagined as having a carefully maintained moustache and love of model trains. She would let the children choose what film to watch, and Daniel, being the elder but still too young to understand the importance of kindness, would insist on something scary like *Indiana Jones*. Callum would agree, not wanting to appear like a baby, but also determined to enjoy the same things as his older brother. It made me uncomfortable, imagining the life that had occupied Breach House before we – Blythe – arrived.

Hazel chose a black-and-white movie about a gang of thieves planning a bank robbery. They had guns but it was meant to be funny I think, the leader often getting hit around the head with heavy objects, including a bird cage. One by one we sat down. The sofas were only large enough for three or four people so the rest of us sat on the floor, our legs crossed like schoolgirls. Hazel complained about her back aching and leaned against me for support. The warmth of her leaking through the fabric of my shirt.

After a while someone got up to make snacks, came back with a bowl full of leftover cherries which we slotted into our mouths and sucked on, spitting the stones at each other like we were no better than the locals. Molly claimed she could tie a cherry stem with her tongue and put one in her mouth to demonstrate, the swell of her tongue rolling against her cheek. Finally she opened her mouth and showed us, a perfectly formed knot. After that we all wanted to try, forever desperate to outdo one another. I found I was surprisingly good at it, nimble-mouthed and patient, working to thread one end of the stem into the other.

'It's not fair,' Hazel told me, throwing her stem on the carpet. 'You're good at everything.'

I searched her face for signs that she was mocking me. There couldn't exist a world in which Hazel considered me to be better than her. But she had turned away, this revelation confessed and forgotten like it was nothing. How I swelled with pride.

When the film finished some of us stood to go back outside. There was still work to do, and hours before our evening meal. Others lingered, wanting to carry on watching television. Blythe and Sarah had only been gone a matter of hours but already it felt like we were losing our sense of discipline. I looked to Hazel for a cue and sat back down when she did. We made eye contact and she pulled a face, somewhere between defiance and indifference. We were teenage girls, sneaking into our parents' alcohol cabinet, stealing sticky mouthfuls of cooking sherry.

*

Evening came. Hazel found an old packet of Butterkist popcorn in one of the cupboards and sprinkled it with so much salt it was inedible. I'd learned her palate was in constant flux, that she either ate food which was extremely spicy or entirely bland, scalding hot or stone cold. Gobbling down roast potatoes still bubbling with oil so they peeled the skin from the roof of her mouth, or else waiting until the gravy on her plate had cooled to form a pale rind and breaking it open with the heel of her spoon. This exactness was one of the reasons I was convinced she would outlast a nuclear holocaust. She was the kind of person made to endure the extreme.

After the first film, we put on another, and then another. A children's cartoon about a group of dinosaurs who came back to life and wreaked havoc on New York City, their carnage interspersed with songs about environmental awareness. Then an action movie about saving the president from terrorists. We watched with a kind of detached fascination, our eyes glazing over, no longer able to absorb the information on screen. Hazel gradually emptying the bowl of popcorn, her breath turning starchy. She looked around for something to pick the kernels out of her teeth with, resorted to a fingernail.

We didn't notice the lights at first, confusing them for an explosion on the television that lit up the entire room. But the sound that followed was unmistakable, a car door being opened.

'They can't be back already,' Molly said, fumbling for the remote, the others scrambling to stand, their faces bright with panic. Hazel and I exchanged a nervous glance, her fingers still inside her mouth, pouching the skin of her cheek.

'Maybe they forgot something,' Ambika suggested, although we knew that made no sense. Something must have changed. Perhaps Blythe's meeting had gone well and they'd concluded their business sooner than anticipated. Or maybe it had gone badly and she'd come home to the farm expecting to be comforted by us – her hardworking, obedient women. Either way we were in trouble.

Pearl got up and peeked behind the curtain. 'It's not them,' she said. 'It's not Blythe.'

'Who is it then?' Hazel asked, butting Pearl out of the way to look. 'Oh,' she said. 'Oh.'

Our relief at not being caught by Blythe turned to curiosity. We jostled for space in front of the window, elbowing each other out of the way. Desperate, now, to see.

More car doors slammed closed. I recognised them immediately. The men from the village.

*

Scott was tall. I'd known that before, but something about being up close to him now made me realise just how much taller he was than me. I only came up to his collarbone so that, when he hugged me, I felt myself pressed up against his armpit, the damp smell of sweat. He must have been in his early thirties but already had the gentle hump of a beer gut, skin that felt hard to the touch. There was a hyperactiveness to him, an excitement that was infectious, or at the very least charming.

'Hi, girls,' he greeted us. 'Hope you don't mind us dropping in.'

He was with the same friends who loped after him, Matthew, Aaron and someone they called Trout – either because of his surname or the bottom lip which protruded from his face and looked as if it had been stung by a wasp, pink and wet-looking. They formed a huddle, taking turns to light their cigarettes. As strange and familiar to us as a pack of wild animals.

They'd brought us gifts. Hazel called this premeditation but didn't refuse anything that was offered to her. There were gossip magazines and tubs of strawberry ice cream, an oversized stuffed animal that looked as though it had been won at a fair. The kind of things sitcoms and romantic comedies made out to be universally loved by women. Scott even went around handing out cylinders of lipstick, a cheap brand I didn't recognise. Make-up wasn't prohibited on the farm but we tended not to wear it for practical reasons. Foundation would run to paste after a couple of hours working outside, clog our pores with oil. Mascara hardening on our lashes, making it painful to remove. Still, the other women took the lipstick offered to them, turning it over in their hands as if unsure what to do next. For hours afterwards I caught them walking around with cherry mouths, their tongues peeking through the incision of their lips.

'This is trouble,' Tanya said quietly, watching the men continue to unload the boot of their car. With Sarah gone, she was the oldest among us, which seemed to add weight to her words, made them true. Pearl was talking to Scott, forming her hair into braids, twirling a strand around her finger and giggling. 'Blythe would kill us if she knew what was happening.'

'But what do they want?' Ambika asked. 'Why are they here?'

'How should I know?' Tanya said.

But it seemed obvious to me: they wanted us.

'Pearl here said it might be okay if we stopped by,' Scott said, addressing us with that smile. 'She told us what you're doing out here. We think it's great. We want to learn more, that's all. Would that be okay, do you think?'

We looked around at each other.

'You invited them?' Hazel asked Pearl.

Pearl hesitated, stealing glances at each of us. Trying to gauge our anger. She separated herself from Scott and came close. 'I mentioned Blythe was going away the last time we were in the village.' She added, defensive: 'They're just curious. They want to learn more about us. Isn't it better to include them in what we're doing rather than shutting them out? The more secretive we are, the more people want to see behind the curtain. It's human nature.'

'That's not your decision to make,' Molly told her. 'I can't believe you would be so stupid.'

Pearl stuck out her bottom lip, peevish. 'Well, they're here now. Let's just show them around. They only want to see where we live, and then they'll go. That would be okay, wouldn't it? If we just showed them around quickly.'

Molly looked at the rest of us. I opened my mouth, closed it again. I couldn't decide what made me more uncomfortable: the presence of the men or the fact that we were defying Blythe by letting them remain here. I kept looking behind my shoulder, half expecting Blythe to appear. Wondered if perhaps it was even some kind of test, a trap we'd all fallen into.

'I'm telling them to go,' Molly said. 'This isn't right.'

But already a crowd was forming around the men, those who were easily plied with trinkets and flattering words. Who talked to the men as if already well acquainted, guiding them around the side of the house towards the allotment. Words coming silky out of their mouths as they gorged themselves on strawberry ice cream, already half melted.

*

We decided to give the men – and in turn, Pearl – the benefit of the doubt. So they wanted to see how we lived, they were curious. Okay then. Hesitantly at first, and then with the kind of confidence that came only from fear, we led the men into the allotment. If there was any place on the farm that could be pointed to as the perfect iconography of who we were, it was here. We took them by the arm and guided them along the rows of cabbages and beetroot, the caned wall of garden peas weighted with their green cocoons. Pleated nests of kale, lettuce, fennel. Ground uneven with onions. Everywhere, the smell of growth. The men must have seen the pride on our faces, how we each pointed to a plot of land and revealed our connection to it: this is where I learned how to propagate rosemary, this is where I almost cut my thumb in half. Why shouldn't we boast? We'd worked hard to achieve what we had. Wasn't that worth talking about?

But I could see Scott and the others didn't understand. Their mouths trembled, on the cusp of laughter. Careful not to look at one another in case it set them off. Pearl must have noticed it too but decided the only way to correct their behaviour was to push through it, keep talking until they came round. She babbled about a new variety of chilli pepper she'd grown, so hot she'd almost choked to death the first time she ate one. If you want to try some, she told them, then you're only allowed the smallest mouthful. A lick from the tip of a toothpick.

Scott smiled politely and asked if it was time to go inside yet.

We led the men from the allotment towards the house, a silent procession. Each of us waiting for the other to say something, to put a stop to whatever was about to happen. But we were stubborn women, who'd been fatted on Blythe's belief that we were stronger, more capable than others. We told ourselves that we would take control of the men, cajole them into good behaviour. We would be in charge of the situation.

Once we'd let the men inside the house, though, it was

clear they had no intention of being controlled. A seal had been breached, a line overstepped and in the process erased, never to be crossed back over. They disseminated, splitting off into different rooms, eager to uncover our secrets. Picking items up at random and acting as if they'd never seem them before: a pocket mirror, playing cards, someone's hairbrush. The women laughed at the men's eagerness. Determined to treat the situation as something they still wanted. I pressed my back against the wall, chewed my nail down to the quick. A burst of pain, blood welling around the skin.

'My mum used to dip my fingers in nail varnish remover.' I looked up and saw Trout watching me. 'I'd bite my nails as a kid,' he explained. 'It drove her mad.' He took one of his hands out and showed it to me. His fingers were stubby, only a thin line of nail left.

'It didn't work then,' I said.

'Nope,' he replied. 'It's a hard habit to break.' A bead of saliva shone on his bottom lip. 'Or I'm just weak-willed. One of the two.'

18

We crammed into the conservatory, bodies piled on top of bodies. A bottle was passed around, something sweet and strong. I hadn't drunk in months. Alcohol wasn't allowed on the farm, although nobody pointed this out when Scott and his friends ferried a box of it from their car inside the house. This was a night of broken rules.

The women took turns swigging from the same bottle, making a big deal out of licking their lips and gasping. They were hyped up on their own rebellion, trying to outdo one another, liquid running down their chins as they took increasingly larger mouthfuls. Even Molly and Ambika joined in, although there was a sense of subterfuge about it, as if they were only doing it so they could remain in the room and bear witness to whatever was about to happen next. When the bottle came round to us, Hazel offered it to me first. Another one of her tests. I realised my decision would impact the rest of the evening, determine how she would treat me. I scrutinised her face, searching for the right answer, but she was stoic. Her mouth a placid line. I lifted the bottle to my mouth and drank. She took it from me and did the same.

It didn't take long for the men to make themselves comfortable. They raided the kitchen looking for glasses and something to eat, cutting chunks from the loaf Sarah had baked before leaving, crumbs speckling the floor. How quickly they were able to carve a space for themselves at Breach House. At first they'd been afraid to touch us, as if we might bite (who was to say we wouldn't?), but their courage soon grew. Small gestures at first, gently repositioning us when we got in the way, their hands featherlight on our waists and backs. Brushing imaginary lint from our clothes. And then, as we grew loose with alcohol, picking us up and spinning us around the room, tickling us until we sobbed.

Aaron found a deck of cards and taught us a few drinking games. There was one where we each had to pick a suit and then those suits would 'race', inching across the floor depending on what card was drawn next from the deck. Every time your suit was drawn, pushing you further towards the finish line, you drank. By the time diamonds overtook hearts, and then clubs and spades, I could no longer feel my face.

The women stamped their feet and screamed for a rematch. Their ferocity frightened me a little. I'd seen them behave like this before, still thought about Beltane and the disregard with which they'd hurled themselves across the bonfire, but something about this was different. I didn't like the way their eyes seemed to roll around in their heads, unable to focus on any one thing. Even Tanya, usually dependable, had begun to slur her words, drinking along with the rest of us.

But if Beltane had been a demonstration of relinquishing control, this was a theft – something taken from us. We were losing our grip.

There were silver linings. The press of Hazel's body against mine, how she kept lifting the bottle to my lips, urging me to drink. Wiping a spilled drop from the corner of my mouth with her thumb.

'Your arms are so tanned,' Pearl was saying to Scott, rolling his sleeve up and brushing a hand along his skin with practised nonchalance. He looked down at where she was touching him, a look of wonder on his face.

'I went to Greece a few weeks ago,' he told her. 'Have you ever been?'

Pearl laughed sweetly.

'Did you know,' Matthew piped up from the corner, 'if a person dies on a flight, they can't legally declare them dead until the plane lands?'

'Bullshit,' Scott said, a snap in his tone. Upset that he'd been interrupted.

Oblivious, Matthew sat up straighter. His words smeared by the alcohol. 'It's true. Flight attendants aren't even allowed to use confirmatory language. If the person next to you dies and you ask a flight attendant if they are in fact dead, all they can reply with is "It appears so." They leave the body in their seat and put a blanket over them. Only they don't cover up their face because then the other passengers might start to freak out.' He glanced around at us, clearly hoping to have horrified us, but we were not women who scared easily.

'Are you telling me the other passengers wouldn't notice if someone on board died?' Hazel said.

'It's not exactly the kind of thing you'd be keeping an eye out for, is it?' Matthew replied. 'Although if you're ever on a plane and you hear the flight attendants start talking about a Jim Wilson, that's code for a dead body.'

I looked over at Scott and Pearl, who'd sunk back into their own private conversation. She looked narrow beside him, a waif, her skin in the harsh strip lighting rendered a sickly translucent. Her fingers continued their glide along Scott's hand, each inch of him spelling disaster.

'What happens if the person sitting next to you dies?' Ambika asked Matthew. 'What if you're just sitting there and then you look and notice they're no longer breathing, what do you do then?'

He shrugged. 'A flight attendant would move you to an empty seat.'

'But what if it's a full flight?' she pressed.

'Well,' he said, carving the word into two syllables. *Weee-lll*. 'Then you'd have to wait until the plane landed.'

*

I met Nathan two days before Christmas, at a house party, wearing a dress that was too small for me. I'd gone on a whim, on my way home from work when I realised I was round the corner from the person who'd invited me. The apartment building was a new-build, anonymous and angular with green-tinted windows. Something about the rigidity of it comforted me, the straight-talking beams and parapets. I needed structure. I lingered outside the front door, breathed in the smell of alcohol, the change in temperature as bodies crammed together.

I'd never gone to a party alone before. Usually I relied on Nessa, who was good at talking to strangers. She always knew what questions to ask, how to keep a conversation going. I floundered under the pressure, stumbled over my words. Still, there was something exciting about being on my own. A possibility of reinvention.

After greeting the host, I poured myself a glass of wine and stood against the wall, taking delicate sips, the way another kind of woman might drink. The room teemed with people, an electric disco ball throwing coins of light around the room. No one looked at me.

After I'd drained my first glass, I poured myself another, and then another. Drinking until the wine no longer tasted like wine, but something blander, the saliva of my own mouth.

In the end there was only one person who talked to me. Nathan. He was slimmer back then, before he'd started going to the gym, and I remember looking down at his hands and thinking how similar they looked to mine. He asked if I wanted another drink and went to fetch one, returned with a plate of food. Starchy things, like bread and crisps. It was a kindness, I realised later. He was trying to sober me up.

We talked about the things that seemed important. He asked about my job (I worked in customer support for an online travel agency at the time) and whether I'd ever been to Thailand. He had. He'd been to lots of places, all over the world, Thailand and Bali and Australia. I felt embarrassed that I was the one who worked in travel and yet he'd seen more of the world than me, although he didn't draw attention to that. Instead he found topics of conversation I was able to talk about: who I hated most in this room, whether I'd be interested in having dinner with him sometime. I loved him for that.

At some point I excused myself to go to the bathroom and somehow ended up on the balcony. There were a few stragglers scattered around, a small group laughing among themselves. As I drew closer, I saw they were concocting something horrible, pouring what they could find into an empty pint glass. Leftover beer, vodka, orange juice. Cigarette butts, mince pies, a hawk of phlegm. The glass frothed with their brew, turning the colour of stale apple cores. They passed it to a young man who received it with reverence, as if he were taking communion. I wondered what he had done to deserve it. Cheated on his girlfriend, stolen money from one of them. Or maybe they had just dared him to do it and he was too afraid to say no. I couldn't move. Was suddenly held to the spot, waiting to see if this boy would drink it.

He raised the pint to his lips, took a sip. Someone tipped the glass, forced him to drink more. I watched as the first cigarette butt slipped into his mouth. His eyes scrunched and for a moment I thought he might choke, but the tobacco was moist enough by then to slip down his throat. They began to cheer him on, in support of him or not, their feet stamping the ground. He hunched over, trying not to spill any, but some escaped the glass and trickled down his cheek, his neck. Stained his white T-shirt, which looked brand new. I watched with a mixture of horror and fascination, wondering why he would agree to such a thing and then knowing absolutely why: because he wanted to impress these people. He wanted to be one of them.

They coaxed him into drinking every last drop and erupted when he did, hollering and chanting his name. He held the glass on top of his head, danced in a sickly circle. One of the men slapped him on the back. And then the group dissipated, already moving on, leaving the man behind with the dregs of his pint glass, wondering what had just happened. Across the courtyard we made eye contact. I felt sorry for him, that I'd been witness to his humiliation. He straightened, feigned bravado as he threw the glass against the nearest wall, but I could see him wince as it shattered. He strode past me back into the flat, a little unsteady on his feet.

I looked up again. One of the neighbours across the way was peering through the curtain, looking to see what the noise had been.

*

More bottles were passed around. The radio was turned up full volume, cheap speakers fraying the music, distorting it so we experienced it as a series of detonations through our bodies as opposed to any real melody. Someone knocked over a glass, screamed. I was that liquid level of drunk where my legs felt detached from my body. It hadn't taken me long to get there: my tolerance was so low now. Stumbling into the bathroom and barely making it in time to the toilet. The colour of my piss like melted butter.

When I went back downstairs I noticed Scott had a camera, the kind tourists wore around their necks. I asked him why he had it with him and he said it helped him remember.

He began taking pictures: of Pearl dancing on top of the table, the tendons in her delicate ankles flexing. Quiet Moira, lifting up her shirt. Tanya passed out on the sofa, her mouth wide open, revealing several fillings.

'I hate how they make women look in magazines,' he said, his voice damp behind the camera. 'It's not real, you know? I want to see what's real.' I knew he meant it as a compliment – the fact of his own benevolence, like not Photoshopping women was a radical kindness – but there was an air of rebuff about him. Angling his camera to mask Moira's double chin as he snapped another picture of her.

When the lens finally swept towards me, his finger hovered over the shutter.

'What's wrong?' he asked.

I held a hand up in front of my face. 'I don't really want my picture taken,' I told him.

'That's okay,' he said. 'Why not?'

I forced a swagger into my voice, held myself like Molly or Hazel. 'I don't have to give a reason.' Still, though, I wondered: was I uncomfortable with the idea of people seeing me drunk, or in the commune?

Scott was visibly irritated but soon went back to photographing the other women, who either didn't notice the camera or slyly played up to it. Pretending to fight with the men, their voices loud and shrill, filled with mock outrage as they were picked up and spun around. In one corner I saw Trout was talking to Lucy, repeatedly gesturing to his hands. I wondered if he was telling her the same story about his mother and the nail varnish remover, briefly jealous that it hadn't been just for me.

It was getting too loud. I could feel the alcohol curdling in my stomach. I hadn't eaten much that day. I went to move but the room suddenly slipped on its axis, churned around me.

'Whoa, are you okay?' Matthew asked, grabbing my shoulder to steady me.

'I think I just need some fresh air,' I said. 'I don't feel very good.'

'It's the alcohol. We found it at the back of some guy's garage.'

My mouth kept filling with saliva, a feeling in the base of my stomach like I'd swallowed something still alive. I staggered outside into the garden, took deep breaths. In through the nose and out through the mouth, like my father taught me when I used to get carsick. I could hear the chickens, gurgling in their sleep. Did chickens dream? That seemed like the kind of profound question someone who'd had too much to drink would ask.

I heard the conservatory door open. Felt something drape around my shoulders, a blanket. Hazel released a slow breath, shivered a little. The alcohol had thinned our blood, made the night feel colder than it truly was. Her hair was wild around her face, framing her mouth, which pursed as if she were about to say something. I waited, knowing better than to try and rob the words. She would speak when she was ready.

'It's okay if you need to be sick,' she said finally, rubbing circles into my back. 'I will rub your back.'

'I'm trying not to be,' I told her.

She nodded and held me close. She could be so kind when she wanted. 'One time when we were teenagers, my sister and I threw a party,' she told me. 'My parents didn't really care about stuff like that. I think they were worried we wouldn't make friends at school so they let us do things they shouldn't have. We weren't even sixteen at the time. Anyway. My sister drank way too much. Like, paralytic, embarrassingly drunk. She ended up getting into a fight with her best friend. It derailed the whole evening, became all anyone could talk about.'

I focused on the sound of her voice. 'Why were they fighting?' I asked.

Hazel made a noncommittal noise. 'I can't really remember. It was probably something stupid. I think my sister had forgotten to get her a birthday present. Anyway, she hit her friend over the head with a bottle. It didn't shatter, but there was still blood. The next week, a rumour started going around that my sister let some guy from another school finger her while she was on her period. People started calling her dirty. It was horrible. She stopped getting out of bed.'

'Why are you telling me this?' I asked.

'To make you feel better about yourself,' she said. 'And because I would never do that to you.'

Her lips were rougher than I'd imagined, when she kissed me. A moment of clashing teeth. I'd never kissed another woman before and was surprised by how different and similar it was. When Nathan used to kiss me, there was a split second of conference; a question asked. He was always looking for ways to protect me, especially early on in our relationship. Packing an extra jumper in his bag in case I got cold, removing the chillies from a recipe. With Hazel, there was no warning. She felt no need to be gentle. She wanted to kiss me and so she did. I placed an experimental hand on her cheek, because it seemed like something that might happen in a movie, but I could sense immediately it wasn't the right thing to do. We weren't those sorts of people. Hazel gently brushed my hand away, bit down on my lower lip.

I realised we were being watched a moment before I heard the sound of the shutter clicking. Scott whispering *Hey* gently so we would look up, the camera's flash momentarily blinding. My mouth opened as if to say something and then clacked closed again. He'd already taken the picture. There was no way of asking for it back.

19

In the morning I woke feeling as though I'd rotted into the bed, my bones moulded around the springs. My tongue was furred and thick in my mouth. It took me a moment to realise I was in Hazel's room, not my own, although she wasn't with me. I had no explanation for what had happened last night. There were blank spaces in my memory, disconnected images with no way to thread them together: the flash of Scott's camera, a group of women leading the men into the barn, Pearl wrapping her arms around Scott's neck, Hazel. Hazel.

I got dressed and went downstairs. The kitchen was a mess: a pile-up of plates and cups in the sink, rimmed pink with dried lipstick. Empty bottles on every surface, someone's mucky shoes, a VHS copy of *Goodfellas* with the tape unspooled. There was a bad smell coming from the living room. I nudged the sofa with my foot, turned over one of the cushions only to find someone had thrown up on the underside. A couple of women were asleep on the floor, oblivious.

Outside there were more women in the allotment, those who had managed to rouse themselves to work. The day was already uncomfortably hot. It was no surprise to find them stripped down to their underwear, the sway of their bare breasts. There was a time when the sight used to shock me.

Now I struggled to remember why I'd ever been so uncomfortable with the idea: they were just bodies. Hazel was among them, rinsing the ground to soften it for planting. She looked up at me and nodded. I wondered if she remembered our kiss from the night before, knew I wouldn't be the first to mention it.

'I put you in with me last night,' she said. 'You were kind of out of it. Most of the girls slept in the living room anyway. Pearl and Scott were using the coach house.'

I looked in the direction of the coach house as if I might be able to see them. 'Did they . . .' I asked.

Hazel drove her shovel into the earth. The skin on her chest was mottled pink, nipples which were darker than the rest of her. I watched while she dug. 'Yeah. She's a real screamer.'

The knowledge that Pearl had slept with Scott shouldn't have surprised me, and yet I felt anxious. Letting the men on to the farm had been breaking Blythe's code, but fucking one felt like a breach of our own. There were women here who had homes and lives on the outside, but those of us who lived on the farm held a different set of expectations for one another. An unspoken agreement that we were different, and therefore must be held to a higher standard. We were icons of Blythe's vision, and that required sacrifice; restraint.

'What happens now?' I asked Hazel.

She continued her excavation. 'Why are you asking me?'

'I'm sorry,' I said, the urge to apologise to Hazel never far from the surface. 'I just don't know what any of this means.'

Hazel knelt and began churning the bucket of compost she'd prepared. An unctuous smell punctured my nostrils. We curated the compost pile ourselves, filled it with the detritus of our leftovers. Potato peel, apple cores, the excess skin from charred peppers. Lawn trimmings, toilet paper, pig shit. For a time, a stray cat kept appearing on the farm, left us offerings on our doorstep in the form of macerated voles and mice. We added those to the pile as well, their bodies visible for a few days afterwards on top of the heap, meat softening on the bone, making them appear flattened, like they'd been run over. Hazel scooped the compost with her bare hands, sprinkled it into the hole she'd dug.

Finally, she spoke. 'If Blythe finds out what happened, she'll make us leave. I know she will. So we'd better hope she doesn't. Did you bring me something to eat?'

I told her no and she went back to work.

I spent some time helping out on the allotment. If I thought my hangover was bad, it was nothing compared to the state of some of the others, who kept having to stop what they were doing to run behind the bushes and be sick. A funk rising from their bodies as the mounting heat sweated the toxins out of their skin.

After a while I looked up and noticed we were being watched. Scott was stood in front of the window at the top of the coach house. From his position, he must have had to step across my bed. The thought of him brushing against my sheets – my things – made me uneasy. The way he looked at us made me uneasy. Like he was on safari, seeing for the first time an exotic species of animal he'd only ever read about in books. His eyes on us, on our naked bodies. Seeing too much. One by one the other women sensed his gaze and stopped what they were doing. For the first time, I felt their embarrassment. In the corner of my eye, Ambika covered her breasts with one hand. Scott raised a hand at us. His other was holding something, an apple from the orchard. He took a bite and for a moment I thought I could hear the crunch as his teeth sank into the flesh.

*

It took us almost an hour to get the men to leave. Hungover, they were slow and ill-tempered. Kept asking if there was something for them to eat. They wanted bacon sandwiches. 'To soak up the alcohol,' Matthew explained. And then, like it was a stroke of genius, 'Didn't you say you had a couple of pigs on the farm?'

We helped them get dressed, guiding their hands and feet into their clothes. Their bodies felt foreign to us, too heavy and rigid in comparison to our own. I tried sitting Trout up to put his T-shirt back on but was surprised by the heft of him, by how much of him there was. He slipped out of my grasp, his head slapping back down on the floor with a thunk.

'It was fun last night, wasn't it?' Scott asked us, taking his time to put on his shoes. Pearl had been following him around like a dog all morning, kept touching him on the neck and shoulder. She wasn't expecting some great love out of him. She just wanted us to know what she'd done.

Hazel made a show of rolling her eyes. 'Sure it was, real fun.'

In the light of day, we just wanted them gone.

I was not the sort of person well equipped for confrontation. In arguments, I either backed down immediately or argued my point beyond rationality, refusing to admit I might be wrong even when I knew I was. I found it difficult to regulate my emotions and would often begin to cry, which was unfair, because who felt good arguing with a crying woman? I knew Nathan thought I did it on purpose. Cried to get my own way, to make him back down. When really it was like there was this stone inside of me that began rising to the surface every time something bad happened. I could physically feel it, notching its way through my intestines, up the rungs of my ribs. Into my throat, where it lodged, preventing the right words from coming out.

But I was a woman of Breach House now. I'd asked for this.

I approached Scott while he was loading the car. Tapped him on the shoulder. 'The photos,' I told him, feeling myself redden as he turned to look at me. 'Of me and Hazel. I didn't say you could take them.'

He gave a distracted smile but kept on packing. I urged myself to be like Hazel then, loud and angry, able to make demands. Could even feel myself pushing my chest out, standing how she did. But my voice shook as I spoke. 'Look, just delete them. It'll only take a second. I didn't say you could take them.'

'Calm down,' he finally replied. 'We had a good time, didn't we? Just relax.'

'It's not fair,' I said, immediately regretting the words. Both of us hearing how feeble I sounded, how shrewish. Just another woman who didn't know how to take a joke or have some fun.

He slammed the car boot shut and gave the house one last appraising look. The chance to delete the photos slipping through my hands, and shouldn't I have guessed it would? I was not like Hazel. I didn't know how to be.

Pearl hovered by the front door as the other men got into the car, smoothing one hand over her shorn head again and again. Was she expecting a kiss goodbye from Scott? She was being pathetic and yet I felt sorry for her. She didn't seem to understand the situation.

They didn't say goodbye to us. There was no thanks for our hospitality, or apology for how they'd left the house. Even Trout, who had seemed nicer than the others, remained silent, although I caught his eye for a brief moment and sensed – what? Regret, pity? Instead, they finished loading their things into the car and got inside, drove back down the driveway. We watched until the dust had settled, until we could no longer hear the press of the engine.

Molly was the first to break the silence. 'We have to clean the house. Blythe and Sarah could be back any minute. We have to tidy it all away.'

When no one moved she gave Pearl a hard shove. 'Go and get changed. And whoever threw up on the sofa can clean up their own mess.'

*

Blythe returned in the afternoon. We'd put the house back in order by then, buried the empty bottles at the back of the farm. Done the washing up and put it away, everything in its rightful place. We'd taken showers and put on fresh clothes. The crops were watered. But still I was certain Blythe could sense something had happened. As she got out of the car, she raised her head. Nostrils dilating as if she'd caught a scent. Sarah fetched an overnight bag from the back and went inside the house. We followed her into the kitchen.

'Place hasn't burned down then,' she remarked to no one in particular. She was always saying things like that, the kind of phrases our own mothers might have said.

'We missed you,' Molly told her. 'We're so glad you're back.'

Sarah seemed touched by this, bundled Molly into her

arms. 'Silly girl,' she said, not unkindly. 'Have you eaten enough? You look pale.'

Molly nodded but Sarah went to the fridge anyway and began chopping tomatoes. 'I'll fix us something to eat.'

'How did the meeting go?' Ambika asked.

Her hand paused and then began cutting again. She shook her head, a quick movement that invited no more questions.

Blythe came into the kitchen, sat down at the table. Her hand traced the grain of the wood, a furrow in her brow. We watched her with pent-up breath, waiting for the moment when she'd look up at us and ask what we'd done. I flinched as she raised her hand, but she only gestured vaguely and said: 'One of you put the kettle on.'

20

It was easier to pretend it hadn't happened. A collective dream in which alternative versions of ourselves behaved in ways we never would, made decisions that – in the staggering light of day – seemed unfathomable. Better to leave it well alone, resign all of it to a dark corner of our minds and go on as normal.

And yes, that meant erasing what had happened with Hazel. It seemed fitting that the moment I'd been waiting for – not the kiss specifically, but a breaching of Hazel's boundaries – was now consigned to hearsay, no different from a rumour or particularly vivid hallucination. Did she ever think about it? I tried searching for proof of that night in the corner of her eye, the way she pulled her mouth to one side as if trying to clear a blockage between her teeth. But she remained stalwart, back to her regular unknowable self.

I kept myself busy. Practised stretching in the morning, contorting my body into uncomfortable shapes. My skeleton had begun to feel brittle, difficult to manoeuvre. Like there was something gritty covering my bones. Sometimes the other women joined in and we'd form a small ring in the coach house, sweating into the wood, making a contest out of whose joints could pop the loudest. A new habit developed of eating apples afterwards, cutting each other segments with a sharp knife and passing them around. The sound of our chewing. We needed the camaraderie, fawned over each other with a new kind of intensity. Desperate to paper over what had happened. Pearl in particular was generous with her time, absorbed our chores so we could spend the afternoon sunbathing around the back of the barn. Brought us cold elderflower cordial when we asked.

'I don't know what game you girls are playing,' Blythe said, catching us out one day. 'But it isn't right to let her run around like that after you.'

How to explain: that reparations had to be made. Pearl owed us.

*

Over the next few weeks, several unfortunate things happened in quick succession. A pipe in the bathroom burst, soaking the upstairs landing. Sarah dropped her favourite baking dish. And then there was the family of magpies we found dead in the chimney. We hadn't needed to light a fire in months, so that couldn't have killed them. Perhaps they'd got stuck, blocked the flue somehow. We only knew they were there at all by the smell, which began to seep into the house and drove us gradually mad before we realised what had happened. When we scraped the chimney clean, we found a litany of objects the magpies had used to build their nest with. Twigs and vegetables from the allotment, clumps of our hair. Fragments of milky-blue shell preceded the soft, withered bodies of the magpie chicks, dead before they'd had a chance to grow feathers.

The worst thing, though, happened one afternoon in the allotment. An accident, a mishap. Ambika had been replacing broken roof tiles up on the barn when she slipped. By the time we found her, blood streamed from her hand, watering the earth. She'd been clutching one of the broken tiles when she fell, some instinct telling her to hold on to it rather than let go. The jagged clay protruded between her thumb and forefinger, piercing skin and tendon and what must have been a nerve, because her fingers twitched like someone had attached strings to them. It was obvious she needed to go to the hospital, that her injury required professional attention, but I also knew Blythe wouldn't allow it. As with everything else, what happened on the farm was for us to deal with alone. And, if I was honest, I think we were waiting for her to perform another miracle. We'd heard the stories of how she'd rescued Sarah from the brink of death, had even watched her breathe life back into Molly. But after what had happened with the men, we were in need of her power now more than ever. To witness it, be a part of it.

We watched as Blythe knelt beside Ambika, speaking calmly. Whispering things like *quiet now* and *just breathe* and *it will only hurt for a moment.* Unflinching when Ambika screamed, her hand wrapping around the jagged tile and pulling it clean. From where I stood, I was able to see inside the wound, how the meat of Ambika's hand was no different to an animal's, jewel-red and finely grained. The band of tendon underneath.

Fresh blood spurted on to the ground. 'Please,' Ambika sobbed, and it was impossible to know just then what she begged for: help, mercy or forgiveness.

*

The wound got infected, obviously. A smell seeping out from under Ambika's bandaged hand, a gaminess that woke something primal in me, teetering between disgust and hunger. She developed a fever, began speaking in breathy half-sentences. Cradling her hand against her chest like a babe, not letting anyone get too close in case they accidentally brushed up against it. She needed to see a doctor, someone who knew what to do in situations like this. But it was never suggested – by the other women or Ambika. I think she felt as if she deserved what was happening to her, like her wound was a physical manifestation of her guilt. She'd been a part of the men coming to the farm and now she was in pain, and how could those two facts not be inextricably linked?

The women's sufferance had begun to grate on me. I felt bad for what we'd done, but not on the molecular level they seemed to feel it. They were just men. It's not like we'd stolen anything. But the fear of what they'd allowed to happen – defying Blythe – sank into their marrow, made them unreasonable. Sometimes I had the urge to say something, comfort the other women and tell them that it would be all right, it was just a mistake. But their fear was infectious and if I thought about it too much, I began to worry they were right, that we did deserve something horrible.

When Blythe finally took Ambika's hand and pressed it to the hot stove, cauterising the wound and sending up a waft of burnt-pork smell, there was a physical sense of relief. Like the rot was being burned out of us all.

*

And then there were the chickens. Slaughtered by some creature that roved slyly without our notice on to the farm and cleaned out the entire coop. Feathers scattered the farm like snowfall, catching in spiderwebs and rosebushes, dander that we'd be finding for days to come. Whatever had killed the chickens clearly did it for sport, had taken nothing with him. Growing up, I was led to believe only foxes did that kind of thing, when really there were lots of predators who shared the same instinct to wring necks. Dogs killed animals smaller or weaker than themselves, regardless of whether they were hungry or not, while cats brought the lifeless bodies of birds back to their owners for praise. Violence was hard-wired into plenty of species.

I volunteered to clean the coop, fuelled by a sense of duty. I'd fed the chickens most mornings and felt as if I owed it to them to put their bodies to rest. Hazel offered to come with me and walked around the coop's perimeter, trying to find the vulnerable spot where a predator might have got in. She crouched down and worried at a corner of fencing until it began to peel away, revealing a gap large enough to have let something in.

'Could that have been it?' I asked her. My voice sounded muffled. I held one hand over my mouth to keep the smell at bay.

'Maybe,' she said. 'I had to yank for it to come loose. But I don't know how else something would have got in.'

It was one of the first times since the men came to Breach House that Hazel and I had been alone, and our interactions felt stilted, out of sync. Every so often we would both go to say something at the same time and then stumble, waiting for the other to speak and, in the end, both fall silent.

'You can go back inside,' she said after a while. 'I can deal with this.'

'It's fine,' I said, a little more harshly than I'd intended. 'Let's just get it over with.'

We placed the hens in bags, scooped up fistfuls of feathers. One hen looked perfectly preserved, still huddled on her perch like she was asleep. Hazel said she probably died of fright once she saw what was happening to the others, that her heart most likely gave out. That, more than anything, upset me. The futility of it.

We set the eggs still intact aside and fetched the garden hose, blasting the coop with jets of cold water. The blood sank into the ground and we exhaled, let the relief whistle through our teeth. Hazel swatted the air, irritated by the horse flies that had been drawn by the blood. I watched as one crept up her leg, pausing to rub its hands together gleefully, searching for the softest part to take a bite. Feeling the tickle of it, Hazel slapped herself, hard. Almost immediately her skin began to welt.

'What would you have done,' she asked me, cleaning her leg off, 'if it had been you in the coop last night?'

'Are you asking me how I would behave if I was a chicken?' Hazel nodded. She was looking at me seriously. I imagined myself as a feathered thing, waking in the middle of the night to the glint of teeth. 'I'd be the one who died of fright.'

'If it was me in that situation,' she said, 'I would have learned to fly.'

*

Blythe told Sarah to cook the leftover eggs for lunch. Waste not, want not. We watched as she boiled the vat of eggs, clouds of sulphurous steam filling the kitchen, before transferring them to a bowl for mashing. The wet sound it made, like lips sliding over teeth. We sat nervously at the table, not wanting to eat the sandwiches and yet lacking the vocabulary to refuse Blythe.

'This is gross,' Pearl said quietly.

Molly shrugged, but I could tell she felt uncomfortable. 'We've never had a problem eating eggs before. Why should now be any different?'

'Because,' Pearl said. 'What happened to the poor hens. It's just weird.'

Sarah placed the sandwiches in the centre of the table. Blythe put one on my plate.

'Eat,' she told us, the tone of her voice leaving no space for argument. For a moment I wondered: did she know? Had she found some evidence of the men that we'd failed to clear away, worked a confession out of someone? Was this revenge? I searched her face for proof, but there was nothing, no truth to be found in the slit of her mouth or unblinking eyes. She was stone.

The egg was tough and tasted of iron. Sarah had used too much mayonnaise, causing the bread to slide apart. I didn't have the stomach to chew and instead swallowed the mouthful whole, a rush of nausea in the pit of my stomach rushing up to meet it. The other women seemed to be waging similar battles, pinching morsels of bread and pushing them to their lips. I swallowed hard, tried not to think about my father.

The first few days after he died were steeped in casseroles and lasagne. It was the first thing people thought of when someone died. What will the grieving eat? They took to their ovens, kneeling in front of them to make sure the cheese melted correctly, formed an even crust. Knocking on our door armed with heavy Pyrex dishes, using them as a shield so they wouldn't have to make direct physical contact with us, as if bad luck were contagious. If you were clever and well prepared, you could deliver your casserole before the horde of other commiserators, when it would actually be appreciated. I couldn't tell you how much food I had to throw out that first week. There was only so much space in our freezer.

I was in my second year of university when my mother phoned to tell me what had happened. I was given compassionate leave and went home to look after her, did the things she could not. Took out the bins and paid the gas bill, fed her endless squares of shepherd's pie and macaroni cheese, which she chewed without thinking, pliant and slack jawed. I refused to eat anything the neighbours had made, convinced I could taste the pity in their recipes. Instead I ate my father's leftover food in the fridge. His mackerel and pâté, tins of corned beef. I made myself sick eating a half-finished plate of smoked salmon, a mineral taste hitting me in the back of my throat. It was the only time I remember crying, weighed down by a feeling of incompletion. These were meals he should have finished himself, and now he never would.

But this was different. Eating the eggs felt like a massacring, bordering on dishonour. I looked up at Hazel and found her already watching me. She'd changed into a loose-fitting T-shirt, scooped low to reveal the scaffolding of her neck and shoulders. When she swallowed her sandwich a ripple broke across her skin, the way a horse shook to rid itself of parasites.

21

Sometimes it was easy to imagine my mother as a snake and that I was the skin shed from her body. We were so alike. Not necessarily in a physical sense, but in other ways. The rash that spread along our necks whenever someone spoke over us, our hands which made neat little fists every time we bungled the telling of a joke. I felt her in the inside of my elbow, which I pinched sometimes to stop myself from screaming. The quiet assumption that we were better people than we actually were.

I thought, when I moved to Breach House, that I wouldn't miss her. That I would be too distracted by my new life – my new sense of self – to dwell on what had come before. But her habits and behaviour lingered in my musculature, and I found that I thought of her often. When Sarah mentioned a new market had opened near the town where I used to live, I took it as my opportunity to go home.

There was no rule that said I couldn't. Plenty of women went in and out of the farm. But I couldn't deny the unease I felt as I stood in my mother's kitchen – the familiar sticky floor underneath my feet. Perhaps there was an element of goading about the situation, too. It was the first time I'd been properly separated from Hazel and I wanted her to miss me. I wanted her to experience my absence as something debilitating.

My mother greeted me at the front door, peering at me through slitted eyes as if I'd caught her in the middle of a nap. She took a step back to let me in. Neither of us acknowledged our previous phone call or the fact I'd been gone for months, filling the awkward gaps with small talk instead: wasn't this weather unbelievable? Had I seen the latest episode of the music competition we used to watch together? There was a man on it this year with an incredible voice who used to be homeless. Wasn't that a turn of luck? As she prepared our tea, I caught her crouching down to check her reflection in the oven door. Where I had gained weight, she'd lost it, as if I'd siphoned it from her. The taut bow of her clavicles jutting as she preened. I could tell she was pleased with her new appearance, the ring of fat underneath her bra vanished to rib.

We quickly resumed our old routine. I helped carry the tea into the dining room, where we sat at our usual places, our faces only inches away: the perfect distance to examine one another. My mother fiddled awkwardly with her saucer, didn't know what to say. I could see the small resentments and unresolved tension clinging to the corners of her mouth, pulling it into a deep frown. When I was younger, she'd found it difficult to be separated from me. She would suddenly call my name if I was in a different room of the house to her, worried that by letting me out of her sight I might come to harm or cease to exist altogether. A Schrödinger's kitten. When I'd explained I wanted to go to university, she began to cry, the kind of wrenching tears you didn't expect from your parent. She would have crammed me back inside her if it had been possible.

But that urge was clearly lost to her now. I'd been gone for weeks, and there was nothing about my mother that suggested she'd been unable to cope without me, our umbilical pull severed. I realised I'd been planning to confess the niggling fear that was growing in a shadowed corner of my brain – tell her about the things that had been happening at Breach House – but that now I would remain quiet, refute any suggestion that things might not be okay. Proud creature; stubborn.

She looked around, clearly trying to scrape her brain for something to say.

'They're building new flats down by the river.' She offered me a biscuit without taking one for herself. 'You know where the old paint factory used to be. The construction company posted a leaflet through the door. There's going to be a cinema and restaurants.'

'When was the last time you went to the cinema?' I asked. It wasn't meant to sound confrontational, but somehow did anyway.

'There's never anything on I want to see,' she said, defensive. 'But maybe there will be now.'

The windows began to fog with condensation. This house had always been greedy, keeping itself warm even at the peak of winter. Air growing stale, potted plants wilting on the windowsill. I tried to covertly wipe the sweat from my upper lip, felt my backside sticking to the leather of the chair. Maybe it was the heat or the simple fact of being back home, but I couldn't stop thinking about my father. He'd been gone so long and yet I'd never managed to shake the feeling that he might walk into the room at any moment, smiling in that way of his, like he'd just told a joke you didn't understand the punchline to.

It was unfair of me to bring it up, but I suppose I was feeling redundant. Wanted to get back under my mother's skin. 'I had a dream about Dad the other night,' I began. My mother took another sip of her tea, hiding a flinch. 'It's funny, whenever I dream of him now it's always how he looked the last time I saw him, before the accident.'

'I'll go and get the leaflet,' she replied. 'You can see for yourself. There's a computer-generated image of what the area will look like when it's done.'

'I just want to talk about it,' I told her. 'I want to understand why.'

She swallowed and would not look at me.

Some traumas were collected during a lifespan, others bred into us. Genetic information as banal as whether we will be able to curl our tongues or if we are more likely to have high cholesterol. It was difficult to know whether the degradation of my relationship with my mother was hereditary, a disconnect passed down from mother to daughter, mother to daughter. Or if our past was a ghost that still haunted the corners of our mind.

*

The story of how my father died has been perched on my tongue long enough. To understand what happened is to understand what he left behind.

It went like this.

My father came home from work one day and had a shower. There was nothing inherently suspicious about this: that was his routine, the first thing he did after stepping through the front door. You learned quickly to wash in the early evening before he'd had a chance to drain all the hot water. I was away at university. By then I was friends with Nessa and we were planning to move out of halls and into a house together, the tender mass of my future beginning to form, possibilities laid out in front of me. While he was showering, my mother prepared something for him to eat. I mentioned before she wasn't a good cook, and so it was likely she made lamb chops or a baked potato, food that didn't mind being overcooked. It embarrassed her, the fact she was so incapable in the kitchen. All those movies about aproned mothers who baked biscuits fresh for their children, held secret recipes that were passed down generations. My grandmother had only ever helped to compound this humiliation, presenting deep dishes of rhubarb crumble and beef Wellington whenever she was invited round.

Maybe if my mother had learned to cook, my father wouldn't have found an excuse to leave that night. As it was, he ate his lamb chop or potato and claimed he was craving something sweet, that he would drive to the supermarket and buy one of their cakes. His coat was on before my mother had a chance to think of something to say.

Three hours later two police officers knocked on the door and delivered the news that my father had been killed in a car accident. I wasn't there and so I can only guess how my mother reacted, the thousand little atrocities that must have rippled across her face. Sometimes I imagined her crumpling to the ground, screaming. Clawing at her face in a theatrical display of grief. In reality she most likely nodded her head and thanked the officers for coming. My mother didn't have it in her to make a fuss.

There were inconsistencies to my father's story that revealed themselves in trickles. Like how his car had made it halfway down to the coast before slipping under the wheels of a lorry, miles in the opposite direction from the shops. Or the flowers and children's toys first responders had found crumpled in the back seat. When I asked my mother what it meant, she remained quiet, refused to answer me. It was only after the funeral when his sister told me he'd been on his way to see another family. His other family. *Sorry, darling*, she'd said, a little gleeful. *I thought you knew.*

I realised my father's infidelity came as no surprise to my mother. That she had absorbed his secret years ago like a tumour, let it travel the length of her body in a slow infestation. She'd known. She'd known and I hadn't. A better daughter would have felt sorry for her, tried to lift the burden from her shoulders. Or if not that, then at least share in it. But I was angry. Angry at her for not telling me herself, angry that she hadn't been enough for my father. Perhaps it was the fact my rage had nowhere else to go except for her now that he was dead, but all I kept thinking was: how could she have let this happen?

*

We finished our tea and went into the living room. Everything looked familiar and yet I noticed several changes. A hardback book on the coffee table about something called quantum wellness, an expensive-looking tub of hand cream scented with rose and geranium. A set of pillar candles on either side of the television, a yoga mat tucked into one corner. New curtains. Small things that were just enough to unsettle me, make me feel out of the loop. It had been naive to think that life outside the farm wouldn't move on without me, that things wouldn't change.

When we couldn't find anything on TV to watch, my mother brought out a pack of cards. The same deck we'd played with since I was a girl. I used to love watching her shuffle them, the quick flurry between her hands.

'Let's hope you've got better at playing,' she said, dealing.

We played our own version of poker, which was not like poker at all but that's what we called it. It involved dealing five cards each with the aim of making pairs or sets of the same suit or number cards; the first person to get rid of all their cards was the winner. It was something my mother had always been good at, slapping down her cards so hard it hurt my ears.

We began to play. She won the first round, and the second. I won the third before she had a winning streak that lasted the next five rounds. 'Don't you want to bet with something?' I asked her.

'Like what?'

I shrugged. 'Money.'

She replied without looking up at me, gaze fixed to her cards. 'Do you have any money to bet?'

Her barb surprised me.

'Something else then,' I said. She placed another pair on the coffee table: a Jack and seven of hearts. 'How about if I win this round, I get to ask you a question. And if you win, you get to ask me one.'

'Oh Iris,' she sighed, putting her cards down to look at me. 'Nothing like that, please.'

I laid down three fours. Now I only had two cards left, and she had three.

'Just a question,' I said. 'It can be anything you want.'

If I could pick up another spade, I'd win. I had my question ready, balancing on the tip of my tongue.

She laid her remaining cards down. A set of hearts. She looked a little sadly at me.

'Fine then,' I said, all bravado. Tossing my cards away and leaning back with my arms folded. Deepening my voice until I almost sounded like Hazel, brash and mean and impenetrable. Never mind the tremble in my leg. 'Ask me something.'

Eyes blurring with wetness now.

She smoothed a hand along her jaw, gathering the loose skin. She smiled and for a brief moment I saw the woman she must have been before the yoga retreats and SlimFast. Before she'd met my father.

'Are you hungry, love?' she asked.

Mother's mercy.

22

Blythe was waiting for me when I returned. Took me by the arm and led me into the kitchen. The other women had made themselves scarce and I began to panic, wondering if something bad had happened. I didn't know where Hazel was.

'Is everything okay?' I asked.

Blythe said nothing, nodded for me to sit down.

'Where have you been?' she asked.

I scraped a nail over the wood of the dining table, accumulating a dried crust of something. 'I visited my mother,' I told her. There was no sense in lying.

She nodded. I noticed she was holding something in her hand, what looked like a rock. But then I saw her squeeze it and the structure gave way. Clay, then. When she didn't say anything else I sat back in the chair, let my gaze drift to anywhere that wasn't her face. Plates drying on the rack, a curl of onion skin on the floor that had managed to escape being swept away.

The words were out before I realised I was going to speak them. 'I'm sorry,' I said, sounding a little bewildered, a little manic. I didn't know what I was apologising for, only that I wanted Blythe's forgiveness for whatever I'd done wrong.

A slow, long breath between her teeth.

'You shouldn't have gone today,' she told me. 'It's like

you're picking at a scab. You want to see what's underneath. You want your wound to bleed again. If you don't want to be here on the farm, then you should go.'

Her logic was elastic, something that could be twisted and stretched and bent out of shape. I found it difficult to follow, that what had been permissible before no longer was. That this new rule had sprouted like a mushroom, an elusive morel, its roots already hard-wired into the ground; impossible to shake loose. I had been allowed to leave the farm whenever I wanted and now I wasn't.

Blythe's gaze crept along the edges of me, so that I felt almost like a shadow. Not quite real. 'I just want to keep you safe, Iris,' she said. 'I don't want to see you hurt again. The reasons why you came to Breach House haven't gone away, they're still out there waiting for you. When you give in to them, it causes you pain. It causes us all pain. I have a duty to the other women, too.'

I wondered how much of Breach House had gone according to plan. It was clear Blythe was proud of what she'd achieved here – with us – but it was difficult to know how much she'd had to compromise in the process. She'd always told us Breach House was a refuge from the outside world, which implied undisclosed trauma, something she herself had wanted to get away from. And perhaps she found that she couldn't, that the outside world still had the power to get in.

I remained quiet, not wanting to say the wrong thing. She continued shaping the ball of clay, a tacky sound as her thumb pressed into its centre. Opening the indentation wider until it gradually took the form of a cup.

'I'm putting you in charge of helping Sarah around the kitchen for the next couple of weeks. She could use the help and it'll be good for you to do something other than work in the allotment.'

The implication was clear. She wanted Sarah to keep an eye on me, to stop me from leaving the farm again.

'Did I do something wrong?' I asked before I could help it, more desperate to please her than upset she'd reprimanded me. 'I didn't think it was a problem, seeing people outside of the farm.'

A tear opened up in the clay. Her hands were too strong. 'It's true there are women here who have their own lives on the outside. They come and go as they please, and yes, they contribute to our existence. But let's call them what they are: they're tourists.' She gave up on the clay, squashed it against the table. 'Your life is here now. I'm just asking you to remember that. Now let's go outside, the pigs need feeding.'

*

Blythe's warning seemed like a precursor for what would happen next. As if she'd looked at the shape of the clouds or the entrails of animals and plucked the future straight from them.

*

Our secret was never going to last. It couldn't. We were not its sole custodians. A secret is only good if it belongs to you, with no other witnesses or perpetrators, but of course this one didn't. It belonged to them, too.

Sarah offered to drive us into the village. She told us she had business to attend to and we knew better than to ask questions. 'I will pick you up later. Try and sell as many of the courgettes as you can, they won't last in this heat.'

We stacked the boxes between us, made short work of it. The appeal of my new body hadn't worn off yet, how easily I was able to heft the weight of the vegetables. Muscles grown thick around my arms and shoulders. Nathan had always made fun of my weakness. He liked that about me, I think. The fact he always won a game of arm wrestling or was called upon when a stubborn jar needed opening. It wasn't that he wanted to overpower me, he wasn't that sort of man. Rather, it made him feel important, like he had to protect me. He enjoyed the idea of having someone he could tuck under his arm or carry over his shoulder. Sweet Nathan, with his microwave burgers and matching socks.

Hazel was next to me, propping the metal tables up to display the vegetables. I bent to help her and our shoulders butted, knocking me off balance. We were still trying to find our regular rhythm after what had happened.

'You're bleeding,' I noticed, her hand scraped in red.

She wiped it against her leg without looking. 'It's fine,' she said. 'You worry too much.'

I dropped one of the crates on to the table from a great height, the vegetables inside rolling around. In minutes their skin would start to peel and bruise. 'Usually when someone checks up on you like that, it's because they're making sure you're okay. Because they care.' The words came out in a rush, too loud and stilted. I wasn't used to being angry with her. Molly and Ambika, writing prices on squares of cardboard with black markers, went quiet.

I braced myself for Hazel to bite back, say something nasty like she usually did when caught out. Surprise, then, when instead I saw her cheeks turn red, her eyes begin to gloss.

She lifted up her hand. 'It's just a splinter,' she said, her voice trembling a little. 'It doesn't even hurt. But, thanks.'

Molly cleared her throat. 'Sorry to interrupt this magical moment, but could you hurry up? People are starting to trickle in.'

We knew something had changed within the first hour. We were used to people looking at us, but not like this, wide-eyed and staring, their contempt barely contained. I reached for Hazel's hand and grasped it, hoping she would squeeze her reassurance into me. But she remained limp, jellied, as if someone had reached inside and removed her bones and tendon.

I opened up a jar of honey. The rosemary bushes that hemmed the farm were still in bloom and the bees flocked to them en masse, forcing themselves into the delicate lilac petals. The result was a deep-tasting honey, smoky and earthen. Not necessarily pleasant, but compelling: the kind of thing you tasted in your mouth for hours afterwards. I dipped a cocktail stick into the jar and offered it to the first person who walked past.

'Locally made honey,' I said, the patter familiar to me by now. 'Perfect to soothe inflammation, colds and flus. Would you like to try some?'

I recognised the woman; she worked at the petrol station. I made my face wide and open, gave her my best smile. Usually people couldn't help but take whatever we offered to them. They were curious about the farm, wanted to taste a little piece of us. Eagerness winning out over suspicion. But, now. The woman looked at the cocktail stick as if it were a weapon. She took a step back, lip curling with derision and then continuing its path upwards into a cruel smile.

'I'm fine, thank you.'

A bead of honey slipped down the cocktail stick on to my finger. I flicked it on to the ground and turned to look at Hazel and the others. They shrugged, but I could tell they were spooked.

It continued like this, us offering passers-by something to eat or drink, asking if they would like to come closer so we could show them what was for sale, our hopes dwindling as the crates of vegetables began to rot.

'What is going on?' Ambika asked after a while. Her hands were neon pink with beetroot juice, jewel crusts underneath her nails. 'People are acting so weird. It's like they're worried we have something contagious.'

Pearl gave one of her girlish laughs. 'That's ridiculous. It's just a slow morning.'

'It's almost lunch and we haven't sold a thing,' Molly said. 'Ambika is right, something's off.'

Hazel was still trying to excavate the splinter from her finger. It was buried deeper than she'd thought. 'Someone else can tell Blythe we didn't manage to sell anything, because I'm sure as shit not doing it.'

'I'm not doing it either,' Molly said.

Pearl bit into one of the apples, a spray of juice flecking the back of my neck. 'It will be fine, it will be fine.'

As they continued bickering, I looked across the market and noticed a small crowd gathering at one of the stalls. They were hunched over something, whispering among themselves. Heads turned in our direction, followed by mean brays of laughter. It was like being back at school, the segregation of the popular and unpopular: them and us. My discomfort began to morph into something else, a feeling gathering low in my body.

A small gap opened in the group and I saw what they were looking at.

I saw.

*

The seconds before a roller-coaster drop
When your heart jumps up into your lungs
And you begin to tip;
The point of no return.

*

I didn't notice myself at first. Gleaned only the familiar shape of the farm, the hills which scaled the background, as familiar to me by now as my own hands and feet. And then, like an optical illusion, my body gradually revealed itself on the page. The angles and folds, drag of my naked breasts as I was caught mid-bend, pulling an onion from the ground. I was racked by a feeling of displacement, uncanniness: surely this couldn't be me. Please don't let it be me.

Photographs. Taken the morning after the men came, when we'd been too hot and hungover to work. It hadn't even occurred to us that we should look behind our shoulders before we took our clothes off: it was second nature. Our bodies were tools, neutral territory. As I forced my way further into the crowd I saw there were also photos of the night before: Pearl dancing on top of the dining table, dropped low on her haunches so you could see the gusset of her underwear. Molly in the middle of blowing a bubble with a stick of gum, the obscene pucker of her lips. We were just having fun, but there was something about the photographs which skewed their meaning, smeared everything in a layer of debauchery. We did not look beautiful. Our bodies were not alluring or desirable. We looked unhinged, disgraceful.

Among the photographs was the picture Scott had taken of Hazel and me kissing. It was at an awkward angle, so that Hazel's shoulder took up the bulk of the shot, but I could still make out the sordid blur of our mouths. How my hand reached for her waist. I kept trying to make Hazel look at me now, if not to force her to acknowledge this violation, then to remind her of what had happened between us. But she kept staring straight ahead, vanishing in that way of hers.

I searched for Scott in the photographs, but of course he wasn't there: he'd taken most of them. Even the other men were only half visible, shadowed creatures lurking in the background. In one of the photos Ambika was being carried over someone's shoulder, a sliver of their face turned towards the camera, although I couldn't make out who it was: it might have been Matthew, or Trout, whose mother had dipped his fingers in nail polish remover to stop him chewing them.

'They can't do this,' Molly kept saying. They'd all seen the photos by now; there'd been no hiding it from them. She slammed her fist down on the table, toppling a carefully stacked pyramid of carrots. 'We need to tell someone. The police, or something.'

'What could they do?' Ambika asked her. 'Everyone's seen them now. It's done.'

The crowd of people had dispersed, although I still felt their eyes on me. I felt ashamed without precisely knowing why. Hazel stood next to me, was still groping at her finger, trying to pick the splinter out. Fresh blood seeped from the cut.

'It will be okay,' Pearl said, her voice trembling.

'What would you know?' Molly spat. 'You're useless. You're a stupid fucking idiot.'

'People will forget them after a while,' Pearl went on. 'And then it'll be like it never happened at all.'

Anger flushed through me. None of this would have happened if she hadn't invited the men on to the farm in the first place. I could have hit her just then. But, no. Pearl hadn't taken the photos of us: Scott had.

'If Blythe finds out she'll make us leave,' Ambika said, beginning to cry. The realisation passed over the others' faces, that they might be forced to return to their old lives. The horrors they'd done their best to escape from.

'We need to make sure there aren't any others,' Molly said. 'We can't let Blythe find out.'

*

As it turned out, the photos were all over the village. Taped to lampposts and letterboxes, the windshields of people's cars. In shop windows, advertisements for cleaners and landscaping companies interspersed with images of ourselves. We tore down as many of them as we could find. Shredding them between our fingers and setting them loose on the breeze like confetti. Grains of our half-naked bodies littering the ground. We raided the farm shop and post office, ripping them down before anyone could stop us. Baring our teeth and snarling at anyone who looked. They thought we were nothing but animals? Then that's what we would be.

A pair of schoolgirls waved at us from the opposite side of

the road as we continued our search. 'Nice tits,' they cackled before running off.

'It's not like any of them wanted to be our best friend before,' Pearl said, breathless as she tried to keep up with us. 'Everyone's always treated us like freaks.'

She wasn't wrong. It was true that we'd always been considered Other. Our choice to live at Breach House meant certain things, that we had chosen to live apart from the rest of the world and the scrutiny that invited. But up until now, the village had treated us with a mixture of caution and awe. They'd bought our produce and held conversations, hired us to clean their gutters and mow their lawns. But the photographs had changed all of that. They still desired us, but their desire was marked now with greed, possessiveness. It was like the worst possible image they'd had of Breach House had been confirmed and they were both relieved and disappointed, like they'd seen behind the curtain and thought that granted them a kind of power over us.

It was late afternoon by the time we finally stopped. My feet were raw from walking, the heat causing them to blister. We'd left the rotting produce behind at the market, but Hazel had kept a couple of apples and gave one to me now, pressing the skin against my lips. I took a bite, swallowed. 'What's going to happen now?' I asked quietly, so only she could hear.

She took a bite from the same apple. 'I don't know. All you can do is wait and see. Have another bite. You need to keep your strength up.'

We went to the spot where Sarah said she'd pick us up. Each of us hoping that we'd torn down the photos before she'd had a chance to see them. We'd been thorough, scrupulous.

Our heads turned at the familiar sound of the estate's

engine. Sarah pulled over at the side of the road, left the car running. We got inside without a word, crammed into the back. She didn't ask us about the market, whether we'd managed to sell everything. Simply pulled away from the pavement and began the familiar journey back to Breach House.

A small stack of photos burning on the dashboard.

23

Early the next day, before the rest of the women arrived, we were summoned from the coach house and told to wait inside the kitchen.

The discovery of the photos hovered over us. I'd barely slept, switching between crying and plotting until eventually, exhausted, I struggled into a semi-consciousness. When I woke a few hours later Hazel was sitting at the foot of my bed, holding my ankle. We didn't speak. Words were tricky just then, the right ones slipping back down our throats before we had a chance to speak them. What was there to say? It was done now. I lay there on my back, watched as she stroked slow circles across my skin. She could be gentle when she wanted.

Eventually I sat up, the bones in my neck cricking. Hazel had worked her way up to my knee and gone no further. I opened my mouth to ask if she would like to lie next to me, just for a little while, but she shook her head before I'd even spoken, her eyes narrowing as if to say: not now.

Sarah had shown the photographs to Blythe, of course she had. She was the most loyal of us all, Blythe's first follower. We couldn't blame her, not really. Any one of us would have done the same in her position. Still, it was difficult to look Sarah in the eye when we gathered in the kitchen. She'd made tea and set some biscuits down on the table but I made a point of not eating or drinking anything, even though I was hungry. Next to me, Pearl nibbled on the end of a biscuit, making annoying little rabbit sounds. Molly slapped the biscuit out of her hand and nobody said a thing.

We felt Blythe before we saw her, her anger preceding her like the tide. She walked into the room holding the photographs, slammed them down on the table between the tea and biscuits. Her gaze swept the room, disassembling each of us into our most basic parts.

'What's to be done?' she said to no one in particular; to all of us. She began pacing the room, the flagstones grinding underneath her feet. 'How can I make you understand? Back in the outside world, we are treated like animals. We earn less than men for doing the same amount of work. We are raped by them on a daily basis. We are murdered by them. And most of the time it's our fault. We weren't wearing the right clothes or didn't scream loud enough. And women are no better, fighting each other over promotions and boyfriends. Blaming each other. It's filthy out there. And yet you still decided to invite that world into our home. The shelter that I provided for you. You let those men on to my land and allowed them to humiliate you in the process. It's disgusting. It's desecration.'

Her rage was a physical thing, like a bruise being pressed. We huddled against one another, feeling as though we were running out of space with Blythe in the room. Her angry mass. In the corner, I heard one of the women – Moira, I thought – stifle a sob.

'And maybe you don't like me for saying all that. Frankly, that's not my priority. I am creating something here. I am on a journey, a mission. Let me ask you something: if you knew what you were doing was wrong, why didn't you say something? Come on, girls. One of you speak.'

I looked around at the other women. Hazel sat with her fist in her mouth, as if that would prevent her from being called upon, Moira openly weeping now. Meanwhile Pearl was playing with the edge of another biscuit, her head pointed low so no one could see she was trembling.

'We were afraid,' Ambika spoke up. 'We were guilty. And we were worried you would make us leave.'

Blythe nodded slowly. There was an undercurrent of ridicule in her voice. 'Yes, exactly. And so now I'm stuck. Because you have a lesson to learn, and I must teach it.'

*

We waited for Blythe's decision the same way you waited for a hospital test result. Trying not to think about it, conducting yourself with a sense of bravado as if you weren't bothered either way. We went and sat in the conservatory, distracted ourselves with feeding the magpies. They were brave birds that came all the way up to the open door, pecking at our feet and chatting to each other in their horrible language.

'I remember when I was in school,' I said to Hazel as we took turns scattering breadcrumbs, 'a magpie flew straight into the window while our class was in the middle of a test. It was so loud, we all screamed.'

She made a noise that was not quite a laugh, not quite a grunt. 'People say birds are meant to be intelligent, but I don't know.'

I could still recall the greasy imprint it left on the window, like a Rorschach. 'My father told me birds fly into windows because they see the reflection of trees in the glass and mistake it for the real thing.' That they flew towards it with confidence and were surprised when their necks broke.

Hazel shrugged. 'That makes sense, I guess.'

When the magpies began shitting all over the patio, Ambika shooed them away and closed the door. No one spoke for a time, the room filling up with our regret. What was there to say now, anyway? We'd been found out, our lies exposed in the worst way possible.

Eventually, Pearl wiped a hand across her face and let out a tired sigh.

'What do you think Blythe will do now?'

Ambika grazed a hand through her hair. It had started to grow out, thickening into a soft-looking down. Mine was still too short. 'If she tells us to leave, I don't know where I'll go,' she said, banging her head gently against the conservatory window. 'I can't go back to living with my father.'

'At least you have someone,' Tanya said. 'I have nothing if Blythe decides to turn us out.'

'It won't come to that,' Molly told them, her impulse to defend Blythe outweighing the need to comfort Ambika, then turned to the rest of us: 'I'm not saying we're going to get away with it. We made a colossal fuck-up. But she's looked after us so far.'

It was difficult, in retrospect, to understand why we had done it. Let the men into Breach House. I knew at the time it had been wrong, but the danger had felt shapeless then, distant enough that I could pretend nothing would come of it. That it would not eventually materialise into this black mass sitting between us now.

'We haven't exactly been a shining example of what she

hoped we'd be,' Hazel said. I noticed her lips were exceedingly dry, watched as she paused to peel a flake of skin away before continuing. 'If she got rid of us now, she could start all over again. Find better women who will actually follow the rules.'

'We will follow the rules,' Molly said, biting the tip off each word, blunting them. 'It was just a stupid mistake. We'll never do it again.'

'It'll be better when she decides what to do with us,' Pearl said. 'When we can prove to her we're sorry.'

None of us spoke about the photographs, how Scott and his friends had embarrassed us in such a specific and cruel way. That seemed almost secondary to the fact we had upset Blythe. But I let it soak in now, the indignity and treachery and – fuck. Wasn't our humility punishment enough?

I imagined what my mother might have said if she were here now. She would struggle to understand why I was so upset. She would say something like *They're just pictures*, which would be her way of shrinking the matter into something unimportant. Her understanding of what constituted abuse restricted to the wholly physical. *It's not like you were raped.*

'We should see if Sarah needs help with lunch,' Tanya said, getting up. 'May as well be useful while we wait for Blythe to make her decision.'

*

But none came. We made lunch and ate it. We worked in the allotment, fed the pigs our leftovers and watered the rosebushes. Doing everything haltingly, jerking our heads up at any small noise, poised to hear our names called. When Blythe continued not to seek us out, we reasoned we should go to bed. I couldn't sleep, was consumed with thoughts of my old life, the items I had left behind at my mother's house, which now seemed to take on a new significance. The can of Dr Pepper I'd left on the kitchen counter before coming to Breach House. My hairbrush, still furred with strands of my hair. The box of tampons under the bathroom sink, which, in hindsight, I really should have taken with me. I imagined all of these leftover items combining into some kind of homunculus and felt like laughing, pictured it crawling across my bedroom floor and down the hall.

*

The next morning, Blythe greeted us at the dining table for breakfast, the same as any other morning. Afterwards, the women formed a circle and wept with relief, convinced that we'd been forgiven. I wept along with them, but secretly I couldn't help but feel a great sense of apprehension, like in the horror films I used to watch with Nessa. Those heavy, drawn-out moments right before a jump scare.

24

Summer dragged on. I began to feel perpetually uncomfortable, my skin resembling map contours as layers of it peeled from sunburn. A hot feeling in the back of my throat. Every night I tossed and turned, trying to find a position that was comfortable enough to sleep in, but the other women's body heat was suffocating.

Sometimes when I was in the bathroom I peered in the mirror and thought I saw someone different. I was beginning to look like my mother, I realised. My eyes ringed with alarm, a gravity to my mouth that seemed to drag my lower lip down. If I could just sleep properly, I thought, I would start to look better; more like myself.

We began spending whole afternoons down by the stream, running into the water with a religious fervour, baptising ourselves over and over again. Sometimes the surface of the water would ripple with mosquito larvae and I would try to ignore the fact that I'd probably swallowed hundreds of their squirming bodies, reasoning that it was a fair price to pay to escape the heat for a few hours.

One afternoon after we'd finished swimming, Hazel took a small bottle of varnish from her bag and told us she was going to paint our nails. It occurred to me that perhaps she was trying to restore some normality to the group, return us to the women we'd been before the photographs. She gave the pot a vigorous shake, the click of a ball bearing as it blended the liquid.

'Do mine,' Pearl said, but Molly lumped her foot into Hazel's lap before anyone could stop her.

'Wait your turn,' she said. Pearl pouted and slunk back into the water.

A chemical smell rinsed the air as Hazel unscrewed the lid. The varnish was dark, the colour of a bruise. My head began to swim with the solvents, a pleasant dizziness that caused me to slump backwards.

Hazel was steady-handed, thorough as she lashed stripes of varnish on to Molly's nails. I watched her face closely, her tongue pinched between her lips in concentration. Eyes moistening as she resisted the urge to blink. When she was done, Molly gently shook her hand to dry the varnish.

'What do you think, ladies?' she asked us.

We made mewling noises of approval.

'Want me to do yours?' Hazel asked me. I glanced over at Pearl, but she was busy in the water. I nodded, and Hazel gestured for me to come closer. She took one of my hands and balanced it on her knee, warmth underneath my palm. I felt heat prickle in my cheeks, the urge to pull away like I'd been branded. She shook the bottle again and I felt the action through her body. 'Hold still,' she said, swiping the varnish on to the nail of my index finger. Immediately I realised the colour didn't suit me, sucked the life from my skin.

Hazel carefully manipulated my hand in hers so she could paint my thumb. 'I wish I had your nails,' she said. 'Mine are impossible to grow.' I shook my head, amazed she could want anything of mine.

Hazel swapped my hands over and painted the remaining nails. When she'd finished, she leaned over and blew on the varnish. 'What do you think?' she asked. 'Do you like them?'

I thought it looked like my hand was bleeding, like I was squeezing something raw between my fingers.

'Thank you,' I told her. 'They look good.'

She nodded, satisfied.

I lay down on the grass, carefully so I wouldn't smudge my nails. Overhead, just visible through the trees, was a bird of prey. A honey buzzard, I thought, or perhaps an eagle. The woods had always felt wilder than Breach House, filled with rare and dangerous creatures, birds and snakes and badgers (my mother once told me if a badger caught hold of you, it wouldn't let go until it felt your bones break). There was a prehistoric thickness to it, paths of gorse and holly that were near-impossible to cut through. Only a narrow footpath made the stream accessible at all, and that was after years of Blythe and the other women trampling their way through.

I closed my eyes and thought of all the ways you could be marked, the same way we had made our mark on this land. The rash you got on your thighs if you wore underwear that was too tight. Lines of pink scar accrued from a wound. Sometimes there was scar tissue on the inside of your body too, marks that could not be seen but still felt: a private pain.

I felt marked by what Scott had done. I felt the photographs burning a hole inside me. Sometimes the pain of it was so bad I forgot how to breathe, a collection of seconds in which the knowledge of what had happened winded me. The other women seemed determined to forget all about it, worried that by bringing it up they might incur Blythe's wrath again, but I could see the effect it had on them. How their eyes shifted quickly left and right as if expecting something to jump out at them unexpectedly, the little piles of pebble and eggshell my bedmate Lucy had begun keeping on our windowsill.

Maybe if I took a break from Breach House, went and saw Nessa, I would start to feel better. She would be tough on me, but sensible. We would order a takeaway and eat it on her sofa, and afterwards she would tell me I could stay with her. I knew she would help me if I asked.

Guilt rushed through me. Breach House wasn't a job I could just quit. It went beyond that: it was part of me now. And things were not so bad. So Scott had leaked the photos of us. Hadn't we deserved it? We knew what we were doing by inviting the men inside Breach House and we'd done it anyway. When my mother's dog pissed on the carpet, she rubbed his nose in it. You cannot have an effect without the cause.

My loyalty to the other women – to Blythe, and Hazel – outweighed any doubt or rationale. Like a body, I buried it.

*

I must have fallen asleep because when I opened my eyes again the light had changed direction, grown treacly. Pearl was still splashing about in the water, picking up rocks and looking underneath to see if she could find any limpets or mud snails, while the other women passed around an old music magazine. It was the same magazine I used to beg my mother to buy for me when I was a teenager because it came with free pots of eyeshadow, a different colour every issue. I managed to fill an entire drawer with them by the time I got bored with it.

I stood up and walked around a bit, the ground nice and

cool under my feet. Somewhere in the distance I could hear a dog barking, and it would have bothered me if I hadn't known about Breach House's mystical sound vacuum. The dog and its owner were most likely miles away.

'I think Jack White sings like a serial killer,' Molly said, flicking through the magazine. 'I like his music, but I'm just saying.'

'You know him and Meg aren't actually brother and sister?' Pearl called over. 'They just want everyone to think that.'

'They look like brother and sister to me,' Molly said. 'Anyway, come out now. It's getting late, we have to head back.'

I was still stretching my legs when Pearl splashed water over Molly, causing the magazine to disintegrate. It had surely been meant as a joke, but suddenly Molly was dragging Pearl from the water and Pearl was screaming that it hurt, Molly was hurting her. I saw Hazel move out of the way so she wouldn't get wet.

'What is wrong with you?' Molly said. 'You soaked me.'

'It was just a bit of water!' Pearl cried.

Molly let go of Pearl and I thought that would be the end of it, but then she grabbed a handful of dirt and lobbed it at Pearl. I saw a clod of it hit her in the face. I opened my mouth to say something, but I wasn't sure what was happening any more, the sudden rupture of peace. Molly had gone bright red.

'You stupid girl,' she told Pearl. 'You clumsy idiot.'

I looked at the fragments of magazine on the ground and then at Hazel, who shook her head at me like she didn't get it either. But of course it was obvious what was happening.

Ambika came between them before Molly could throw any more dirt. 'She didn't mean it,' she said, putting her hands on Molly's shoulders. 'It was just a bit of water, like she said. She didn't mean it.'

'She never means it,' Molly said, straining so hard against Ambika it caused her to stumble a few steps backwards. We watched as Ambika splayed a hand out to steady herself, tried to grab Pearl's shoulder. But it was her bad hand, which couldn't grip as tightly anymore, was mangled now with scar tissue and severed nerve endings, so that she lost her footing and fell sideways on to the ground. I'd never seen Molly so much as raise her voice at Ambika before, and the shock of it, the transgression, stunned me.

'Someone help her,' I said.

'Now look what you've done,' Molly said to Pearl as though I hadn't spoken. For a moment, I was certain she was taking some kind of pleasure from this whole situation. Anger feeding anger.

'This is so unfair.' Pearl wiped the dirt from her face.

Finally, Molly bent down to help Ambika. I could tell by the pinched expression on her face that Molly was handling her too roughly, picking her up from underneath her armpits. 'You don't get to talk about what's unfair,' Molly grunted, pulling on Ambika.

'That's enough,' Hazel said suddenly, splintering the tension. 'You're all giving me a headache. Stop fighting, grow up. It's time to go home.'

Later I would wonder if Blythe had somehow planned this. If this was our real punishment: degeneration, picking each other apart. Had she known if she left us long enough, we would do the hard work for her?

25

Nathan wasn't there when my father died. We wouldn't meet for years after the fact, but the way he spoke about my father and how difficult it was for me to cope, I began to believe that I'd remembered it all wrong. That he must have been there after all, hovering at the edges of my memory. He spoke about my grief with more authority than I felt I'd ever had, pointed out the ways in which his death had changed me.

It's made you distrustful, he said one day in IKEA. We were shopping for a new sofa, or I was trying to persuade him to buy a new one – he still thought his uncle's old sofa with the assprints was fine. The shop floor was divided into several showrooms, each appealing to a different demographic: bachelor who enjoys cooking and entertaining his friends, professional couple with a penchant for DIY. I began to make up my own categories, rattling them off as we went. 'Single woman who talks to her dog like it's a child. Well-paid lawyer who needs plenty of storage to keep the chopped-up bodies of all the hookers he's killed. Lesbian couple who fell out of love years ago.'

Nathan stopped in front of a sofa and patted its cushions. 'How about this one?' he said.

'Are you just picking the first one you see?' I asked. 'Or

are you deliberately picking an ugly sofa so I give up and say we're better off with what we already have?'

He smoothed his hand along the back of the sofa. 'I just like this one. Can't I like it without there being an ulterior motive?'

I laughed. 'No one with the correct prescription lenses would like this sofa. You're fucking with me.'

Nathan looked for a genuine moment as if he might sit down and cry. Something shot through me, dreadfully close to satisfaction. 'You sound just like your father,' he said.

A family came into earshot, drawn to a sensible-looking drinks cabinet. I could tell the wife was trying to listen to what we were saying, recognising the stiffness in our smiles as we desperately clung to the veneer of well-functioning couple. I stared at her until she turned away, gesturing for her children to follow her into the kitchen section.

'How do you know what my father sounded like?' I said when we were alone again. My voice had risen, a hysteria that I was immediately embarrassed by. If I had sounded like my father before, I no longer did now. I swallowed and began again. 'You never even met him. If you had, then you'd know he'd tell you you've chosen the ugliest sofa in this entire warehouse.'

Nathan pinched the bridge of his nose, squeezed his eyes shut. It was a gesture reserved strictly for me: exasperated by the overbearing girlfriend. 'The way you and your mother talk about him, everything I've heard, I think it's okay for me to say that sometimes you act like him.'

'And how am I acting?' I said, talking too loudly again.

He smiled gently, sadly, like I'd just told him I was ill. Always a kernel of pity to be found in him. 'Like the only way to get what you want is by belittling me. You can't just accept I like this sofa. You need to make me feel bad about it.' I blinked, dumbfounded, and saw him take some satisfaction from that, walking away from the sofa without a second look. I followed him through the maze of kitchens and bathrooms until we reached the restaurant at the other end, and refused to answer when he asked if I was hungry. Convinced that my indignity outweighed anything he might have felt.

It was only now that I recognised this lineage of cruelty. Nathan was right. I'd spent years emulating my father without realising it, trying to capture his charm and power and disliking myself for it in the process. The more I struggled to understand why he'd betrayed me and my mother, the more I inadvertently behaved like him. Hiding myself behind a mask of superiority and dissatisfaction, telling myself again and again that I was destined for something greater.

*

'They overthink things,' Hazel told me. 'Not every thought needs to be acted on. You can be angry or heartbroken or scared without having to let everyone else know about it.'

We were sat on Hazel's bedroom floor, clearing out her wardrobe because she'd decided she no longer liked any of the clothes in it. 'I don't know how half this shit ended up here,' she said, smoothing one hand over her head. Her ponytail was pulled so tight her forehead shone pink. 'I'm sure most of it's not mine.'

I was sat close enough that I could tell she hadn't brushed her teeth yet, the sourness of morning breath. I liked being this close to her, able to detect the parts of her that usually remained hidden. The birthmark under her ear, a jagged pleat of keloid along one shoulder.

'I hope Ambika's okay,' I said, speaking the words quickly, before I regretted them. I knew Hazel wanted to forget about what had happened.

'She's fine,' Hazel said. 'It was just a stupid fight that got out of hand.'

And yet, the memory of Ambika falling over, of Molly handling her like an unloved pet, had engraved itself at the forefront of my mind. I didn't like how quickly the fight had broken out, different from the other times I'd seen the women argue. This had been nasty, spiteful. There was an unhappiness that lingered, made it difficult to maintain eye contact.

'Are you listening to what I'm saying?' I blinked at Hazel, who rolled her eyes. 'I asked you to pass me my cup of tea.'

'Oh.' I went over to her bedside table and retrieved the lukewarm mug, watched as Hazel took a long sip. She never complained about the cups of tea I made her anymore. I knew just how she liked them (with too much milk, which had to be poured before the water or else she wouldn't drink it) and took pride in seeing her swallow. Lately I had begun imagining doing these sorts of things – clearing out wardrobes, making cups of tea – somewhere away from Breach House, although I found it was difficult to picture Hazel with me. She didn't fit into restaurants or churches. I couldn't envision her sitting next to me at the local pub or buying stamps from W. H. Smith. Even when she'd first come into the off-licence where I'd worked, she had seemed so out of place, as if her image was tied to the farm. Still, I couldn't help but wonder.

Hazel scrunched up several dresses without even looking at them. She'd cut her clothes down to the bare essentials, leaving several gaps in the wardrobe. We could leave in a hurry, if we wanted to.

She looked up at me then – sharply, like she could tell what I was thinking. I stood, stepping over the pile of clothes to get to the window, where there was a slight breeze. I didn't know why I suddenly felt so guilty, or what it was I really wanted – only that Hazel was looking at me in that way of hers that meant I was not doing a good enough job of hiding.

'My first boyfriend's name was Lloyd,' she finally said. I was not expecting her to say this and so for a moment I thought I had misheard. 'This was when I was in sixth form,' she continued. 'He used to eat two packets of ready salted crisps every lunchtime, so his breath stank and then he'd try to finger me. His hands were always oily. Eventually I got a UTI.'

'That's horrible,' I said.

She nodded in agreement. 'One morning he pulled me aside before class and told me we were better off as friends. And then he shook my hand as if he'd just agreed to sell me a car.'

I tried to imagine Hazel as a girl, tender and uncertain, wearing a jumper two sizes too big for her. There was still so much I didn't know about her. Even in these rare moments when she talked about herself, there was a sense of uncanniness, as if the story had happened to someone else, not her.

'Why are you telling me this?' I asked.

She closed her eyes and exhaled.

'I'd like you to know something about me that no one else does.'

It was impossible to know whether she was telling the truth, or if it was some kind of trap, a way to keep me on the farm. Could I really be bought so easily, with stories of ex-boyfriends and urinary infections?

Yes. Always, yes.

*

In the end we'd bought the sofa Nathan wanted. It was ugly and awkwardly shaped, so that we skinned the wallpaper of the living room trying to get it in. Still, I was careful not to say anything, silenced by the residual guilt I felt. I was a bad person, and bad people deserved to be punished with ugly furniture.

26

We were woken one night by a noise. I roused to it easily, sat up in bed with the covers knotted around my legs. Lucy was already awake, our beds so close I could see the whites of her eyes in the dark.

'You heard it?' she asked. I nodded. 'I'm sure it's nothing.'

We pressed our faces up against the coach house window. Motion down on the ground, slippery, as though something was moving through water. I tried not to think about frilled sharks and viper fish, ugly deep-sea creatures that relied on the dark to capture their prey. Living on the farm meant a baseline of wildlife. It was probably just a fox come to find its next meal, despite us never getting around to replacing the slaughtered chickens.

One by one the other women in the coach house woke up, came to the window. 'What do you think it is?' Pearl asked.

'It's probably just a fox,' Tanya said.

And yet none of us moved. There came a percussive rattle as one of the bins was knocked over, the pigs sending up a fearful screech from the barn. It was becoming increasingly difficult not to feel like we were being hunted, that whatever was lurking outside had a taste for woman-fat.

The lights in the main house went on. A moment later I saw Hazel at her bedroom window. Our eyes met briefly before

I saw the front door open and Blythe go storming out, her torch casting wild slices of light across the ground.

'What is she doing?' Lucy whispered.

I shook my head, was compelled to keep looking.

'This is private land,' Blythe called out. 'We won't stand for trespassers here.'

The bellow of her voice rang through the farm, our bones. I held my breath, pushing my forehead hard against the glass until I was certain it would shatter, a sickness seeping into me as I saw Blythe's torch answered by several more sweeps of light. Phone screens, their blue glow illuminating the chins and mouths of teenagers. In the past I'd seen them lingering on the outskirts of the farm, drinking in the fields that connected the village to Breach House, their roving eyes as we passed by them in our car. But they'd always respected our boundaries, either out of disinterest or superstition. Their broaching of our land was a line redrawn, a kind of dismissal. Whatever power we'd held was suddenly thrown into question.

Their laughter rang out. 'Lesbos,' one girl yelled before lobbing a can of lager at the kitchen window. It was empty, bouncing off the glass easily enough, but the impact of it still made me jump. I felt Pearl grab my arm.

Someone threw a second can, and this time it was not empty, an arc of liquid spraying the air before it hit Blythe's shoulder. A third got her in the face, just below her nose. I could have sworn I heard the metal whack a tooth. Her head whipped back and she let out a cry of pain, the sound echoing across the farm. We gasped, held our faces in symbiotic agony. For a moment it looked as if Blythe would lose her footing.

She staggered sideways before steadying herself against the wall.

The group were gone before she had the chance to run after them, the light from their phones blinking out one by one. Blythe sank on to her haunches, ran a hand across her mouth. It was strange to see her that way, out there on her own, the dark and distance diminishing her largeness, reducing her to just another vulnerable woman. She looked up at us, saying nothing, although I was sure I could see her lips moving.

*

The next day we gathered the full extent of the damage to the farm, beer cans strewn across the ground, cigarette burns on the tomatoes and peppers. The smell of their charred flesh. The teens had sprayed graffiti along one side of the house and all over the conservatory windows: it would almost have been funny if it wasn't so difficult to scrub clean. I kept expecting more visitors to show up, found myself staring down the driveway every few minutes. And some women did arrive, taking a long time getting out of their cars, peering at the wreckage from last night with a mixture of shock and wariness, but it wasn't like how it used to be.

There'd been fewer visitors since Blythe had learned about the men coming to the farm. Fewer women to work the allotment and bolster our numbers. Perhaps they'd sensed the shift in Blythe and didn't want to get caught up in her anger. Or maybe being on the farm meant something different now, its appeal quashed by how the villagers had sneered at the photos of us. Maybe, analysing the reasons why they'd come in the first place, the other women had decided to go back to their friends and family.

I told myself it was better this way, that only the truly committed should remain.

The sun cast a heat that wound its way into the marrow of your bones, burst capillaries. A breeze stirred the trees and I lifted my chin to capture it, watched as it filtered through the pastureland. I had always loved the wildness of the landscape – the vastness of it, the views, the brackish taste of the water – and my appreciation had never seemed to run short. I recognised that, until I'd moved to Breach House, I had lived only adjacent to the wilderness, a visitor to it rather than a resident. But now I felt cowed before its expanse, the fistfuls of thorns and nettles, hidden crags that could snap your ankles clean in half. We could be dead in our beds and no one would know.

I could tell the others were coming to the same realisation, moving around the farm with a new vigilance, spooking at any loud sound.

'But what did they want?' Pearl asked, her voice breathy as she attempted to remove the paint from the window with an old brush. 'Why would they come and scare us like that?'

'It stinks of piss. They've pissed over everything,' Molly said.

'Did you see Blythe?' I asked the others, not knowing I was going to speak until the words were out. 'When they hit her in the face, she almost looked scared.'

Maybe I was being unfair. I would have been scared too if I was hit in the face. But, if I was honest, I expected more from Blythe. The others did too, I could tell. She'd built herself into this monolith, something that was untouchable, separate from the rest of us – but last night had punctured that image. Last night she'd been just the same as any of us: soft and frightened.

'She still chased them off,' Ambika said, although that was not strictly true. They'd left because they wanted to, not because they'd been afraid of Blythe.

I watched the other women fill bin bags with empties, Pearl's whole body shaking as she tried – futilely – to scrub the paint away. Most of them had come to Breach House fleeing something – Ambika's father, Pearl's boyfriend. They came because they believed they would be safe here. I wondered whether they still believed that, or if they had already managed to twist what had happened last night, mangled it into somehow being their fault.

By the time we'd finished, it was so hot I could no longer touch the brick wall with my bare hand. Hazel piled her hair on top of her head, revealing the sweaty nape of her neck. As I fell into step with her, I could make out the beginnings of a heat rash creeping down her shirt.

'Don't you wish you'd cut it?' Molly asked her.

Hazel shrugged. 'It doesn't bother me.'

The front door, when we reached it, wouldn't open. I thought perhaps the wood had expanded from the heat, become trapped in its frame. Molly anchored herself with one foot against the wall and gave it a good tug, her hand winching the door handle up and down. 'I think it's locked,' she said after several attempts, wiping the sweat from her forehead. We looked around at each other, acknowledging the strangeness of the fact but trying not to let it spook us.

'Let's try the other door,' Ambika said. We followed her

round the side of the house but found that the conservatory door was locked as well. The sweat was beginning to make my forehead sting, a stripping feeling as I wiped it away.

Molly knocked on the glass.

'There must be a spare hidden somewhere,' Pearl said.

'Do you really think Blythe would be the kind of woman to risk leaving a spare key lying around?' Hazel answered.

That familiar feeling was starting to creep back in. A jump scare, right around the corner.

Sarah appeared at the conservatory door. I could tell by the look on her face that she wasn't going to let us back in. 'Blythe has instructed me to keep the doors locked until she says otherwise,' she told us.

'What do you mean?' Ambika asked.

Sarah sucked her top lip into her mouth, regarded us with a mixture of irritation and sympathy. When she spoke, her voice was muffled by the glass, etching her words in condensation.

'You girls know what I mean.' A small shake of her head. 'She was never going to forget.'

'What are we supposed to do now?' Pearl asked.

Sarah gave a helpless shrug. 'Enjoy the weather.'

*

At first I thought it was some kind of bluff, a joke. I kept waiting for someone to point and laugh and say, *Got you.* When that didn't happen, I told myself Blythe would relent. She couldn't keep us locked outside like animals. But the house remained sealed, left us with no choice but to do as she commanded.

Later I would wonder why I agreed to any of it, this

humiliation, instead of leaving. The truth is, you'd be surprised what you're willing to go along with when everyone around you acts like you deserve it.

*

We loitered outside the farmhouse, trying to find somewhere that wasn't in direct sunlight. The heat was immense. If I looked in the mirror, I was sure I'd find the hairs on my body scorched away, the skin underneath thin and red as if I might be able to peel it clean in one long strip. I could tell Hazel and the others felt the same, shiny and flustered, swatting the flies away from their faces. Our self-preservation telling us to go back inside, but of course we couldn't.

'This is stupid,' Pearl whined. 'She can't do this – we could collapse. We could get really sick.'

'She'll let us in soon,' Molly said. She struck a hand against the side of her face, splatting a midge. I could see the dark smear of it on her brow, a crinkled wing. 'We just have to wait like she told us.'

'Pearl's right,' Ambika told Molly gently. 'This isn't okay.'

Molly gave a dismissive shake of her head. 'You know why she has to do this. She wouldn't be doing it if we hadn't broken the rules.'

'I'm going to the coach house,' Pearl said. 'I'm not standing out here any longer.'

'We can't.' This from quiet Moira. We stopped to look at her. She wouldn't meet our eye, kept staring down at her feet. Her voice sounded strained when she spoke. 'Molly's right. We're being tested. Blythe wants us to wait outside, so that's what we need to do.'

The women continued to argue, those who felt they didn't

deserve this and wanted to seek respite inside the coach house. Others accepting what was happening to them, even going so far as to work in the allotment, as if eager to prove their devotion to Blythe. Hoping she would see and reward them. Hazel lay down on the grass and closed her eyes, one hand slung over her face to guard it from the sun. Everything about her projecting nonchalance. I interpreted her calmness as a well-trodden path: she had seen this coming too.

*

An hour passed, two. We remained outside, growing so dehydrated it became difficult to speak, the same dry, clicking noises in our throats as we tried to swallow. Although I hadn't drunk anything in hours, I needed the bathroom very badly and ended up squatting behind a bush. An acrid smell rose from me that reminded me of the hospital. I pulled my trousers up quickly, glancing at the farmhouse in case Blythe was watching. I resented the thought of her catching me in the act, seeing what she'd reduced us to.

When I returned I found Molly standing directly in the sun, her face inscrutable. I'd noticed she was able to handle this punishment in a way the rest of us were not. Unlike Hazel, who went about it with an air of indifference, Molly seemed almost determined to suffer, as if it was a game to win. When Ambika's hand had been cauterised, it was Molly who reminded her that she was lucky to have been healed by Blythe at all, utterly convinced that there had been no other option or outcome. She'd taken Ambika's mangled hand and kissed it, gently, which would have been touching if not for the jealous pout of her lips.

'I'm so thirsty,' Pearl said, stamping her feet. She wouldn't stay still, kept walking circles around the house like she could find a chink in its armour, a hidden door she'd never noticed before. Sweat soaking her vest, causing it to cling to her slight body. 'I need something to drink. I need a glass of water.' Her lips were pale and peeling. 'For fuck's sake, I'm so fucking thirsty.'

'Sit down,' Molly told her. 'You're making things worse.'

But she was incapable. I watched as she continued to rave, marching up and down the driveway, talking about how it was unfair, it was so unfair, her words beginning to blur so she wasn't even making sense any more. I looked down at my feet, at the intricate weave of veins, and tried not to think about the possibility that I had found myself in a bad place, with the wrong people.

There was a wet noise. I looked up and saw Pearl had been sick. Vomit all down her front, tinted red from the strawberries I'd seen her eating earlier. Wet chunks clung to her chin. She stood very still, her arms splayed out in front, blinking several times, quickly, as if to stop herself from crying.

We couldn't look at her for long. It was not embarrassment, so much as shame, that prevented us from helping her.

*

Of course, that was when Blythe came to the conservatory door. She must have been watching after all, waiting for a moment like this. We stared at her, seared and desperate, just wanting something to drink. I'd lost count of how long we'd been locked outside for, although the sun had gradually inched its way around the farmhouse. Up close, I noticed there was a red mark on Blythe's chin where the beer can had hit her.

'I've a special treat for you ladies,' she said, stepping aside to let us in. 'Sarah's made some of her famous lemon drizzle. You'll find it on the kitchen table waiting for you.'

We smiled and thanked her; could already taste the citrus on our tongues.

27

And now I began to realise. That I had stumbled into something I didn't quite know the shape of, had misjudged my circumstances. That I was part of something that would mark me for the rest of my life, even if no one knew who I was. That I was in trouble. That if my mother knew what was going on, she would be afraid for me. That I was afraid for myself. That I had to make it stop somehow, but that I wasn't going anywhere without Hazel.

*

After what had happened with the trespassers, new rules were set in place. A night watch was organised so at least two women were awake to make sure no one else tried to infiltrate the farm. That was how it was spoken about – infiltration, like we were part of a military operation. We could only go into the village if Sarah accompanied us and we did not leave her sight. No more coming and going: either you lived at Breach House permanently or you were not welcome. Most of the women with families slunk back to their other lives without complaint. A handful moved into the coach house, cramming the space even further. There were fifteen of us now in total, enough to fit into one room.

None of us dared argue with Blythe, but the apprehension

we felt was clear. This gradual shifting of what it meant to be a woman of Breach House. Whichever way you looked at it, there was a sense of whittling, of conservation: Blythe was paring us back to the bone.

'Doesn't this all seem a bit extreme to you?' Pearl asked a couple of days later. None of us had brought up our punishment, a silent agreement that if we didn't talk about it, we could pretend it had never happened. 'We're meant to be part of a community, aren't we? Not a prison.'

'If you don't like it,' Sarah said, appearing in the doorway, 'I'm sure you know what Blythe will tell you to do.'

Increasingly I found myself wanting to ask Sarah what she thought about everything. Whether the utopian vision Blythe had sold to her years ago was the one we were living in now. Did she ever feel short-changed? Did she miss her children, those tidy grown-ups who had looked at us as if we were dirty? I wanted to ask her, and yet the graph of my doubt seemed to run inverse to her own stoicism. It was as if she could sense the questions on the tip of my tongue and knew any answer she gave would not be the one I wanted to hear. She looked at me as if I were a piece of furniture, loveable in its own small, unimportant way.

Pearl's bottom lip jutted out. She wouldn't leave. She had nowhere else to go.

*

A few days later the farm came down with the flu. It wasn't the first time we'd got sick – living in such close proximity, it was inevitable – but I'd never seen a virus hit the women quite so hard. No, that wasn't true. I'd never seen one hit Hazel so hard. The glands in her throat swelling, reducing her voice to a feeble croak as she asked me to look after her.

I boiled some hot water with honey and chamomile and took it to her room. She was propped up in bed, frowning at me as I perched on the mattress. I was one of the only women who hadn't fallen ill, and I knew my good health irritated her.

She took the cup of tea and sipped noisily. I watched as some of it dribbled down her chin but resisted the urge to mop it away. 'How are you feeling?' I asked.

'The best I've ever felt in my entire life,' she said. 'No one will ever feel as good as I do right now.'

'Can I get you anything else?'

She shook her head. 'Thank you for the tea.'

'I might go and see if the others need anything,' I told her, but she grabbed my arm, tethering me to her.

'Don't bother. They can look after themselves.'

I didn't argue. Truthfully, I no longer felt the sense of camaraderie between us like when I first joined Breach House. That word had always felt wrong to me anyway, the sound of it working in opposition to its meaning. The push and pull of each syllable as though it was trying to tear itself apart. Cam-a-rad-er-ie. Everyone kept to themselves at the end of the day now rather than seeking one another out, the farm becoming a quiet place as we each turned inward. Our community seemed defined by a certain sadness: we were trying to preserve an eggshell peace that could shatter any moment.

I'd even noticed something change between Molly and Ambika. They still slept in the same bed and spent the most time together out of everyone, but they argued when they thought nobody was listening. More than once I heard Ambika try to calm Molly down after some kind of disagreement, only for Molly to hit the wall next to Ambika's head or throw a glass in her direction. Never striking her directly, but it was a violence I'd never encountered before.

I went over to the window to let some fresh air in. Hazel pulled the covers up to her chin. Although I told myself I wished she wasn't sick, there was something about her feebleness that I found pleasing. A wearing down of toughness.

'What did you do today?' she asked me. 'Let me live vicariously through you.'

I shook my head, sat down next to her. 'Nothing particularly exciting. One of the pigs got tangled up in the fence again. It took me nearly twenty minutes to get them loose.'

Hazel readjusted on the bed, edging slightly closer. The skin of her shoulder brushing against mine. 'Is Blythe angry?'

'I don't know,' I said. 'I don't think so. She can't be angry at you for being ill.'

Hazel arched an eyebrow. It was difficult to know what would provoke Blythe now. We were becoming accustomed to her mood swings in the same way I imagined people who lived somewhere prone to earthquakes did: living with a low level of threat in the back of their minds. She hadn't forgiven us for the photos, or for the farm being ransacked. The most mundane thing could trigger her wrath. For example, one night Ambika accidentally left the kitchen light on and in the morning Blythe chastised her for draining the generator and scraped her breakfast into the bin. And then there was the time she found us taking a break from work in the allotment and trampled the ground like a toddler throwing a tantrum, pulling premature carrots out of the ground and hurling them at us. We no longer knew how to please her, although the other women still seemed desperate to try.

Hazel leaned forward and began tracing a letter down my back. I smiled, arched towards her. It was a game we played sometimes when we had nothing better to do.

She drew a rigid right angle across my skin. L.

I sat up a little straighter. Before she'd got ill, Hazel had thrown herself into Blythe's new regime, always the first to put herself forward for night patrol or else working in the allotment until sunset, coming away with her hands resembling raw meat. It had become difficult to spend time alone with her. And yet, I sensed a new neediness in how she found ways to lock our bodies together, walking with her arm threaded through the crook of my elbow, resting her foot against mine underneath the dining table. It was as if two opposing forces were battling for space inside her.

An almost-sensual swoop between my shoulder blades. O.

'If you could live anywhere in the world,' I began, trying to pluck up the courage, 'where would you choose?'

'That's a stupid question,' she replied. I felt her foot under the blanket twitch. 'I live here.'

The point of her finger rested unmoving on my spine. Considering her next letter.

'But if you didn't live on the farm,' I went on. 'Where would you want to live?'

Hazel began drawing the next letter. 'Maybe on the coast. I've always liked the idea of living in one of those town houses painted a bright colour. I'd get a dog and walk it on the beach every morning. Early, before any tourists showed up.'

'That would be nice,' I said. 'I always liked going to the beach.'

'Maybe we'd meet for lunch,' Hazel said. I thrilled at her inclusion of me in her hypothetical life. 'We'd have to go full vegan. I don't think you can live on the coast in a brightly coloured house and not be vegan.'

'I can do that.' Hazel's finger slid down my back. I tried not to shiver. Already my mind was inventing scenarios for this new life, one where it would just be me and Hazel. Perhaps that's what I'd always wanted: to be alone with this person. 'Maybe one day that's what we'll do,' I said. 'After all of this.'

'You planning on leaving?'

'Not without you,' I said, my voice barely above a whisper.

A line met another. I was too distracted to discern if it was a soft join like a G, or something straighter like the beginning of an N. Or even a V. Please let it be a V, I thought to myself. If she wouldn't speak the word out loud, let her write it on my skin.

'Can you do that one again?' I asked. 'I don't think I quite got it.'

Hazel sighed but shook her hand and began again. This time there was no mistaking the soft swell of the letter U. I was glad then that we weren't facing each other, so she couldn't see my disappointment.

She finished with the letter D.

'Loud,' I said. 'What's that supposed to mean?'

She sat back in the bed. A vegetal waft as she finished her tea. 'It's not supposed to mean anything,' she told me. 'It's just a game.'

28

I was in the orchard helping Sarah gather plums. It was a small orchard, grown haphazardly so it was difficult to tell the various fruits apart. They all had soft, beautiful names like Opal and Avalon and Mirabelle de Nancy: names you wanted inside your mouth. Hazel told me one of her favourite things about living on the farm was watching the trees blossom, the way the petals drifted like snowfall, catching in your hair. That was how I liked to imagine Hazel best. Soft as a plum.

By summer the blossom had given way to its fruit, branches bending with their weight. Sarah was a dab hand at picking them, knew just by sight which plums were ready to be harvested and which weren't. She could even tell when one was rotten inside, holding it up to her face for inspection before letting it drop to the ground for the magpies to fight over. By the way she fussed over me, gently slapping my hand every time I did something wrong, I could tell she enjoyed having someone to shepherd: she probably used to do this with her children years ago, before she'd met Blythe.

When Hazel first brought me to Breach House, she'd told me how it had all begun with Sarah. That she'd been recovering from an illness and struggling to find meaning in her life when Blythe appeared, how everything that had come after stemmed from the root of their friendship. At times

I'd wondered if there was something more between them – it wouldn't have changed anything, how we viewed either of them – but I'd never seen a furtive look exchanged, no slinking into the other's bedroom late at night. Truthfully, I struggled to imagine Blythe sexually. That body of hers used for anything other than labour. She was impassive – unreachable.

No, the more time I spent at Breach House, the more I realised: Sarah was proof of Blythe's power, walking among us, cooking us dinner. A mirror held up to each of us, reflecting back our own desire for change.

When we'd finished picking the plums, I followed Sarah into the kitchen, where she began slicing them to make a pie. Their juices soaking into the wooden chopping board. Sarah's mouth slipped open as she worked, the combined heat from the oven and the weather outside causing her to sweat.

'I can't remember the last time we had a summer like this,' she said, mopping herself with a tea towel. I stretched over the sink and threw a window open, for all the good it did. 'When was the last time it rained?'

I shook my head. I couldn't recall.

'There used to be a pond in the garden, when we first bought the house,' she said. I'd never heard her talk about her life before Blythe, was careful not to move or say anything in case I spooked her into stopping. 'It was thick with frogspawn, these disgusting mounds of grey jelly. You could see the babies wriggling inside them.'

'Creepy,' I said.

She smiled, taking the wet towel from me and draping it around her own neck. 'Most of it gets eaten before the tadpoles can hatch,' she said. 'Birds come, or hedgehogs, and hoover it up. But not all of it. Andrew wanted to fill the pond in with dirt to save us the bother. Andrew was my husband. But my boys were fascinated. Every morning they'd wake up and put on their little wellies to go outside, look at the tadpoles through the magnifying glass they begged me to buy them. It was the only time you could be sure they wouldn't argue or fight.'

She seemed pleasantly exhausted by the memory, her toes twitching as if she were walking alongside her two boys.

Oil popped in the oven, making me jump. 'What happened to the pond?' I asked her. 'It's not there any more.'

'No,' she agreed. 'Andrew and I came downstairs one morning and found the boys at the kitchen table. Daniel was hunched over Callum, who was drinking something, his little face all scrunched up. By the state of them, I could tell Daniel had put Callum up to it. He was always egging his brother on like that.'

'What was he drinking?' Sarah looked at me until I gasped, clapped a hand over my mouth. 'The frogspawn?'

She nodded. 'A pint of it. I still remember how it slithered along the glass into his poor mouth, Daniel tipping it back so more would come out. Horrible little boys.'

We looked at each other. I didn't know what to say, caught somewhere between horror and understanding. It would have been a lie to say I never would have done something like that, that Hazel couldn't convince me to do much worse. Tolerance the measure of how much we love someone.

And then we were laughing, Sarah bent over, the towel falling from her shoulders and splatting on the floor. Tears pouring from her eyes. 'That's revolting,' I said. 'That's awful. What did you do?'

'What could I do?' she said. 'He'd already drunk the thing.'

'Did he tell you why he did it?'

Sarah gave a helpless shrug. 'Why do boys do anything? It was a dare, of course. Andrew was so outraged, the next day he drained the pond and filled it in, just like he'd always threatened to. It's where the rose bushes are, round back. It's the first thing I think of every time I walk past them.'

I wanted to ask her then: did she have any regrets? Would she still have chosen Blythe if she knew it meant not speaking to her children again? It was difficult to know what Sarah thought about everything, her allegiance to Blythe putting a distance between us. Impossible to know whether the vision she'd been sold was the one she found herself living now, women being punished and left to burn in the thirty-degree heat.

The kitchen door slammed open and Molly appeared. She was covered in filth from the allotment, her hair nested with debris. I could tell something was wrong, could feel the panic washing from her. Sarah's laughter caught in her throat.

'What?' she said, standing.

'There are people here,' Molly said. 'I think they're police.'

*

The officers wore fluorescent jackets with walkie-talkies strapped to them, milling about on the driveway as they got the measure of Breach House. They'd surely heard the stories from locals, seen the photographs of us paraded around the village and formed their own opinions on whether we were devil worshippers or sluts. And yet, it was a very different thing to see the farm in person. How it looked so unbelievably normal, just another house. One of the officers depressed a button on his radio and muttered something into it, his gaze trained on the upstairs windows.

The other women trickled in from the allotment, including Hazel, who came and stood next to me. 'What's going on?' she whispered. I shook my head and she reached for my hand, held it tight.

I looked around for Blythe, but she was nowhere to be seen.

'Can I help you?' Sarah asked.

The officer who'd been fiddling with his radio spoke. 'Are you the owner of this property?'

Sarah held up one hand. 'I'm afraid I must ask you not to come any closer. We don't permit men here. Where you're standing is far enough.'

The officers exchanged a glance, as if they found Sarah charming more than anything. He spoke again. 'All right then, I'll just raise my voice so you can hear me. Are you the owner of this property?'

'Yes,' Sarah said.

'Your name is Blythe Roberts?'

'No.'

'No?'

'What is this about?' Sarah asked.

Someone had called them, the officers explained. A complaint had been made and now they were here to investigate.

'What complaint would that be?' Sarah said, careful to keep her voice calm, unsuspecting.

Neglect. Coercion. Emotional and physical abuse. 'Where is Blythe?' they kept asking, looking at each of us in turn. Where is she? Are you her? Are you, are you?

We formed a ring around the officers, us women streaked with filth. Heat baked into our skin. Pearl kept shifting her weight from foot to foot, chewing on the sleeve of her blouse until I saw the fabric begin to dampen and fray. It was difficult to know where her nervousness came from, if she had something to do with what was happening now. Could she have brought chaos to the farm a second time? I could tell the other women were thinking the same thing, eyeing her up.

Sarah instructed someone to go and find Blythe. The officers came closer, even though we had asked them not to, inspecting the gables and cladding, pressing their faces up to the kitchen window. What were they expecting to see? Signs of debauchery, witch's brew bubbling away on the stove? They'd already formed their opinion of us. I could see it in the rigidity of their shoulder blades, the dilation of their nostrils. As if to compensate, we gave them our best smiles, asked them if they would like some tea while they waited, or maybe some biscuits. There might be fig rolls in the pantry, perhaps someone could go and check. But the officers didn't want to eat or drink, treating us with a level of detached hostility that was difficult to comprehend.

'If they're investigating anything, it should be the photographs,' Hazel whispered, and wasn't that the truth? The officers hadn't even mentioned the photos. They hadn't once asked if we were okay.

Blythe arrived carrying a basket of kindling. She couldn't have been far away, might even have heard the car arrive. 'Hello,' she greeted the officers, setting the kindling down on the ground as if it weighed nothing. I was pleased the officers were there to witness her strength, her mass. Forced to take a step back so they could look her in the eye. We still deserved their awe. They cleared their throats and explained the situation again to her. An anonymous complaint had been made citing grievous neglect and harm, did Blythe know anything about this? Could they see some identification?

Blythe held up her hands in a conciliatory gesture. 'I don't know anything about this,' she said. 'Look at these women. Do they look neglected to you?'

We flinched from the officers' stares, uncomfortable under this new scrutiny. More than anything, we were tired, unsure of what was being asked of us. Whether we should lie outright or twist the narrative, refocus it on the men who'd come and sown discord among us. Surely it was a crime to photograph someone without their permission, let alone disseminate the images among the public. If they hadn't done any of that, there would have been no need for Blythe to punish us. But the police wouldn't see it that way. They'd find some other reason to blame us.

And yet, this was perhaps the only opportunity we'd get to voice our fear. That life here was spiralling out of control. That we needed help. I saw the same realisation dawn on the other women's faces, that all we had to do was confirm the police report. Open our mouths and speak the words. In that moment we held a kind of power over Blythe. I think she knew it too, that everything she had strived to create could be undone by us in a moment.

If I expected that to soften her though, I was mistaken. If anything, I felt her harden further, pinning us in place with a metallic look.

'Ask any of them,' she told the officers. A challenge – to them, and us. 'Go ahead.'

The officer with the radio looked me over. If I squinted he could be handsome, like a television actor. I felt him take me in and knew what he must see. A woman who hadn't brushed her hair in days, who, if he came closer, would exude an earthly reek.

Pearl made a noise high in her throat, her tongue poking between the gaps in her teeth. The other women swallowed her into their midst, hiding her from the officers. It wasn't out of love or protection, I knew: they were simply preventing her from saying anything. As they formed a circle, it became impossible to tell them apart. When we'd first got our matching haircuts, I'd enjoyed the communion of it. It had felt as if we were part of something, sharing an experience. But I realised how it must have looked to the officers: a homogeny of women, an indistinguishable swarm of us.

I licked my lips, tasted the possibility of telling the officers myself. They would surely escort us away before Blythe had a chance to react, punish us further. But, really, what was there to gain from telling? Most of these women had no lives to return to. And I could not imagine returning to mine, back to my mother and Nessa and a shitty, pointless job. It would be too much of a defeat. This was our life now, our entire existence.

Above all, I didn't want to be separated from Hazel.

And so, we remained loyal. No, we told the officers. We didn't know anything about these claims. No, we said. We are looked after here. We are a family. No, we said. No.

*

None of us went to bed that night. We gathered in the living room, Sarah passing around cups of chamomile tea, the air swamping with it. The women sipped slowly, unfocused and afraid. Crying was rare on the farm – at least in public – but now some of them broke down, pressing their faces into each other's shoulders, inconsolable. The rest of us remained silent. But, I knew, in all of us lurked the same fear.

At some point Blythe came into the room and stood in front of the empty fireplace. She loomed larger than usual, her anger maximising her body, allowing it to dwarf the room. She smiled at each of us, tilting her head to the side as though deep in thought. Looking every bit the peacemaker, here to make it all okay again. But I knew it was just another role she was playing, a way to crack us open. In one corner of the room lay the fragments of what had been the telephone. After the police officers had left, Blythe had cut the phone line and thrown it against the wall. I could still see where the impact had left a chip in the plaster.

She asked only one question: who had made the phone call?

When nobody spoke, she looked around the room. We were unnaturally still, prey hiding from predator. She placed her hands on her hips, revealing the shape of her muscles. She could knock out a tooth, fracture a bone, without breaking a sweat.

'Let's call this what it was. It was a mutiny. One of you has tried to usurp me, tear everything I've worked so hard for to shreds. They'll be back. The police, the others. They always come back. And now they'll be looking for ways to do us over. Our time here is limited.'

I looked at Sarah, wondering what was going through her head. If the commune failed and we had to leave, where would she go? This was her home. She stood behind Blythe's right shoulder, appearing nothing but resolute. I saw Blythe lean back and whisper something in Sarah's ear, who gave a short nod. Outside, the sun was finally setting.

Molly was the first to speak. 'I want to be clear that I am

only speaking for myself right now. I am as responsible as the next woman for letting those men on to the farm. I knew it was wrong, but I didn't do enough to stop it from happening. I knew I'd failed in my duty to preserve peace here. And so, when you punished us' – at this she turned to Blythe – 'I was able to cope with it. Because I knew there would be consequences to our actions. Because I knew I deserved it. But it's clear not everyone felt the same way.'

'Speak freely,' Blythe told her, offering a smile to grant Molly strength to carry on.

Molly pointed a finger at Pearl. 'None of this would have happened if it wasn't for her. She's the one who invited the men here, who told them to come. And now she's trying to ruin things even more.'

A few of the other women made noises of agreement – Lucy and Tanya, and even Moira, clustering close to Molly as if to shield themselves. Pearl gave an incredulous laugh, her eyes widening as if to say *Can you believe this?* But the look on the women's faces made her laughter shrivel up. 'You think I called the police?' she asked. 'I would never do that. You can't actually be serious.'

'Who was the one complaining about being punished? Who was the one who said the outside world was just curious about us, that we should let them into our home? You've always wanted an audience, and now that you've got one you can't handle it.'

Molly's words ricocheted around the room. 'Is this true?' Blythe asked, whisper-soft.

Pearl shrank against the wall, looked as if she wanted to sink into it. Poor, foolish thing. 'You're making it sound worse than it was,' she whimpered. 'I didn't mean for it to go so wrong. I know it was a stupid thing to do. But, I swear. I didn't call the police.'

'You're a fucking liar,' Molly told her. 'Lying cunt.'

Ambika placed a hand on Molly's arm. 'She's still one of us. She deserves for us to listen.'

Molly snatched her arm away. I could see the violence of it shocked Ambika, who recoiled as if Molly had slapped her across the face.

'One of you is to blame,' Blythe said, oblivious to their exchange. 'I want a confession. I won't even consider next steps until someone comes forward.'

A ripple of nervous muttering went around the room. Hazel was perched on the arm of the sofa, arms crossed. Watching us all closely. There hadn't been an opportunity for us to speak alone after the police had left, and I wondered which side of the fence she sat on. Whether she understood why someone might do it, or if she considered it a betrayal. Her eyes lit on mine, the ferocity in them shocking me. A glimmer of something that looked almost like hatred.

'You cannot build a house in the eye of a hurricane,' Blythe went on, her voice rising and, in the process, silencing ours. 'A home is only as strong as its foundations. If we cannot trust one another, we are doomed. The only chance we ever had at succeeding here was to respect the sanctity of this land, but now it has been tainted. Maybe it would be best if you all left. Maybe that's what needs to happen.'

A swell of noise shook the room, women both outraged and frightened. That they might lose their home, that they had been put in this position in the first place. Pearl was sobbing now, insisting through wet plosives that she didn't understand what was happening, that she was a good girl. I could sense a fissure gradually separating the room, parting us into those who believed her and those who didn't: those who wanted justice and those who sought mercy.

Blythe's gaze picked over us, eventually landing on me. She came forward and took me by the shoulder, marching me to the front. I could feel myself withering under this new scrutiny, all eyes turning towards me. A hot rash spread up my neck. For a moment I thought Blythe meant to accuse me of betraying the commune, but it was more than that. She wanted to use me, force a stake in the ground. There would be no coming back from whatever was about to happen. 'You came here to be a part of something,' she told me. 'To be part of a community. Isn't that right?' I told her yes, that was right. 'And if someone sought to threaten that community, what should be done? What would you do if you were me, Iris?'

Hazel leaned forward, waiting for my response. She looked softer now, more open – the same Hazel who'd lent me her jumper so I wouldn't be cold, who had pulled me into the river with her. I wished it could have been just us, that it had always only ever been just us.

I knew then the only way to keep her was to cling tighter to the commune, and to Blythe.

'I would do whatever it took to find the one responsible,' I said.

Blythe nodded slowly, clearly pleased. I would be lying if I said it didn't feel good to win her approval, the way she gripped my arm with her thick fingers. Something about it that made me think of my father. 'That's exactly it,' she said.

The noise from the women escalated again, reached a new pitch as they threw accusations and threats at each other. *I saw you on the phone the other day. I heard you two talking when you thought no one was listening. I know you never believed in any of it.* How quickly we all went for each other's throats. I felt Blythe let go of my shoulder and was drawn back into the mass. An elbow jutted painfully into my side as I was jostled about, panic rising through me until Hazel slipped her arms around my waist and whispered into my ear that she wouldn't let anything bad happen to me.

It went on like that for some time. We argued and knocked things over, a deafening clobber of sound so that we didn't notice what was happening at first. It was only when the glow of the fire lit the room that we realised Blythe had gone outside. Sarah was the first to follow, the rest of us close behind.

She'd set the car on fire. Columns of greasy smoke obscured our vision, frightened the dunnocks and sparrows out of their nests. We staggered backwards, afraid of the engine exploding, and begged for Blythe to do the same, but she kept pouring more white spirit on to the flames, until the fire was blinding. For a dreadful moment I pictured it spreading, catching the dry grass and sending the entire farm up in flames. All our work, ash-soaked. But it was a still night and there was no breeze to carry the flames. Only us and Blythe and Pearl in the corner, still crying.

2018

The tenth anniversary came and brought with it a fresh wave of obsession. A documentary came out on Netflix and was the second most watched thing that week, falling behind a show about teenagers with superpowers. True crime was back in vogue, particularly with women who enjoyed watching or reading about it. They became a dating archetype: true-crime feminists who didn't have time to fuck with men, were too busy guarding themselves against the various methods serial killers used to murder them. Countless podcasts were released in which wealthy white women discussed famous murders and kidnappings, calling the victims sweet baby angels. Our story featured on a couple of them, usually once the presenters had rinsed Jonestown and the Manson family for all they were worth, but we were not considered sweet baby angels. No, we were something else. Bad women, disturbed women: psycho bitches.

Scott crawled out of the woodwork around this time. In all honesty, I was surprised it had taken him this long, almost admired his self-restraint. He was interviewed for the Netflix documentary, unable to look at camera lens at first, but then warming up once he began talking. He'd put on weight and chipped one of his front teeth, but other than that had the appearance of someone who hadn't suffered much in life. He'd shared the photographs he'd taken of Breach House with the documentary makers, the ones he'd strung up around the village all those years ago and which we'd worked so hard to destroy. Pearl dancing, Tanya passed out drunk in the corner. Hazel and I kissing. The possibility of the photos resurfacing had always frightened me, but when I finally saw them again there was only a sense of disassociation. I'd grown my hair long since leaving the commune, could hardly recognise the shorn woman in the photograph, how her eyes peered sideways at the camera, caught out. After the documentary aired, I began seeing Scott's photos all over the internet – people seemed to love how vulnerable we looked in them.

There was one benefit to the attention we received, a sordid silver lining: learning things about each other in the aftermath of Breach House. Finally being able to pick apart what was and wasn't bullshit. For instance, I learned Molly's real birthday was actually in December – not in June, like she'd told us. Ambika's mother wasn't dead either, but a dental hygienist living in Scotland. She cropped up once in an article online. I thought her hair looked very neat.

I learned things about Blythe, too. Nothing concrete – nothing that could demystify her entirely, but morsels which still felt like ammunition. I took what I could get, dined for weeks on discovering her middle name (Patricia) and the house where she was born (a three-bedroom terrace, with a pond at the end of the garden). While listening to another podcast, I learned Blythe's mother had been admitted to a psychiatric care ward when Blythe was seven years old. The presenter had managed to dredge up some transcripts, where she mentioned a boyfriend who had mistreated her daughter, duct-taped her hands to a radiator. I thought about when I'd first met Blythe, how proud she'd been of her hands, thick and scarred. Only now did I realise they were not just a symbol of her power, but her endurance.

Ten years passed and people still wanted to know what she had to say. She continued to receive letters from fanatics, although perhaps not as many as before. According to the internet, at least thirteen people had asked to marry her. She entertained a couple of them, insofar as she let them buy her things until they ran out of money, and then cast them aside without a second thought. Silly. They should have known she'd never let another person share the warmth of her spotlight. She looked older now, although age had not weakened her. She was still a large woman; formidable. Those hands which could crush you to pulp. Do you regret anything, people asked. Would you do it again. What is your favourite colour. Her answers were always vague, deliberately steeped in mystery.

I had no desire to speak to her. There was nothing left she could say.

Around the same time as the documentary, property developers bought Breach House and its surrounding lands. Up until then it had been used as a playground for bored teenagers, throwing parties at the desiccated farmhouse. Covering the walls in graffiti, starting fires in the empty living room. The usual mess made upstairs in the bedrooms. It felt like more than just proving something; it was as if they were trying to burrow themselves into the house, comprehend it on a cellular level. Even after the developers tore everything down and built apartments over it, people came. Just to see.

No longer rebellious teenagers, but adults now – teachers, electricians, parents. They brought their children and pointed to the land and warned them what would happen if they misbehaved. You could end up like those women, they'd say, if you aren't careful.

Ten was a good number, often considered the angel number. It signified wealth and power, good luck and prosperity. Ten little monkeys, ten bottles of beer on the wall. Ten lacerations across the torso and abdomen, ten separate puncture wounds to the arms, legs, cheek. Ten years was a good amount of time to make amends. And I did, to a degree. I continued writing manuals for the furniture company and began to make more of an effort with my colleagues, joining them for Friday-night drinks and participating in office gossip. One woman there, Jenny, even invited me to her birthday party, and I went. I began taking a cooking class, where I learned to make lasagne and slice an onion so fine you could see through its skin. I dated. Some of them hung around for a while, a teacher in her early thirties who had an annoying habit of burping in public, a man named Stephen who was a carpenter and knew how to make coffee just the way I liked.

But there was something about the number ten, the completeness of it, that threatened to unravel me. It became difficult to focus. I left chores half finished, kept forgetting basic things like locking the front door and eating lunch. Autumn was nearing its end and already winter had sunk its teeth in, my dahlias shrivelling in a premature frost before I could store their tubers. Something disturbing about having to empty them into the compost bin, the futility of it.

The only things that really kept me warm were thoughts of Hazel. Normally I was able to tamp her down into a hidden corner of my mind, cover her in the rubble of everyday occurrences – when to pay the council tax, whether the new mole on the inside of my elbow was normal or something to be worried about. But lately she kept finding her way through the cracks. When this happened, it was like falling into a bottomless pit. Or like trying to fill one up. I would repeat behaviours I knew were unhealthy, cancelling social plans to stay home and mine the internet for information about her. Analysing Scott's photo of us kissing, how the angle of Hazel's shoulder reminded me of an iceberg, impassive and tipped with her socket.

If I knew her address, I could write to her. Dear Hazel. Ink sinking into the page. Dear Hazel, how are you? Tell me the truth. Dear Hazel, do you ever think about me? Dear Hazel, I think I blame you for everything.

PART THREE:

AUTUMN

29

2008

It was as if the farm had been wrapped in gauze. Sound no longer seeming to carry beyond the trees which leaned over the farm, keeping us contained, interned. It almost came as a relief, the knowledge that the only thing that could inflict damage now was already here, among us.

I'd spent the entire night outside watching the car burn down. The smell of engine oil thick in my clothes and hair. When I blew my nose, what came out was dry and flecked with black. If I closed my eyes and tried very hard I could almost convince myself it was Beltane again, that the warmth I now felt came from the bonfire. That any moment Hazel would take my hand and we would vault over it together. It seemed so long ago now.

A groan of metal as something gave way and one of the car doors collapsed on the ground. I hugged my knees, rocked slowly back and forth. Out of the corner of my eye I could see Molly, walking in a small circle, her eyes chipped with burning coal reflected from the fire. She hadn't said anything since Blythe set the car on fire, no more accusations or threats, but I could sense something had changed in her. She was recalibrating.

Images of my father disturbed my train of thought. I couldn't help picturing his final few moments, driving to see his other family. Whether the collision had killed him instantly or if he'd had time to understand what was happening to him, comprehended his own death. There had been toys in the back seat for a child that may or may not have been biologically his. According to police, one of them had been an electric train set addressed to Joseph. A boy, then. Just as well. My father had never really known what to do with a daughter. He'd always been so exacting of my love, constantly demanding I prove how much I adored him without ever really offering anything in return. That's what he'd always wanted, I understood now. To absorb my admiration, a vitamin for some internal deficiency. And when it wasn't enough, he took it from other women, other families. The irony wasn't lost on me. I'd spent most of my life trying to escape what my father had done, only to end up in the exact same position. Blythe, the commune, Hazel – they were just more of the same. Demanding unmitigated fidelity to satisfy their own lack.

*

The glow from the fire was dulled by the dawn, a yolked sun blotting through the trees. Another day had come. I stood along with a few of the other women, who shook their heads as if snapping out of a trance. I noticed Pearl wasn't among them. She must have retreated to the coach house, away from accusing eyes. Hazel came over to me, her hair matted in several places.

'Hungry?' she asked.

'Yes,' I lied.

She looked over my shoulder at the car, gave her head a small shake. I could still remember how she'd looked at me the night before, like I might be the one to blame. Her suspicion cut deep, that she still believed I had the capacity to betray her. Even if she'd sensed my doubt, even if I'd confessed I wanted us to leave Breach House together, surely she knew I never would have done anything without her permission.

A high-pitched keening snapped me out of it. It sounded like a kettle left too long on the stove, shrill and inescapable. I looked at Hazel. 'It's the pigs,' she told me. 'They can smell the smoke.'

'We should go and see if they're okay,' I said, struggling with the idea of them suffering in their pen, convinced they were about to die.

'We will,' Hazel said. 'But first let's find something to eat.'

I followed her inside. It was only once we were in the kitchen I realised I was shaking, my hands wrought with cold. Fingers stiff and unbending. Sarah was at the stove, frying up a big pan of mushrooms and onion. She had remained by Blythe's side throughout last night's conflict and yet I sensed remorse in her now, guilt in the way she spoiled us with large portions and pots of freshly brewed tea.

As I sat down at the table, slotting myself between Ambika and Hazel, it struck me how few of us were left. When I'd first joined Breach House, there'd been a constant struggle for space; too many names to learn. Where were those other women now? I wondered. The ones who'd gone back to their children and families. Did they miss us? Did they even think about us?

'Where's Blythe?' I asked no one in particular.

'She went walking,' Sarah replied, mopping her plate with a

slice of bread. Her hand was red around the knuckles, looked as if she'd been scratching herself.

Molly sat a little straighter. 'When will she be back?' Panic constricting her words. 'Is she coming back?'

'Of course she is,' Sarah said. 'Eat your food.'

'What about Pearl?' Ambika asked.

'Who gives a shit,' someone else replied.

Gradually, each of us testing the other's boundaries, we began to pick apart what had happened last night. Trying to make sense of it, twist the events into something we could convince ourselves was acceptable, proportionate. It went beyond loyalty to the commune. It was self-preservation, a way to stop ourselves from catastrophising. None of us questioned how Blythe had behaved. Instead we focused on the practical: who made the phone call to the police, whose turn it was to empty the bins, how we would ration the toilet paper and toothpaste now we had no car. We could still walk into the village. It was a difficult trek through bramble and nettle, but it could be done. Blythe's burning of the car had been more of a symbolic tethering, a way to ensure we were unable to go anywhere she could not easily bring us back from.

I left the last mushroom on my plate, imagining it as a kind of offering: if I abstained from eating it, perhaps things would get better. Fool's errand, dreamer's logic.

*

It turned out to be an overcast day. We sat in the conservatory waiting to see if it would rain. There were only two sofas, and the women fought over them, playfully at first and then turning nasty, scraping their nails across each other's arms and showing their teeth. Outside, a squirrel ran across the lawn, cunning-quick, its head shaped like an almond. It had something in its mouth, kept touching it with its paw to make sure it was still there.

Pearl appeared in the doorway, carrying a plate of biscuits. She held them out to us, smiling with her mouth closed so we wouldn't see the dark gape of her gums. I thought about the first time I'd met her, how giddy and alert she'd seemed. Always wanting more of everything, one of the first to leap over the bonfire at Beltane. I thought about her then and how she was now, little more than a girl. Doing her best to hide her trembling.

'Does anyone want one?' she asked, still offering the plate. A couple of us took a biscuit, everyone else pointedly turning their heads to look anywhere that wasn't at her.

'Fuck,' Molly said, pointing to the window.

I looked up just in time to see a crow swoop down on the squirrel. The squirrel made a beeline for the fence, its mouth still stuffed with something – even now, not wanting to let it go. We pressed ourselves close to the window, watching as the crow made another dive, its talons knocking the squirrel on to its side. I willed it to get up, felt a measure of satisfaction when it did, but then the crow came back and caught the squirrel by its neck and after that it seemed like the end. The squirrel lay flat on the ground, twitching as the crow began picking it apart.

'Oh god, someone sort that out,' Ambika said. 'Otherwise it'll be there for hours, chipping away at the poor thing.'

We looked around at each other, not wanting to be the first to volunteer. Finally, Pearl put down the plate of biscuits. Perhaps she felt obliged, or thought it might restore some sort of harmony between us. Make us like her again.

She stepped out into the garden with her hands raised in a placating gesture, visibly frightened as the crow clapped its beak at her. The rest of us stood and watched from a safe distance as Pearl finally chased the crow off but then faltered, confronted with the squirrel's body. From where I stood I could see its intestines had spilled out like grey vermicelli, its heart which was smaller than a kidney bean. Pearl shook her head, unable to go any further.

'Just leave it,' Hazel said. 'The crow will carry it off eventually. The allotment needs seeing to. Everyone get up off their fat arses.'

Her capacity for kindness always caught me off guard, just as her bouts of cruelty did. The problem was I never knew what to expect from her, and how do you care for someone who only ever shows you half their face?

*

The afternoon tore on. A heaviness, palpable and sucking, drew the moisture from our skin and left us feeling weighted, a sense of foreboding with every fought-for breath. None of us said it but we were all thinking the same thing: plague, pestilence, was on its way.

We worked in the allotment for as long as we could bear it, pulling chives from the ground which had shrivelled to straw. Rows of lettuce which all had the same lax quality to them. Afterwards we staggered back inside, our eyes impotent in the half-light. Hands outstretched, looking for something solid to hold on to. Blythe had returned from her walk a little while ago and was still being preened by some of the other women, who offered her glasses of cordial and wiped her feet with a cool towel. She swatted them away when she'd had enough of their fussing, sat back in her chair and watched Sarah prepare dinner. She made no mention of what had happened. It was difficult to know how deep her anger went or what might trigger it again. I became hyperaware of myself, sneezing pollen into the crook of my elbow as quietly as I could, pressing myself into the wood of my chair, not wanting to do anything that might gain her attention, turn me into an object of scrutiny.

Dinner was unusually quiet that evening, not even the scrape of forks to cut through the lack: none of us was particularly hungry. The thought of eating felt gargantuan, too much of an effort. I pushed the peas around on my plate. Beside me Pearl asked Ambika if she would pass the bread, but before she could Molly snatched it for herself, handed it down to the opposite end of the table. The same women who'd sided with her last night piled their own plates high, Tanya's wrist popping with the weight, even though I knew they had no intention of eating the bread. This was about deprivation, a line being drawn.

Pearl knew better than to argue. Or perhaps she was too frightened, staring at her hand as if the bread might magically materialise in it. Her chin wrinkled and for a moment I thought she was going to cry, but then she swiped a hand across her mouth and the moment had passed. I could have said something, given her the bread off my plate. But I didn't want to put myself in the middle and risk upsetting Blythe, self-preservation pulling any tenderness I had by the root and stem. It frightened me, how quickly derision overtook sympathy. The sudden urge to pour water all over Pearl's plate.

The bread made its way to Blythe. She took two slices for herself and then, after a pause, slid the plate back to Pearl, who took it gratefully. Stuffing her mouth full before anyone else could stop her. It was impossible to tell whether it was kindness that had provoked Blythe's generosity, or if she was simply trying to even the playing field.

Suddenly, there came a rendering noise from outside. A sound so loud it rattled the windows, made us jump. We looked wildly at one another, our feud temporarily forgotten as we struggled to place what was happening. For a moment I wondered if the men had come back to wreak more havoc. Pictured Scott getting out of his car, looking up at the farmhouse with the same mixture of wonder and derision. The heft of a rock in his hand. But, no. This noise was something else; elemental. Thunder, I realised, a second after it came again, followed by the sound of rain. A few drops splashing against the patio tiles before gaining confidence, tipping into a surge. We'd gone so long without rain, I couldn't even remember the last time I'd seen it fall.

'It's so loud,' Ambika said.

'It's about time,' Sarah remarked, holding her chin in the cup of her hand. 'God knows we needed this heat to break.'

Blythe picked gristle from between her teeth, her tongue making wet sucking noises. I wanted to go outside and stand under the rain, feel it soak into my clothes, but something about her face stopped me. The churning of her jaw chewing the weather's blessing to cud.

*

It rained all through the night, a sound rich with static. I'd asked Hazel if she wanted to share a bed with me, hoping we could listen to it together, but she'd turned me down, made some excuse about how she always slept better in her own bed. I told myself it was less about her being upset with me and more about her needing to withdraw, that there were times when she had to make herself impenetrable. I made do on my own, wrapped the blankets tight around myself until I felt safe and secure. The coach house was quiet except for the other women's snoring and farting, no susurration of late-night confessions, which was what I usually fell asleep to. I noticed before switching off my lamp that some of the women had moved from their regular sleeping spots and were bundled together in new configurations. Tanya and Moira together in one corner, a few others sleeping head to toe. Even Lucy had pushed her bed further away from mine. Factions continuing to form. I assumed, judging by the fact neither of them had appeared in the coach house, that Molly and Ambika had gone to bed together as normal, although this might have been out of habit more than anything else. I recognised well the need to maintain appearances.

I lay very still and tried to sleep. But my exhaustion was the unhelpful kind that couldn't be solved by simply closing my eyes. My legs became restless, electric charges that caused them to kick under the covers until someone told me to knock it off. I turned over the events of the past few months in my mind, imagining them as being attached to the same length of string, making each individual event part of something larger, inevitable. Maybe it was always going to happen like this. The men coming to Breach House. And maybe we were always going to welcome them inside. Was that easier to accept than the possibility we'd brought this on ourselves, that we'd chosen our fate?

Something smacked against the window above my head. The wind had begun to pick up, howled its temper at us. My mother was afraid of storms. Even when I was a child I'd been the one to comfort her, our roles reversed. Holding her tight as the room lit with lightning. I hoped she was sleeping through this one now. I hoped she was dreaming well.

Eventually something like sleep took over, a soupy trance that dragged me, finally, into morning. Some of the other women were already awake and gathered at the window, the soft slope of their backs to me.

'What is it?' I asked.

'It's like a monsoon out there,' Tanya said. 'Doesn't look like it's ever going to stop.'

Pearl approached the foot of my bed and after a moment perched on the end. 'It's like a Greek myth or something out of the bible, isn't it?' she said, playing with her bottom lip, pinching and twisting it. 'How it appeared all of a sudden, just like that. Like an omen.'

She looked frightened, inconsolable. Pulling at her lip until I saw a seam of red appear. I sat up and gently pulled her hand away. It was easy to forget sometimes how young Pearl was, her age betraying her naivety. I had to force myself to remember that, or else my anger – the need to place blame at someone's feet – would be overwhelming.

'Oh my god!' Lucy cried out, stumbling away from the window.

Pearl and I exchanged a quick look and scrambled off the bed. 'What?'

'Just look. I think I'm going to be sick.'

I elbowed the other women out of the way.

There, in the gutter running alongside the window, were the remains of the squirrel from the day before. Sodden from the rain, its mouth still open, revealing the stained yellow of its teeth. The crow had made an excavation of its body, a flap of grey fur covering the worst of it although I could still make out the unnatural hollowness underneath. It occurred to me that I had never seen a squirrel up close before. Its size surprised me, even in this state.

After a brief discussion, it was decided we couldn't leave it where it was. That it would block the gutter and so perhaps cause structural damage to the house. We opened the window and wedged a wire clothes hanger underneath the squirrel's body and flicked, sending it flying, the impotent sound its body made as it hit the concrete below.

30

Once the sky had been torn open, nothing seemed able to sew it back up. Veins appeared in the ground and formed tributaries, which ran their way downstream towards the farmhouse. The wind pressed its fingerprint on to the surface of the water, forming messy pleats. It didn't take long for the coach house to succumb to the weather. It was an old building, poorly maintained. I attempted to catch the worst of the leaks in repurposed saucepans, littering the floor with them like some weird art installation. The women were good sports about it at first, dancing around like it was some kind of game – a glimmer of their old selves coming back – but when we ran out of pans and the smell of damp spread, they soon lost sight of any silver lining. And when water, bright with rust, began to drip on to our bedsheets and soak through, there was nothing to be done about that.

It was decided we'd all move into the main house, where it was still relatively dry. Transporting what bedding we had left, we set up camp wherever there was space: in the living room, conservatory, the kitchen floor. Sleeping on top of each other like cubs, the air ripe with our smell. Sometimes, late at night, I'd catch myself wondering about Scott and the other men. What they would think if they saw us now, reduced to this. It was difficult not to envy them, warm in their own beds, sleeping the sleep of self-satisfied men, who had nothing to worry about except work the next day and their receding hairlines.

The allotment flooded on the third day. We went outside layered in raincoats and woollen jumpers, the wind whipping at our faces. Blythe led like Moses, her body the only thing we were able to focus on in the midst of the storm, although it was clear even she struggled to part a way through it.

I felt myself stumble into someone as the party came to a sudden halt. Gathered by the familiar smell of peat that we had arrived at the allotment. I wiped my eyes, trying to rid them of their underwater feeling, and looked.

What had once been the nucleus of the farm was gone. In its place was a miniature sea, a reef of leek and garlic, islands of cabbage which were the only green thing left I could see. Everything else had been submerged, drowned. Root systems turned soft, pulled apart like wet tissue. A soapy smell undercutting the peat, oil released from the rosemary bushes which bees had once flocked to for pollen. A pane of glass was missing from the greenhouse, more water flooding through the gap, destroying the trays of seedlings I'd planted only last week. Everywhere was wreckage, ruin.

I saw Sarah break apart from the group and wade further in, until she was almost up to her calf in water. One hand foraging under the surface to retrieve a handful of cherry tomatoes. They came apart between her fingers, the skin sloughing away to reveal pale pulp inside. We looked around at each other, like we couldn't believe what we were seeing. Someone shouted something, but it was snatched away, reduced to a primal noise that meant nothing. I looked down at my feet and saw they were submerged. 'The river must have burst its bank,' Hazel said, or maybe it was Molly. It was difficult to tell.

The thought of the allotment being gone after all the work we'd put into it was so unthinkable as to be untrue, a group hysteria conjured by stress and guilt. Let it be a dream, I thought. Something we could wake up from in the morning and discuss among ourselves, laughing in that way survivors who narrowly avoid a disaster must do, unable to believe their good luck.

A roar of thunder rattled the farm, a cruel reminder that this was real. This was happening to us.

'What are we going to do?' Moira asked, her gentle voice barely audible. 'What will we eat when the pantry runs out? There'll be nothing.'

'We'll have to go into town,' Ambika said.

Blythe, who up until now had been incredibly still and silent, spoke. 'There's no way of getting there now. The road will be too treacherous.'

I looked in the direction of the village. Up until what had happened with the photographs, I'd always enjoyed going to the market. Even taking a kind of pleasure from being scrutinised by the locals, the way their eyes skulked across us, wary and wanting. It had also given me the chance to spend time with Hazel away from Breach House, when she was usually softer, more willing to let her guard down. And yet, I'd be lying if I said I didn't feel some kind of relief now that we'd been cut off from it all. No threat of being woken in our beds by the locals playing a trick on us, or of stares of pity and fear from Sarah's boys. I knew it was no longer safe at Breach House, that it was filled with its own chaos, and yet was it any less safe than what lay outside it?

'I can go,' Molly said, interrupting my train of thought. 'I can at least scout the route.'

Blythe shook her head. 'You mean until you twist your ankle in a ditch and end up drowning in two inches of rain-water. And don't think any of us will risk our lives to come and fetch you. Your body will be trapped on that road for days, maybe weeks, before anyone would think to come. The birds and bugs will have a feast.' Her conviction was so strong it was difficult to argue against, our minds filling with all the terrible ways we could die away from the safety of the farm.

I looked back at the allotment, considering its annihilation in a new light. For a moment unable to believe it was anything other than Blythe's fury unleashed, yet another way to prove the power she wielded over us. Despite the rain-haze, her eyes appeared bright and in full focus, picking over each of us: waiting to see who would speak next. When no one did, she reached below the surface of the water and retrieved a handful of earth, mashed it between her fingers.

'Whatever is meant to come next will come. Nobody is leaving. We are still bound to this land, even if it no longer provides for us.' Was there a kind of pleasure in her voice as she spoke? Her anger laced with satisfaction, that we'd broken her rules and now look what had happened. There was a gruesome noise as she let the earth plunk back into the water. 'I'm tired now. I need to rest.'

We watched her go. After a couple of minutes Sarah followed without a backwards glance. The rest of us looking from the allotment to the house to the edge of the woods, unsure what to do next. There was a breach in the sole of my boot; my sock felt wet. I shifted my weight, felt it squelch.

We were going to starve.

'Who did it?' Molly turned around, glaring at the rest of us. I began to laugh, thinking she was accusing one of us of flooding the allotment. Hysteria jumping up my throat. Hazel reached over and pinched the underside of my arm, where the skin was pale and sensitive. Her fingers twisting until I stopped. 'Who called the police?' Molly asked. 'You might as well just say.'

I took a few steps away from the other women, making some quick mental calculations. With the pantry as it was, there was about a week's worth of food: more if we could be persuaded to ration. It wasn't so bad. The weather couldn't last much longer. Eventually the river would slim back to its original depths, the roads would become safe again, and we could rebuild. Perhaps we'd make the allotment even better than before, so that we never needed to worry about starving again. It would be all right. We would be all right.

Sentiments of the damned.

I felt myself being grabbed, spun around. Molly was up in my face, so close I could see the stains on her teeth. She sank her nails into the skin of my arm, her desire to hurt me writ plain across her face. 'This is about more than just pissing off Blythe now. This could mean the end, for all of us. Whoever the traitor is, they should come forward so we can deal with them.'

Molly was one of Blythe's most loyal followers, clearly keen to emulate the power she wielded over others, although she always fell short in her efforts, an air of desperation in the way she tried to make others fear her. Not seeming to understand that one of the reasons Blythe was so easily able to lead us was because she made it clear she could live without us. That if we disappointed her, all she'd need to do was go out and find a new group of women, another legion of dissatisfied souls who believed she held the key to their redemption.

'Let go of me,' I said as calmly as possible. 'You're hurting me.'

'I've seen the way you look at us,' she said. 'You think you're better than everyone else?'

I shook my head, my stomach pitting with fear. Her nails were going to tear through my flesh, I could feel my skin beginning to give. I looked wildly at the other women, expecting at least one of them to come forward and take Molly by the hand, redirect her anger elsewhere, but no one did, simply carried on watching. I twisted my body to an uncomfortable degree until I could pick Hazel out of the crowd. A beat passed – two – and then she took a step forward.

'Let her go, Molly. There's enough drama going around without you adding to it, for fuck's sake. The rest of us are freezing our tits off.'

Molly released me with a sudden, jerked movement, as though she'd branded herself on my skin. Her face a twist of disgust. 'Fine.'

The women began to disperse, trickling back inside the house. The leak in my boot had worsened; I was wet up to my ankle now. The hem of my trousers had caught the wetness as well, and the skin underneath felt too soft, like I'd be able to poke a finger through the muscle.

I made to follow the others but only got as far as the barn when Hazel stopped me. Now would come her reassurance – that she knew I wasn't to blame, that Molly was just afraid. We would laugh about it, to make what had happened smaller, insignificant. Instead she pushed me back against the wall, one hand at my neck. Her thumb on my larynx. When I swallowed, I could feel the outline of her nail against me.

'If I find out it was you,' she said, squeezing until no more air came, 'I will hurt you worse than this. I will never forgive you. Do you understand?'

An agony to nod.

When she let go I did my best not to gasp, instead taking small sips of air until the dark spots receded from my vision. A bruise already beginning to form around my neck, a ring of roses in the shape of her fingers.

*

Over the next few days the pantry was emptied by some of the women, all with the same idea in mind: to take something for themselves before they were beaten to it. By the time I'd had the idea myself the pantry was already barren, only a few jars of pickles left. A bad smell hung in the air. Something had toppled, spilled, festered. Weevils hatched inside the bags of flour. It seemed impossible that this was the same pantry I'd once hidden in during a game of hide and seek, Pearl and I taking turns to feast on apricots. Our mouths fermenting with the sugar.

After that we began to starve. My body became a betrayal of noise, the liquids and gases inside me roiling expectantly, sending saliva into my mouth. I licked my lips almost obsessively, thought I could taste the salt of bacon or egg, but it was just my own gathering staleness – the sweat on my skin. I caught Hazel hunched over the kitchen sink, filling her stomach with water. She drank until it ran down her chin, wiped it away with the back of her hand.

Without the allotment or orbit of meals to keep us busy,

we struggled to pass the time. A game of poker was started, fought over, ended before anyone could get hurt. Ambika tried to teach me how to knit, manipulating my hands until I was holding the needles correctly, but it felt too strange. My fingers didn't know what to do. I purled the beginnings of a grey scarf, but it came out crooked and I soon gave up, unravelling the yarn until it was all gone.

The women became increasingly ritualistic in how they passed their time, looking for far-out ways to keep themselves busy and in the process reverse the damage that had been done to the commune. Fashioning little poppet dolls of themselves out of spare fabric and twine and sticking pins into them, as if the punishment to their physical bodies wasn't enough. Molly took to piling the windowsills with a litany of mismatched items: pretty-shaped stones, a broken clothes peg, an earring. Claiming, when someone asked, that they were both offerings and talismans, to protect the house. The other women soon followed suit, developing rituals of their own. Hanging increasing amounts of lavender above each door to ward away the evil spirits, the smell becoming so strong it was impossible not to choke on their perfume. Going whole days without speaking or else only speaking certain words: words without the letter W or M or D in them, words with no more than three syllables. Pearl took to smearing the living-room walls in the detritus of the allotment, too-soft peppers and tomatoes which wept on to the floor, and nobody thought to stop her because by that point it made a kind of sense.

And where was Blythe in all of this? Either on the fringes or deep in the centre, offering no comment on the women's actions, or praising them the more outlandish their behaviour became. Although she blamed us for what was happening, I knew she took a certain pleasure in seeing how far we could be pushed.

One afternoon – or morning, or evening – Hazel took me into the bathroom and wedged the door shut. She ran a bath and we both climbed in, my back pressed uncomfortably against the taps. Plug digging into my bottom. It was easy to accommodate both of our bodies now we'd gone a few days without a full meal. The pleasant excess of Hazel's body had been slaked away to reveal muscle and tendon, angles of her I'd never seen before. A birthmark on her hip which – up until now – had been concealed by a fold of fat.

The water was hot enough to scald, my skin flushing lobster-pink. There was a box of bath salts buried at the back of the cabinet and Hazel tipped the entire contents in. The sound reminded me of school, teachers gritting the hallway carpet to cover up a child's sick. What was it about children that made them throw up all the time? I stirred the water, but the granules wouldn't dissolve, rubbed gritty against our skin. Hazel tipped her head back, steam flattening her hair. Her breasts which were asymmetrical and tipped with dark-peach nipples.

'Come here,' she said after a moment, voice throaty and welcoming. 'It's uncomfortable where you're sitting. Turn around, lean against me.'

Since she'd threatened me after the allotment flooded, Hazel had been nothing but kindness to me. I even slept in her bed most nights, our backs pressed warm together: bliss, being away from the other women. I tried not to overthink things, tamping down any feelings of doubt. The niggling suspicion that maybe she wasn't a good person. Maybe she was a bad person, or not a person at all: that behind all the layers she'd accumulated over the years, what was left had already been petrified.

But, oh it felt good to press back against her.

After a while Hazel began to snore. I twisted around to look, her mouth parting, a trail of saliva dripping down her chin. The hot water was thinning my blood, making me light-headed. I turned my head left and right and the movement felt delayed, glued. There was a razor resting on one corner of the tub. It was stiff and rusted, mildew growing along one side of the handle. A dozen different-coloured hairs clogged between the blades. I shook it under the water and began shaving my leg. It had been weeks and my calf was downy, an insulation that I had grown accustomed to. But now I longed to be sleek, bare: to feel everything I came into contact with. When I reached the crag of my knee the razor caught, snagged the skin. Blood beaded, trickling down my leg into the water. I used my thumb and forefinger to widen the cut until I could see the tear properly, and the bleeding began to quicken. I thought about making it wider, dragging the razor around the circumference of my leg and peeling the skin off like a sock.

'Do mine,' Hazel said, awake again. She reached between us and washed the blood from my knee. Stuck her leg out for me to shave. I was more careful with her, lathering shampoo on to her skin first so the razor would glide across. The scum of our hair and sweat skinning the water.

31

Time became a river, ribboned and fluid. No telling any more when the storm had begun and no point speculating when it might end. We simply accepted its presence as another member of the commune. Sometimes I was able to block it out completely, but there were times when the rain fell like shrapnel and I felt all along my body, half expecting to find it pierced with metal, blood-wet skin. I had a constant headache. I was no longer hungry.

The only thing left to be grateful for was Hazel's company, which she doled out in increasingly generous measures. Her mood continued to fluctuate but there were moments when it felt like it had before, in those early summer days when we'd swim in the river, our bodies pressed close. She found ways of being kind to me – offering me the last bite of a cereal bar which she'd stolen from the pantry, massaging my feet with cold cream until it became too slippery to walk. It was clear to me during these bouts of generosity that Hazel didn't remember the other things she had done to me, the threats and acts of cruelty, or perhaps it was that she was unable to comprehend them. I was happy enough to let her overwrite the bad with the good, never once complained when she wrapped her arms around me. This, I told myself, was my prize for staying.

One afternoon a few of us were sat in the conservatory sorting through piles of laundry, looking for old T-shirts we could slot underneath doors, into the corners of rooms to keep the rain from leaking in. Pearl was among us, kept offering to fetch something for us to drink, clearly grateful we'd chosen to include her. She'd shrunk since it was revealed she'd called the men to Breach House, the shine taken out of her and replaced by something duller, more brittle. Panic in the way her eyes kept leaping from one woman to the next, as if we might pelt her with something. I knew it was unfair, that the other women were just looking for a scapegoat. After all, none of us had told the men to leave. There had been those of us who'd protested, but in the end we'd all gone along with it.

'The others hate me,' Pearl said, knotting two T-shirts together. Pulling them taut. 'The way they look at me now, like I'm no better than an outsider.'

'They're upset,' Ambika replied, staring out the window, her skin paled to grey. 'They're upset because Blythe is upset. But it won't always be that way. When she forgives us, things will go back to normal.'

Hazel huffed with laughter. 'Right, everything will magically go back to being hunky-dory. I thought you were meant to be the smart one.'

I said nothing: I knew Ambika needed to believe this.

'Look,' she said, gesturing to the window. 'What are they doing?'

I gazed in the direction she was pointing, saw Molly leading a group of women across the field, their hands filled with various tools. It was difficult to tell them apart, the same rabid expression blending their faces together.

Their journey was slow going. Every so often they were

forced to suck their feet out of the ground or else help a woman stand after falling over, everything made soft and treacherous by the rain.

'Maybe they're going to try and drain the allotment,' Pearl suggested. 'Redirect the water channels or something.'

'I don't think so,' Hazel said.

'They're heading towards the barn,' Ambika pointed out. 'Should we join them?'

But even as she said it Ambika was pressing herself further into her chair, as if to root herself in place. I felt sorry for her. I knew what it was like to feel excluded from the person you cared about most. She held her hand close to her chest, the skin on one side rippled pink with scar tissue. Did she resent Molly for it now, how confident she'd been that Blythe would be able to heal her wound, instead of just taking her to a fucking hospital?

Hazel stood, looked as if she meant to go outside. Fear, irrational in its intensity, surged through me and I stood quickly, grabbed her by the arm before she could open the door. I felt her resist at first – unable to fight her instinct to pull away – before she relaxed, took a small step backwards. 'Leave them,' I told her.

The procession continued, Molly leading the other women into the barn. The lot of them looking like children on some kind of scavenger hunt, an unmistakable air of glee about them. Perhaps it was a new game, something to replace our days of hide and seek.

'I remember the sound,' Pearl said, also looking down at Ambika's hand, the messy shape of it, 'when you fell from the roof. Like a bag of flour splitting.'

'It's not something I particularly want to think about,' Ambika said.

'Sorry,' Pearl replied. 'It's just, I was certain you were dead. And I know what happened was still bad, but you're alive, and I don't know – I guess I just thought at the time that nothing bad could really happen to us while we were here.'

It would have been on the nose, if I hadn't also believed that was once true.

Before any of us could reply, a terrible noise rose from the barn, pickling the air with terror. My heart beat hard against my ribcage, for a moment seeming like it might burst straight through. My vision blotting with dark spots. Pearl screamed at the same moment Hazel asked *What the fuck*, still holding my hand when she stood so that I was half dragged along behind her. As she opened the door, the sound came again, drawn out and keening, before it was eclipsed by – shouting, jeering.

'What is it?' Ambika asked, but I think she already knew. We all did.

The women burst from the barn, hauling the slaughtered pigs between them. The animals' heads lolling against the ground as if keeping time to a beat.

*

The violence of what they had done followed us to the dinner table. Sarah wept when she realised what had happened, having looked after the pigs for almost fifteen years. She kept asking why, why did you do it, but Molly and the others merely shrugged their shoulders and said, we were hungry.

If the rest of us thought Blythe might punish the women for what they had done, we were sorely mistaken. She was pleased, a gratification that bordered on jubilance, as if this escalation in behaviour proved something about their devotion to her. How far they were willing to go. She rewarded them with her smile, handing Molly a carving knife to do the honours. I didn't know who'd cooked the pigs – Sarah had refused – but it was clear they didn't know what they were doing. The meat had been poorly butchered, cut into rough chunks and shoved in the oven for too long. Somehow both under- and overcooked, a wet-looking flap of skin peeling away from the grey flesh. None of them had thought to let the meat rest either, so that when Molly carved into it whatever juices were left flooded out on to the table.

'It was either us or them,' Blythe told the table. 'And now, thanks to the capabilities of these women, we are able to eat. The land continues to provide.'

There was no talk of what we might do after the pigs had been eaten, how we would continue to survive. That was not the point, I understood. Everything now was about subjugation: how far we could be pushed until one of us confessed to calling the police, and thus betraying Blythe and the commune. Our comfort – our safety – was secondary to this. And if dividing us into factions was the quickest way to achieve her goal, then that was what she would do. After all, wasn't that how she'd created the commune in the first place? By convincing each of us that we were better off with her, and not with our partners, friends, parents.

Not all of us ate. Only those who had been part of the slaughter, and Blythe of course. At one point I thought I saw something glisten on Hazel's bottom lip, a slight movement in her jaw which may have been her chewing or simply a simulation of the motion of it. I, personally, preferred to starve.

I watched as the other women fell on to their plates, not bothering to eat with cutlery. The shine of grease, of fat, on their hands. Animals, all of them. Was there a part of me that was jealous, tempted? Yes, of course, yes. I hadn't eaten a proper meal in days. I felt stupid with the want of a full stomach, was beginning to forget how it felt. But I also knew if I gave in, something crucial in me would be lost for ever.

Lucy caught my eye and belched, a meaty gust of air. I saw Sarah cast a look at Blythe and for the first time there was no warmth in her eyes, only disappointment and fright.

*

Later in the evening we could no longer see the rain, but we could hear it, bashing against the window. I was alone with Hazel in her bedroom, the door wedged shut with a chair. For once, it was impossible to tell where the other women were. At one point there had been a great commotion downstairs, the cacophony of their laughing, or chanting, rising through the floorboards, but now the house sounded empty. They might have gone to the barn to revel in their victory, or could be hiding quietly in the shadows, waiting for the next thing to happen. I didn't particularly care, was content to be alone with Hazel.

I perched on the edge of the bed. 'It's a full moon,' I said, gazing out the window.

Hazel didn't look up from her nails, which she was methodically peeling one by one. 'No wonder everyone is acting so crazy.'

'That's just a myth,' I said. 'It used to be a way for people to accuse others with mental health problems of being dangerously insane. *Lunatics*.'

A light sound as one of her nails fell on to the floor. 'Bullshit. My friend's mum would always start acting out right before a full moon. She'd cut all her clothes into shreds and only eat cheese; it was bizarre. Once, my friend covered up all the windows so her mum wouldn't know when the next one came, but the same thing kept happening. She could just feel it.'

I didn't know what to say to that and so kept quiet. In truth, I was thinking about my own mother, how her superstitions had impacted our lives. She'd become a different person when my father died. No. I knew that wasn't true. Her fall had been a gradual one, since she'd first realised what my father got up to when he wasn't at home. It must have ruined her, keeping that knowledge to herself. The weight of it.

Hazel shuffled closer on the bed until our kneecaps bumped up against each other.

'Iris,' she said, my name in her mouth a witch's spell. 'What are you thinking?'

What I wanted to say: We should have left when we had the chance. I should have made you get in the car, when there was still a car, and driven us far away. I don't know how we will survive here now. I am so angry. Sometimes I wish we'd never met. And sometimes I regret that this all didn't happen sooner.

Instead what came out was: 'Nothing.'

She smiled, an agreement to play along. Leaning in closer until our breath mingled and – finally, finally – her mouth swallowed mine.

I had thought of our first kiss often, calcifying it into something I suspected was not true, making it out to be something tender and essential, when really it was probably more like this: awkward and wet and filled with too many teeth.

She pushed me down on the bed. I was careful not to make a sound, was even silent when she began easing the shirt from my shoulders. Biting my lip to stop the noise from spilling out, paranoid that any small thing would spook Hazel into stopping. My skin was clammy and made my clothes stick to me, an awkward manoeuvring as it took her three attempts to remove my bra. I hadn't showered that day. Her mouth clamped over my nipple and I gasped, on the cusp of pleasure and pain. My hips involuntarily bucking. Hazel's body on mine was heavier than I expected, a painful jut as her hipbone sank into my thigh. She smelled of woodsmoke and earth and something indefinable, something so uniquely hers.

Whenever I'd pictured this moment, I'd always envisioned something more reverential. A soft-focus lens sweeping down the length of our bodies, plenty of eye contact. Music, maybe. Instead it was like a burrowing, her fingers searching between my legs and reaching up into me, her mouth which sucked bruised kisses along my chest, neck, stomach. Several times I attempted to undress her, but she pushed my hands away, shaking her head every time I tried to touch her. I told myself it was because she wanted to do something nice for me, rather than experience her distance as yet another denial.

*

In the morning I woke feeling as if I'd gone for a long run, my legs jellied underneath the covers. Hazel was asleep next to me, her spine curved into the perfect C-shape. I thought about pressing my body up against hers but decided against it, not wanting to wake her. She looked so soft, just then. Breakable.

Last night, after she'd crooked her fingers inside me until

I came, I'd tried to touch her again, but she'd climbed out of bed and gone over to the window, opening it so a gust of wind swept everything off the dresser. She'd leaned her head out and taken a few deep breaths, her face hidden by the sash. Had she wondered about everything that had happened up until now? The pigs and the men and the time before that, when we'd unwittingly met on the downs? Did she ever think of that day as I did – life-altering, fundamental? Or had it been merely another ordinary event to her, no different or more profound than brushing her hair?

She turned over in bed now, already awake. 'Did you hear the other women last night?' she asked me.

I shook my head. 'I might have heard Sarah in her bedroom, but it could have been the pipes. I'm not sure.'

'Weird,' Hazel said.

'What do you think they were up to?' I asked.

Her mouth cranked open with a yawn. 'Raiding the shed for rats to roast? Dancing naked under the moon to appease the weather gods? Who knows.'

I shuffled alongside her and smiled, trying to conjure some of last night's intimacy. 'My legs feel funny, like I ran a marathon.' Hazel gave a loose smile. 'You'll have to push me around in a wheelchair. Has your sister still got hers?'

'What do you mean?'

'When she broke her legs,' I clarified, worried now I'd upset her. 'Her trampolining accident. Sorry, it's not the same, obviously. It was just a dumb joke.'

Hazel began braiding her hair, fingers working nimbly against her scalp. 'You must be thinking of someone else,' she said.

I smiled, baffled. 'What do you mean?'

'I don't have a sister.'

I opened my mouth, closed it. Opened it again. Wanting to ask Hazel what she meant, if she was joking. 'You've mentioned her a couple of times,' I began. Cautiously, as though trying not to anger a wild animal.

Hazel made a face, pulling her mouth downwards in an I-don't-know-what-to-tell-you way. 'Not me. You've got me confused with one of the other women.'

She was fucking with me, she must have been. Either that or she had some kind of illness I didn't know about, something that affected her memory. I searched her face carefully for any trace of a joke, half expecting her to turn around and say, *Got you.* But she went on as she was, plaiting her hair and humming quietly to herself, our conversation already forgotten. I pulled the covers tight across my body, feeling suddenly like I might be sick. My legs were no longer shaking. Instead they felt heavy.

So, she didn't have a sister. People did weird things like that all the time, embellished the truth or told outright lies about themselves. It usually stemmed from insecurity. I'd done it before. I'd once told Nathan I was fluent in Spanish, the truth only revealing itself a year into our relationship when he introduced me to one of his colleagues and I couldn't understand a word they were saying. Lying was just something you did. And yet, this felt different. It was worse. The scales had always been tipped in Hazel's favour, ever since I'd begged her to take me to Breach House. Our relationship was like a hill, with her standing at the top and me at the bottom, looking up. When she'd told me about her sister, it had felt like an equilibrium. I knew something about her, something that perhaps the other women did not, not even Blythe. It had made us even, sort of. And now here she was, lying to my face about it. Treating me like an idiot, like I was going to sit there and allow her to rewrite the past just like I'd allowed her to do everything else she wanted.

She finished braiding her hair and got out of bed, her bare feet making sticky sounds on the wooden floor. I watched as she went over to her dresser, took a sip of water. The sound it made as she swallowed. 'That was good last night,' she told me, coming round the bed to duck a dismissive kiss on my jaw.

I knew nothing about her. I never would.

32

Sometimes I imagined my father and Hazel meeting, in a reality where he was still alive and Hazel was something more clearly defined to me: a friend or lover, someone I could point to and say, 'Yes, this is Hazel. She's my . . .' He would have liked her, I think. He would have called her a clever girl, something meant as a compliment but which still contained a barb: the implication that there was something remarkable about a girl being clever.

Whenever I invited friends over from school my father would go out of his way to learn everything about them: what music they enjoyed listening to, if they played any sports. And my friends always answered earnestly, quickly – flattered that this man was taking an interest in them. He had such a way with people, women in particular; of making them feel like they were extremely important. But I knew the inner workings of his mind, how the questions he asked were little more than a way to gather information, ammunition in the battle of dominance. 'Oh,' he might say, smiling and wrinkling his nose as if embarrassed, 'you like listening to *him*? Better not tell the other kiddies at school, or they'll have your guts for garters.' Or: 'Netball, is it? Wouldn't have guessed it from looking at you.' I'd seen him do it time and time again to my mother, picking on her interests and hobbies but managing to say it in a way that made you agree with him. And if you didn't, then it was, 'All right, sweetheart. I was only saying. No need to get upset.' It was something I used to admire about him. That instinctive capability of controlling a situation, a person. Now all I felt was disappointment, having seen behind the curtain one too many times.

Hazel wouldn't have been fooled by him. Yes, it was a shame they never met.

*

I left the bedroom and went downstairs. Having to feel along the wall with one hand, the house plunged into premature darkness. I tried flicking on a light switch, but water must have finally got into the generator because the electricity had gone. My fingers brushed across something wet as I went into the kitchen and I held my hand up close to my face, caught the scent of something foul. A wind whipped across the room. There was a hole in one of the windows, glass constellating the floor underneath.

I didn't know this place any more.

There was no food to eat so instead I sat at the table with a glass of water and took long, slow sips. Trying not to look at the destruction that surrounded me, the strange patterns and sigils smeared on to the walls, rubbish overspilling the bin. Someone had hung one of the pig's trotters from the ceiling. It dangled above me now, looked almost as if it were pointing, or waving. A crescent taken out of it where someone had tried to chew through the gristle.

I didn't know what was worse: the devastation itself or how quickly it had all happened. The ease with which we'd turned feral. There was no one to blame for this desecration other than ourselves.

A sound behind me, and Hazel appeared a moment later, barefoot. I told her to be careful of the glass – there were already red slicks on the floor – but she shrugged her shoulders, walked carelessly over to me.

'Have you seen the others?' she asked. I could tell she was about to take a sip from my glass and moved it away before she had the opportunity. A flash of – surprise, anger? – registered on her face but was just as quickly swallowed up with her usual aloofness. She slumped in the chair next to mine.

'No,' I said. 'I don't know where anyone is.'

'Blythe?'

I shrugged my shoulders. Hazel pulled a face, looked around the room. She didn't seem to register the mess in the same way that I did, her gaze passing over the stains and filth with indifference, as if it had always been there. I wanted to shake her, then. Tell her to look, really look. But I was also tired and hungry and the effort of trying to change anything felt too large now.

Gradually I became aware of music. Looked up to see that the radio was still working. Someone must have found a fresh set of batteries. But it had obviously been knocked about or got wet because the music didn't sound right, was all garbled and distorted. The melody of whatever was playing taking on a kind of underwater quality. Hazel stood and went over to it, whacked the radio with the heel of her hand. It was just like her, to believe a quick bit of violence would solve everything. The radio crackled and then became worse, so she hit it again. It sputtered and then stopped altogether. It was only once the room had plunged into silence – real silence this time – that I realised how much I would miss the sound of the radio. Hazel let it slip from her hand on to the floor. I fought the urge to scream at her.

'It was old anyway,' she told me. 'It's amazing it lasted this long, really.'

I smiled because it was easier that way. But Hazel knew me well, could sense my frustration even better than I could feel it. 'What's the matter with you?' she asked, like I was a child throwing a strop and she was the exasperated parent who now had to make sense of my unhappiness. Everything that had happened before was irrelevant: she saw no reason why I should be upset.

I shook my head, but she persisted, leaning across the table and pinching my cheek with her thumb and forefinger. When I continued not to say anything she pinched again, harder. This was meant to make me cry, or laugh. Zap us back into our usual rhythm. But I snatched my body away from hers, rubbing at the sore skin until the pain faded.

'You lied to me,' I said, surprised by the strength in my voice.

All my life I had believed there were reasonable explanations for the ways people behaved. They were victims of their environment, learned destructive behaviour patterns by watching their parents or friends, or else there was an imbalance in their brain chemistry, a genetic predisposition for certain behaviours. People weren't born evil. It was something they learned through observation and repetition. And so I knew on some level that there was a reason why Hazel was the way she was. A triggering event in her life, some deep-seated trauma that prevented her from getting close to anyone.

But there was another part of me that couldn't shake the feeling Hazel was the exception to all of this, a force unto herself. The only person who could ever give a reason for why she behaved the way she did was Hazel, and prising anything resembling the truth out of her, I realised now, was impossible. She was a void, a black hole. I thought the knowledge of this would devastate me, and yet all I felt was disappointment, like I'd been short-changed.

'You lied to me,' I said again, and this time my voice fractured. There was a lump in my throat when I swallowed and I told myself if I cried now that it would all be over, whatever power I had in this moment would vanish. Swallow again, swallow it down. 'I'm here because of you. I stayed because of you. And now I feel so stupid. I should have just left. I should have left days ago. I don't even know you,' I said, speaking the words slowly, haltingly, as if two parts of my brain were in opposition. One half trying to stop the other.

Hazel's mouth lifted in a grin, searching for the punchline, but when she couldn't find one her face dropped. Skin scraping over wood as she made a fist on the table. She will hit me now, I thought. I relaxed the muscles in my body because I'd heard that stopped it from hurting too badly, but then she stood up and a distance opened between us.

'Well, I know you,' she replied, her words holding all the weight of a threat; a condemnation.

She fled from the kitchen, out of the house, and for the first time I did not follow.

*

For all the people who claimed to have loved my father, his wake was ill-attended. Pale finger food sitting out in the back room of a pub, tuna sandwiches curling at the corners. I asked the woman behind the bar for a Coke but when I took a sip I could taste rum. 'I didn't ask for this,' I told her, but she merely shrugged, said I could probably do with it anyway, no charge. It was sticky-sweet on my lips, went straight to my head. My mother was having a difficult time speaking to the well-wishers, her small talk stuttering to sudden halts with no clear way of how to carry on. She was wearing the dress she used to wear when my father took her out for special occasions, back when he used to do things like that. It was too small for her now and I could tell she felt uncomfortable in it; she kept pulling at the fabric around her stomach. I should have said something nice to her, offered reassurance, but instead I lurked in the corner, sipping my drink and getting progressively more drunk. Half an hour before, when the sausage rolls were still hot and mostly edible, my aunt had told me about my father's indiscretions. His other family. The news sat like pitch in my stomach, dark and heavy and all-consuming. I wanted to do something with it, spend it like money. It bothered me that there weren't more people at the wake, when they'd seemed so charmed by my father. Was it possible they'd seen something in him that I'd missed? Was it possible they knew all along?

'Sweetheart' – my mother came up to me, making that face of hers as she smelled my breath – 'can you talk to one of the bar staff and see if they can do something about the music? The same Paul Weller CD has been playing for the past hour. I'm not sure he even liked Paul Weller.'

She looked so tired, and scared, and overwhelmed. I should have been a good daughter and told her, yes, of course I will tell them. I will find something that he really used to listen to, and I will try to understand everything that has happened. But it was so much easier to be cruel, to foist the blame on to her. 'Ask them yourself,' were the words I said.

Barely a flinch from my mother, who by then was used to such things.

33

After Hazel left I did my best to clean the house, although I could not bring myself to touch the pig's trotter still hanging from the ceiling. Water had got into the walls and saturated the plaster, forming air bubbles underneath which I found deeply unsettling, although I couldn't put my finger on exactly why. I scrubbed the floors, swept hair from the corner of every room. But nothing seemed to help: the house had changed in the storm and would never be the same again. The women's fury had scarred it.

Midway through cleaning I heard a sound rise up from somewhere outside. I would have assumed the pigs, if not for the fact they'd been eaten. It must have come from one of the women. I stood very still, my knuckles whitening around the broom. Waiting. Hazel hadn't come back after our argument and, although I missed her, I was glad she wasn't here now – she'd only make a joke of it, try to dismiss whatever was happening outside as trivial. The noise came again, somewhere between a laugh and a howl. I knew, even as I brought my head low, that I would have to go outside and find out what it was. I'd made the choice to join Breach House, had bound myself to it and the other women: I was compelled to see it – whatever *it* was – through to the end.

Shoes, then. I put down the broom and went into the

hallway, pulled on a pair of wellies and went outside. The ground was wet and tender, a struggle just to walk around the side of the house towards the allotment. The rose bush which Sarah had been so proud of had been stripped bare, its petals strewn carelessly about by the wind. As I walked past it, I pressed my face up to the window of the coach house, half expecting to find the women all curled up together, kittens in a pile. But the building was derelict, had given itself over to the storm. Part of the roof must have finally collapsed too because I could see leaves now carpeted the floor, a layer of grime coating everything. This, the place where we had once slept and laughed, and talked late into the night: gone.

The allotment was still submerged. Only now it carried a stink, of soft roots and rotten vegetables. The kind of smell that got trapped in the back of your throat. I waded further in, felt under the surface for a remnant of a carrot or cucumber, but it was all soft, the same wetness sliding through my hand. It was difficult, now, to remember what it had felt like to eat anything we'd grown here, food that required chopping and cutting and chewing.

A sound, similar to the first, rose up into the air. Closer now so that I could feel it run through me, almost bovine in its appeal. I realised with a sickening dread that I knew where the sound was coming from, and from who.

Someone else must have done the walking for me because I couldn't remember taking the steps myself. I was in the allotment and then suddenly I wasn't. I was standing outside the barn and I could hear the other women inside, the cacophony of their voices obscuring anything specific they might be saying. With hands and feet that no longer felt like mine, I approached the barn door, which had been left ajar.

Pressed my face to the gap, careful not to make a sound. Funny, how I'd spent the past few months wanting nothing more than to be accepted by these women and now here I was – on the outside again, looking in.

It took time for me to work out what I was seeing, an effort to separate the women from the shadows. There was Ambika, leaning against the door of what was once the pig pen, her eyes like two dark holes in her head. And Sarah, who seemed locked in confrontation with the others – Molly and the horde who'd taken her side, helped slaughter the pigs – her hands gesticulating wildly, pointing at something just out of sight. She looked desperate, which surprised me: she'd always been able to wrangle the other women, being Blythe's second-in-command. It was clear, though, that whatever she was instructing – pleading – them to do was falling on deaf ears.

I opened the door a fraction wider, needing to see, a feeling in the pit of my stomach like I might be sick. Acid in my throat. As I pressed myself closer to the gap in the door, a circle gradually revealed itself. Women stood shoulder to shoulder, stomping their feet impatiently as though waiting for something to begin. In the centre stood Blythe. And beside her was Pearl.

She was bleeding. It took me a moment to realise that. A long, red line running from her head to her chin, so perfect it looked as if it had been drawn with felt tip. She was uneven on her feet, had to rely on Blythe to keep her upright, although I could tell even from here that Blythe's grip was too tight, nothing comforting about it.

'I didn't do it,' Pearl sobbed, the words creaming in her gapped mouth so only a selection of consonants made it out: *I idn' do i.* The other women roared in response, pulled at their hair and beat their chests in anger. It was obvious I'd arrived in the middle of something. Clearly there'd been a fight, the excitement of slaughtering the pigs no doubt spurring Molly and the others on to some greater action. They were hungry, and angry, and looking for someone to blame. But it felt different this time, elemental and spiteful and earnest in the way the women showed their teeth, baring them at Pearl.

And Blythe in the centre of it all.

'Now is the time,' she told them. 'To decide what we are willing to accept. Are you willing to accept humiliation? Are you willing to let yourselves be ridiculed, made fools of?'

No, was the resounding answer. Their voices mashing into one brutal drumbeat: no, no, no. I tried picking Hazel out of the crowd. She wouldn't go along with this sort of thing, would she? But, of course, it was impossible to say. She'd gone along with everything else – so had I. I realised now she belonged to Breach House in a way I did not. There was no telling how far her loyalty might stretch. Perhaps it was because she needed it more. Perhaps that's what it had always been about.

Blythe stepped out of the circle, leaving Pearl on her own. A rock was thrown, missed, clattered against something metal. Pearl flinched, arms coming up to protect her head. The other women began to move, leonine in the way they stalked around Pearl, as if assessing the softest parts of her. 'Molly,' I heard Ambika call. 'Molly, please. Don't.'

Molly turned briefly to look at her. 'She has to pay for what she's done.'

This time, when the second rock was thrown, it did not miss.

It was difficult to say, during the next few moments,

whether the women meant to go that far, or if they simply got carried away. Perhaps they'd intended only to scare Pearl, rough her up a bit. Just enough to prove a point to themselves, what they were capable of. I'm not sure they even believed Pearl had called the police; it was simply the excuse they needed for whatever was about to happen.

The rock connected with Pearl's shoulder and knocked her off balance. She fell on to her back with a surprised grunt. After that the women piled on top of her, punching and kicking and biting, unable to help themselves. Their mouths spilling open in a war cry, a combined ululation that could strip trees bare, suck iron from blood. It was a taking sound, their anger selfish. Screaming like children who'd had their favourite toy taken away from them.

I caught Pearl only in glimpses after that, shards of her body revealed through gaps in the other women: a roving eye, her left foot, the pink pulp of what had once been her mouth. Several times I took a step forward as if to enter the barn. I could feel the muscles in my legs preparing the movement, the ringing of blood in my ears so loud it felt as if my head might burst. I wanted to storm inside and rip the women away from Pearl. I wanted to enact my own violence, strike them until they were clear-headed enough to see what they had done, how they had forsaken everything. Can't you see? I would scream at them. Can't you see what's been done to you? There was nothing unique or special about us. Realisation washed over me in a frigid wave, made me shake. Fate hadn't called us to Breach House: we'd just been scared, or bored, or lonely. We'd made a decision to come here – the same kind of decision you make every day, no different from buying a new perfume or finally agreeing to floss. And instead of finding ourselves, we'd been reduced to a single entity, consolidated into one vague woman-shape, moulded by Blythe's whims.

But I didn't do any of this. I stayed where I was, rooted in place by fear and self-preservation.

Through the flurry of fists and claws I saw Molly break apart from the others and vanish into a corner of the barn I could not see. She reappeared a moment later carrying something heavy, a salt lick once given to the pigs. Showed it to the other women, whose screams reached a new, excited volume. They stood back to make room, Pearl on her back like a bug, her legs at a strange angle, and Blythe no longer even there, fled like a ghost, fucking coward, probably deep in the woods by now. Somewhere in the back of my head, I heard my father say: you shouldn't start what you can't finish.

And, for just a moment, what could have been a trick of the light, I thought I saw a glimpse of copper hair.

Molly raised her arms and brought the salt lick down.

I clamped a hand over my mouth – to stop myself from screaming, from being sick. A feeling in the pit of my stomach that went beyond fright or disgust, was something altogether more primordial.

There was a wet sound as bone and tissue were pulverised, before a loaded quiet took its place. A silence that had texture, grated against the skin. I pressed my face closer to the gap in the door but was no longer able to see Molly or Pearl, only the backs of the other women, their hunched shoulders. Had they even noticed Blythe was no longer there, that they were on their own?

Several thoughts came to me at once as the violence of what Molly had done settled: that I would never be able to come back from this moment. That I was frightened and wanted my mother more than I wanted anything else in the world, to hear her tell me it would be okay. That, even now, there was still a part of me that longed to go inside the barn and be among the other women. A terrible muscle memory of wanting to share in their pain.

Slowly, with a great effort, I backed away from the door. Hand still pressed against my mouth, saliva pooling between my index and middle fingers. I heard someone begin to cry as I retreated back down the path, the nausea gradually draining from my body, emptying me out fully, until all that was left was a kernel of something cooler, what I recognised a moment later as resignation.

34

My mother kept a drawer full of takeaway menus and when I was younger, on a weekend, she'd tell me to stick my hand in and choose one without looking. I always wanted Chinese food and so made a point of memorising the texture of their menus. One restaurant in particular used thicker paper than the others, making it easier to find. Sometimes though my mother refused to play along, would sense my trick and order pizza instead. But now she smiled and said, yes, perfect, she was just in the mood for some sweet and sour.

The food arrived sooner than expected. I froze when the doorbell rang, for a moment forgetting where I was. My mother made a gesture for me to stay and returned a moment later with two heavy plastic bags. We took our plates through to the dining room, lined the foil containers neatly in a row. We'd ordered too much: beef in chilli sauce, prawn toast, chow mein slippery with sesame oil. There was a greasy bag of spring rolls that had turned soggy in transit but which still tasted unbelievably good. I ate until my stomach hurt, grease running down my chin, sinking a prawn cracker into a pot of sweet and sour sauce and watching as it gradually disintegrated.

*

There are some things I'd prefer not to remember but which feel unfair to forget, so I will say them here, now.

I left the farm: in the rain, while I still could. Running in boots that were a size too big for me so that the skin on the backs of my ankles was scraped clean. It was getting towards the afternoon – thunder rumbling quietly in the distance at first and then persisting, growing into a mighty sound like a hammer striking an anvil. I struggled to see in front of me, took each step on blind faith, praying that I didn't break my leg and drown in two inches of rainwater like Blythe threatened we would. I only looked back once. Told myself it was because I wanted to make certain I wasn't being followed, but if I was honest a part of me hoped I might turn around and see Hazel. It didn't matter, just then, whether she'd been a part of the violence or not; we would leave together and work something out, start a new life on the coast selling handmade earrings or fish and chips. But it was futile to cling to a dream I'd already woken up from, and she was not standing behind me anyway.

Eventually I made it on to the main road and was picked up by a woman in her seventies. Despite the weather, some people were still willing to drive. She pulled over, cranked the window of her Land Rover and told me to get in.

The air inside the car was stifling, a trickle of sweat running down the curve of my back. I could smell the other woman, how she must live; her home sucked into the fabric of her coat, cooking oil and compost and the faint aroma of neglect. She held the steering wheel low down so her hands could rest in her lap. 'You've got some balls being out in weather like this,' she told me, rolling the window down a crack. 'I thought my medication was playing up on me, making me see things. I said to myself, can't be there's a woman out in weather like this. On her own, no less.'

'Thank you for stopping,' I said.

She sniffed, carried on. After a little while I felt her gaze slip towards me again. I pressed my hands into the seat, trying to make myself as small as possible. 'Where am I taking you then?'

'You can drop me in the village,' I said. 'Or wherever's easiest.'

Outside the window the full extent of the storm revealed itself, the road obstructed in several places by fallen branches and abandoned vehicles, cars that weren't made to traverse this kind of weather and had to be abandoned by their drivers. At one point the way looked cut off entirely by a stream of water that ran across the road, but the woman revved the engine and ploughed straight into it, the undercarriage of the Land Rover sounding like it was scraping along something. I worried the engine would flood, but then we made it out, the woman giving a small grunt of satisfaction.

'Got someone who'll meet you?' she asked. When I didn't reply, she shrugged her shoulders. Truthfully, I hadn't thought much further ahead than getting away from Breach House. I just wanted to put space between me and the women, as if that would absolve me of what had happened. If I got far away enough, maybe it would be like I had never been there to begin with.

The woman leaned towards me and I jolted back in my seat, but she was only reaching for the glove compartment. 'Should have a spare flannel if you want to dry yourself off. It might smell a bit, but it's clean.' I thanked her and dabbed the flannel along the back of my neck. 'I used to live in the village when I was younger,' she went on. 'When I still worked at the post office. I'm retired now, of course. I was never the sort of person who did very well on her own, always enjoyed the company of others. I'm not ashamed to admit part of the appeal was the gossip – who was sleeping with the vicar that week, if Jill the landlady was diluting the lager. But now . . .' She shook her head, sucked on her bottom lip, which I noticed was scabbed and sore-looking. 'It never used to be this nasty. The photos, I mean.'

She raised a hand before I could reply. 'I recognise you from the market. I bought your strawberries a few times, the sweetest I've ever eaten.' I looked at her but said nothing, let her go on. 'Now I'm older, I don't have time any more to worry about other people. Whatever you ladies get up to is none of my business. But I will say, those boys played a horrible trick on you with those photos. They shouldn't have done that.'

Adrenaline flooded my body, sent an electrical pulse through my brain. The humiliation of our bodies displayed across the village – and everything that had come after – felt like a physical scar, a ridge of tissue underneath my breast which I could touch and feel the shape of. We'd spent so long blaming each other for what had happened, it was a relief to hear someone say that it wasn't all our fault.

'Thank you,' I said, grateful and guilty in equal measure.

She nodded. 'So, I'll ask again. Where shall I take you? I'd wager good money you don't actually want to step foot in the village after all of that.'

I gave her my mother's address.

*

Once we'd finished the takeaway we decided to watch a movie, something familiar we'd both seen before. We landed on *Jaws* because the DVD was right in front of us and we loved to shout 'Worst mayor ever!' whenever Murray Hamilton came on screen. My mother patted the seat next to her and I tucked my feet under her bottom to keep them warm. There was something comforting about the percussion, the familiar *dun-dun-dun-dun* as the camera sifted through the seabed, stalking upwards to a shot of a girl's legs. Knowing what was about to happen somehow dampening the horror of it, making it something to anticipate rather than dread.

The woman had parked on my mother's driveway and left the Land Rover running. There was a long hair growing from her chin and she'd pulled on it absent-mindedly. 'You'll be all right from here then?' she asked.

Her kindness overwhelmed me; I wanted to be away from her.

'Yes, thank you. Thank you for taking me. What about petrol . . .'

She waved a hand at me. 'No worries. Call it even for the strawberries.'

I'd waited until I could no longer hear the Land Rover's engine and then knocked on the front door. My mother answered after two full minutes. She looked surprised to see me.

'Iris,' she said. 'Hello.'

'Hello,' I said.

We stayed like that, her on one side of the door and me on the other, an unbreachable space between us. I didn't know what to say to her, had no words to adequately describe what I was feeling. The anger and fear and shame. And so I said nothing, which probably made things worse, until, finally, she took a step back.

'Come on then. Come out of the rain.'

I followed her into the kitchen and nodded when she asked if I wanted something to drink, a cup of tea. It felt surreal, watching her prepare everything, rifling through the drawers looking for a teaspoon. The domesticity of it clashing with what had happened at Breach House, the whistle of the kettle rising to a panicked squeal as my mother got distracted trying to find clean mugs, a sound that made me cower. I couldn't stop thinking about sweet, young Pearl lying on the ground, begging for them to stop, just for a moment, to just stop . . .

'I can't remember if you take sugar,' my mother said, handing me one of the mugs. 'But you look like you need a bit of fattening up. I hope that's okay to say.'

She must have known something was wrong. I'd never been very good at keeping myself private. I was afraid she'd ask me about it, Breach House and what had gone on, why I'd lost so much weight and had a look about me, like I was very afraid of something. I didn't know what I would say if she asked. How did you explain a thing like that?

Instead, she chose kindness: 'Fancy a takeaway?'

*

The rise of several cellos filled the living room as the shark latched itself to the girl's legs, dragging her under the surface. My mother pretended to be frightened, gave a joyful scream as the girl's blood curdled in the water.

*

Certain images lodged themselves in my brain and wouldn't let go:

Hazel tuning the radio until she found a song she liked. 'Easy Lover' by Phil Collins filling the kitchen, which happened to be one of her favourite songs. Something precious in learning this about her.

All of us sunbathing on the lawn, taking it in turns to plait each other's hair, before we'd decided to cut it all off.

The way Pearl would massage the space between your thumb and forefinger if you had a headache and tell you all about the Union Valley pressure points, which were not to be confused with the place in California.

The first stalks of rhubarb in early summer, tart yet oh-so-sweet.

Pearl's arm twisted at an odd angle as one of the women bore her foot down on it.

It was as if I'd experienced so much on the farm, I no longer knew how to come back home.

*

Days passed. I spent much of the time asleep, buried in my childhood bedroom, which my mother had recently cleared out, so that it felt like I was a girl again, my old *Now That's What I Call Music* CDs tucked into a neat stack on the windowsill. After a while she stopped trying to make me come downstairs, took to leaving cups of tea outside my door and taking them away again when they turned cold. Our language gradually whittling down to the bare essentials. Would you like an orange, shall I peel it for you? I've just cleaned the bathroom tiles, be careful when you go in.

I began to write things down on a piece of paper, sat at my

bedroom window looking out. *The couple across the street are having a baby. It is their first, I think. The neighbours on the right have bought a basketball hoop and the father and son play every evening after he comes home from work. There is a basketball-shaped dent in my mother's lavender bush.* These events helped mark the passage of time, although soon felt like a rebuke: life was going on without me. It was as if the stitches that connected me to everyone else had been pulled. I'd been unravelled from the tapestry, had become scrap. Excess. I found myself longing for home, but if home wasn't here – the house I'd grown up in – then where was it?

*

Necessity eventually called me downstairs. I needed to know what had happened to the other women. I waited each morning for my mother to return from the shops with James, and would snatch the paper from her, scanning it for news of Breach House. Afraid yet desperate for any information – whether Pearl's body had been discovered yet, if the other women had turned on each other. It seemed impossible that the rest of the world didn't intrinsically know what had happened, that they couldn't sense Pearl's murder when the knowledge of it felt welded to my skeleton.

It took almost a full week for the police to go to Breach House, and that was only because Ambika told them. She'd waited until the weather cleared and then walked in her bare feet to the nearest station. After that, the story began to snowball, became the only thing news channels talked about. Images of Breach House filling the television screen, something uncanny about witnessing the farm from the safety of my mother's sofa.

Nobody knew for certain what had happened at first, but gradually the story pieced itself together, and then it was all anyone could talk about. What were those women thinking? What led them to behave this way? Trout was even in a couple of interviews, his hands appearing every now and again in frame, the same stubby nails as before. Yes, he'd visited Breach House once. No, the women hadn't seemed normal. Well, yes, he sort of could see this coming.

As the story reached new heights of fame, the specifics of what happened became more vivid, salacious: how the autopsy report concluded the women hadn't stopped once Pearl was dead. That their violence had continued, perhaps for hours afterwards: deep cuts found all along her torso and abdomen, a smell like rot as one of the wounds punctured her stomach lining. I told myself the other women must have been delirious with hunger, that Blythe's goading had changed something in their brain chemistry. But there must have been rage, too. The kind that could only be exorcised on other people, because that's where it came from in the first place. Most of the women there had been running for so long – from bad fathers and shitty exes – that it had become difficult for them to recognise who was truly at fault. They'd been convinced Pearl was the source of their anguish, and so they'd snapped. I understood that kind of anger well, which worried me even more. What would I have been capable of, if I'd stayed?

I learned a few of the women lingered after Blythe fled, including Molly. Wandering aimlessly around the farmhouse, malnourished and dazed, their deep-socketed eyes cringing from the lights of the police vehicles as they packed the driveway. Molly kept insisting that Blythe would come back for them, that she would explain things in a way that made sense. Even after everything, her faith remained unshakeable. While the police continued their manhunt for Blythe, Molly and the others were arrested and drowned in the legal system to prevent further uproar. As for Hazel, there was no sign of her.

My mother must have smelled the guilt on me, seen it every time I opened my mouth or blinked, the truth peeking through like an exposed nerve. I kept expecting her to grab me by the shoulders and shake me, as if all of it would come tumbling out. She deserved to know. I owed her that much. Instead she continued making fresh cups of tea, each with a little bit more sugar in, until my teeth began to ache with every sip.

I loved her very much for that.

*

If I expected to feel relief once Pearl's body was discovered, I was mistaken. And once I learned the truth of it, that it hadn't been Pearl who'd phoned the police, it hadn't been any of us, but Sarah's sons, who'd simply been worried about their mother, I became angry. So angry it hurt, blood running thick in my veins. I didn't understand how I could be filled with so much grief and yet feel completely empty. I took to slamming doors open and closed, ripped the stuffing out of cushions. Wading into the garden in my bare feet and digging around until I found the perfect stone, sucking it into my mouth and clamping down until all I could taste was dirt and mineral and blood.

Sometimes my mother would wrap her arms tightly around me so that it became difficult to breathe, her nails digging into my skin, trying to reach something deep within me. But it felt as if my moment for absolution had come and gone. I'd missed my chance to confess and now had to make do with whatever was left.

When it became clear the police weren't going to show up at the door and arrest me, I tried to punish myself in ways I thought were fair. Pulling a hunk of hair from my scalp every time I missed Hazel or Breach House. Brushing my gums until I spat blood into the sink. I thought of the old science fiction films I used to watch with my father on weekends, sacrificial virgins being thrown into volcanoes. It felt as if it would take something equally primal to make amends. Maybe a therapist would say it wasn't my fault, that I'd been manipulated. I was a victim. You were groomed, they might say, like it was an awful thing. But *groom* was such a soft word, made me think of mother cats licking open the eyes of their new-born kittens. Blythe had seen something in each of us that was worth having, misfits that had never been chosen for anything before – and no matter how far my hatred might extend, it was matched only by a sense of loss.

35

One afternoon I agreed to join my mother's yoga class, because she'd been good to me and denying her any more seemed a step too far. I tried not to think about Breach House as she led me upstairs into a stuffy office room where several middle-aged women and one man were getting ready on their mats. My mother was surprised by my flexibility and even became a little competitive, overstretching herself in Warrior Pose so she began to tip forward, was caught by the instructor who helped reposition her body. I relented after that, wanting her to have something over me. Smiled and thanked her when she whispered to drop my hips lower or else I might strain myself.

Afterwards we drank coffee on a bench outside, even though it was cold. The rain had finally stopped, but I could tell summer was at an end; already the leaves were beginning to change. We split an almond croissant, our lips freckling with crumbs, the butter in my mouth almost euphoric. I was starting to put weight back on, a new heaviness to my body that made me feel tethered, secure.

'You finish it,' my mother said, handing me the last of the croissant. I insisted she finish it and we went on like that until coming to the conclusion we'd just split it. We'd been in a stalemate for so long, for years, that every interaction now felt as if it had to end in compromise. It didn't bother me. I suppose I felt like I owed her.

She smiled at me as she chewed and then clapped her hands clean. 'Your father used to make his own marzipan. I hated it; the house would smell like cyanide for days. He'd warm it up and spread it on his toast in the mornings. It was the reason why he had so many fillings.' She dabbed her mouth with a tissue and threw it into the bin next to the bench. 'About a year after he died, I developed a craving for it. I'd spent my entire life hating the stuff and then all of a sudden it was all I wanted to eat. Even now, I can't eat a croissant without thinking of him.'

She held my hand. I was surprised by the grip of her, so warm and strong, a beautiful weight. 'It's all right,' she told me, squeezing gently. 'To miss something even though you know it wasn't good for you.'

It was the closest she'd come to addressing what had happened – with my father, and with Breach House. I knew she wouldn't ask me directly about any of it, that she understood some things cannot be faced head on. 'It doesn't make you a bad person. You're not a bad person, Iris.'

I took a long time sipping my coffee, holding the polystyrene cup up to my face so she wouldn't see how easily I was overcome. There was so much I wanted to tell her, about how I'd felt so bad for so long and made it all her fault, that I understood now what it was like to love someone who could never love you back, not in the way you wanted. Not in the way you deserved. And that, above all, I was sorry. But I wouldn't be able to say it all at once. Perhaps it wouldn't mean as much if I did, anyway. There were some things that took months, years, to atone for. And that felt okay.

*

Almost a month passed before they finally arrested Blythe. She was squatting in a disused office block by then, had amassed a small group of new followers who tried to barricade the doors, as if they stood a chance against a whole squadron of police.

According to the newspapers, it took three grown men to wrestle her to the ground.

2018

The tenth anniversary of Breach House comes and goes and I am still alive, I am still here. Winter thaws into spring. I start swimming at the local leisure centre, which also has a Mexican restaurant, so the smell of ground beef mingles with the smell of chlorine. On Wednesdays the pool is halved to make room for the local swim team, who are otter-sleek in their caps and goggles and take stretching very seriously. I set myself the challenge of keeping abreast with them. Usually I am able. My body has never forgotten the months of labour working in the allotment, the quiet pride that – even as I get older – I am strong.

There are bad days, of course. Days when I can do nothing except think of Breach House, that final image of Pearl working its way through me, her mouth squeezing open and closed in what might have been a plea or prayer. I often wonder what the outcome would have been if I'd intervened, if I'd tried to save her. But of course such thoughts are pointless. I ran, and I cannot change that now.

There have been other casualties. Several women who passed through the commune have died in sudden, unexpected ways. Lucy, who'd slept next to me in the coach house, drowned in her bathtub one afternoon. And then there was Moira, who'd leaned too far over her friend's balcony and fallen. Molly, a few years into her prison sentence, was found unconscious in her cell and later diagnosed with significant brain damage. It's still unclear whether her injuries were self-inflicted: neither outcome would surprise me. She'd been filled with fury, right up to the end.

And then there was Sarah. The only one I truly missed, whose scrambled eggs I was never quite able to replicate. She was dead in a matter of weeks after the events of Breach House. A sudden decline in health, it was reported. Sarah's sons held a small funeral for her, but of course I didn't go. The thing I hated most were the rumours that mushroomed after her death, as if it was proof of Blythe's power. That she had been the one to keep Sarah alive all those years and as soon as they were separated, Sarah succumbed to illness. And who's to say that wasn't true? Wasn't the fact that we all kept talking about her proof of Blythe's magic?

I try my best not to think of Hazel, but the people who change us have a way of coming back. She is with me at night when I wake suddenly, gasping for breath, a feeling like a great weight has been lifted from my chest. She is the rubble everything that's come after is built upon, every new job and relationship grafted in some way by her memory. I have given up so much because of her. I quit my job at the furniture company after one of my colleagues recognised Scott's photo of me and Hazel kissing, even though it was so long ago, even though I looked different now. He promised not to tell anyone, but I could see his image of me had been spoiled, that there was no coming back from it. I was unable to maintain a relationship longer than six months. There never seemed any point in staying, when the best of me had already been taken.

*

Hazel once told me she wanted to live on the coast, in a brightly painted house. I imagine her walking along the chalky cliffs, a scarf wrapped tightly around her face so only her eyes are visible. She eats in abundance: greasy cones of chips, apple turnovers, battered sausages. No longer restricted to the diet of Breach House. I can never decide if she has a dog, cannot picture her having the patience to care for one.

She has someone who cares for her, though, in this life by the sea. Not anything as clearly defined as a girlfriend, but someone who keeps her back warm at night. It only occurs to me afterwards that, even in my fantasy, Hazel does not belong to me.

What I can never decide is whether she thinks about what happened as often as I do. If Breach House is always at the forefront of her mind, a permanent stain that no amount of scrubbing can clean away. Or if she's managed to compartmentalise, push everything that happened into a dark corner. I don't know which version I prefer: Hazel in turmoil, or the Hazel I remember, who has surely learned to forget.

I still don't know if she hurt Pearl. Some days I tell myself it doesn't matter, when the outcome was still the same.

I have done my best, all these years, not to pry or go looking. Settled with reading through message boards and blog posts, watching the Netflix documentary as if I was just another bystander. But after a decade, I am curious. I have an itch. I want to know where she is. I find myself driving down to the coast on weekends, a different place every time. No plan in mind other than to continue building up my fantasy of present-day Hazel. I want to imagine, in crucial detail, this life I've invented for her. I don't tell anyone where I'm going, especially my mother. Over the years she has managed to worm details out of me: not all of it, but enough that if she knew what I was doing, she'd tell me to stop.

I arrive at another small seaside town, where bakeries outnumber clothing shops. After the recent rainfall, people are only just returning to the streets, peering cautiously up at the sky. Pensioners, mostly – people who no longer need to live near high-speed train lines or cities. It's a place at the end of the road, quite literally. Nothing beyond it but sea and sky. A good place to come to if you want to be forgotten.

The beach, like almost every other in Kent, is shingled. It is slippery after the rain, difficult to walk on. The sea is sucked of colour and churns in grey folds, washing foam on to the shore. There are more people here than there were in town, dog walkers and families who are making the best of the bad weather. Groups of teenagers being too loud and throwing rocks into the water, chucking the polystyrene packaging from their chips on to the ground. A man pushes an ice-cream cart up and down – a tad hopeful, I think, although people begin to form a queue.

I contemplate dipping my feet into the water when I notice a flash of copper hair in the crowd.

Funny. I'd spent so much time wondering where Hazel went, I never considered what would happen if I actually saw her again. Was it possible she'd been searching for me, too? Or that she'd known where I was this entire time, and had been keeping tabs on me over the years? Following me home from work, watching me swim laps in the pool. A witness to drinks with colleagues and grocery shopping, hospital appointments and first dates.

I pull my coat tighter around me, suddenly cut to the bone with cold. This is what I wanted, what I came here for. The possibility of a reunion. And yet all I can feel is terror lodging in my throat, the weight of everything that has happened: the hunger and death and the loss. Pearl's missing smile. Above all else, the memory of how good Hazel was at hurting me, and how I do not want to hurt any more.

Quickly, without looking behind me to see if it is really her, I begin walking back up the beach. I dig my hands into my pockets, lick the chap from my lips, and taste salt.

ACKNOWLEDGEMENTS

I wrote *Spoilt Creatures* under strange circumstances, during the first Covid lockdown in 2020. I owe thanks to many, for helping make this book happen and for keeping me sane throughout.

To my agent, Charlotte Seymour. Always a safe pair of hands, calm and generous: I'm very lucky to have you in my corner and hope we get to do this for years to come.

To my editor, Ellie Freedman. I knew you were the perfect choice to publish *Spoilt Creatures* when you described it as 'fun'. Your relentless hard work and enthusiasm have made this journey a joy. Never stop sending me your horror movie recommendations.

Thank you to the wider Tinder Press and Headline teams, in particular Isabelle Wilson, Mary-Anne Harrington, Elise Jackson, Alexia Thomaidis, Ana Carter, Lucy Howkins, Amy Cox, Tina Paul and Isobel Smith.

I'm grateful to several organisations for their help: Johnson & Alcock, Blue Pencil Agency, Mslexia, Curtis Brown Creative, Justine Kurland, the estate of Vita Sackville-West and Curtis Brown Heritage.

Endless gratitude to Tom de Freston for his wisdom and guidance. Your kindness has meant so much these past few years. And to all the authors who championed *Spoilt*

Creatures early on, especially Kiran Millwood Hargrave, Jennie Godfrey and Alice Slater.

Thank you to booksellers, librarians and book bloggers everywhere. This would be so much harder without you.

To Chloë, Olivera, Carre and Charlie – my own commune of astonishing women.

Thank you to Dexter for the emotional support. Thank you to the TwiHards and board game crew. Thank you to my magnificent Debut 2024 group. Thank you to Gabrielle (and Steve): how lucky I am to know you. Thank you to my friends and family.

Thank you to my parents, who never once tried to discourage me from this path, and who are always proud.

Finally, to Keith. All my stories are for you.